EX LIBRIS

"Come Aboard, Mr. Hands," I Said Ironically.

# TREASURE ISLAND

BY

ROBERT LOUIS STEVENSON

WITH INTRODUCTION AND NOTES BY

GILBERT SYKES BLAKELY

ILLUSTRATED BY

FRANK GODWIN

THE JOHN C. WINSTON COMPANY

CHICAGO        PHILADELPHIA        TORONTO

# CONTENTS

# CONTENTS

## Part IV

### *THE STOCKADE*

## Part V

### *MY SEA ADVENTURE*

## Part VI

### *CAPTAIN SILVER*

# LIST OF ILLUSTRATIONS

# TO THE HESITATING PURCHASER

If sailor tales to sailor tunes,
    Storm and adventure, heat and cold,
If schooners, islands, and maroons,
    And Buccaneers and buried Gold,
And all the old romance, retold
    Exactly in the ancient way,
Can please, as me they pleased of old,
    The wiser youngsters of today:

So be it, and fall on! If not,
    If studious youth no longer crave,
His ancient appetites forgot,
    Kingston, or Ballantyne the brave,
Or Cooper of the wood and wave:
    So be it, also! And may I
And all my pirates share the grave
    Where these and their creations lie.

# INTRODUCTION

THERE is a very natural interest in knowing the story of a book that we like: when and where and under what circumstances it was written. If the book happens to be a great popular success, our interest in its story is much greater. Of such a book much that is told is usually gossip or tradition, interesting no doubt, but not to be depended on. *Treasure Island* is a very popular book, interesting to boys and girls of sixteen or sixty, and the author himself has told us the circumstances of his writing it. Read for yourselves what he has said in "My First Book," found in the volume of his completed works called *Juvenalia*.

In the winter of 1881, Stevenson was living in Braemar, Scotland. Here his stepson, Lloyd Osbourne, came to spend his vacation. Like other small boys, he was sometimes restless for want of something to do. One day his stepfather joined him as he was trying to amuse himself by drawing pictures. From a boy Stevenson had been fond of drawing pictures and he entered into the fun with zest. Presently he began to draw the map of an island, and as he drew he saw an irregular coast line, bays and rivers, hills and valleys, trees and grassy slopes. To this creation he gave the name of Treasure Island.

As his imagination played further, he saw people inhabiting the island and engaging actively in various employments. Like the wide-awake author that he was, he began to jot down notes for the chapters of a story to be connected with the mysterious island. Many times before, he tells us, he had done the same thing and had gone no further. But this time he was interested to go on, and began to write at the rate of a chapter a day. It was, of course, for his stepson that he wrote, and the test of the story's value was whether it was interesting to the boy. But as the author read each night the chapter he had written that day, he aroused the interest of other members of the family. Stevenson's elderly father listened as carefully as the small boy for whom the story was written, and since he had spent a large part of his life building lighthouses along the rugged coast of Scotland, he knew about ships and the sea. There was something in the story, too, that appealed to the old man's delight in sport, in contest, in danger, and in victory, a delight that in many a man does not die even when his hair is white and his strength begins to weaken.

In spite of the author's enthusiasm at first, and in spite of his interested audience, he lost his inspiration after writing some fifteen chapters, and could not seem to go on. His friends feared that this promising story would go the way of others that he had begun, but never finished. Some months later, while in Switzerland, Stevenson took up the thread of his story again

and carried it to a successful and an enthusiastic conclusion.

At first he called the book *The Sea Cook*, from the
principal character, John Silver, in whom he took a
particular interest. For this character, he tells us, he
took an admired friend of his, deprived him of all his
finer qualities and higher graces of temperament, and
left him only his strength, his quickness, and his
magnificent geniality. The story was published serially
in "Our Young Folks," but attracted no special attention. A few months later, in November, 1883, it
appeared in book form and immediately became a
remarkable success. We are not surprised that boys
and girls found it interesting. But men, distinguished
men, judges, scholars, and business men, were as eager
as their sons and grandsons to get the book and devour
its contents. From that day to this, it has maintained
its popularity and proved itself an inspiration and a
delight to hundreds of thousands of boys and girls.
Moreover, it helped its author to go on with other
stories and gave him an ever-increasing audience.

—GILBERT SYKES BLAKELY

TO

## S. L. O.

AN AMERICAN GENTLEMAN,

IN ACCORDANCE WITH WHOSE CLASSIC TASTE

THE FOLLOWING NARRATIVE HAS BEEN DESIGNED,

IT IS NOW, IN RETURN FOR NUMEROUS DELIGHTFUL HOURS,

AND WITH THE KINDEST WISHES

*Dedicated*

BY HIS AFFECTIONATE FRIEND,

THE AUTHOR

# ROBERT LOUIS STEVENSON

When we find a book that interests us, it is natural for us to wish to learn about the author. If he lives near us, we wish to see him; if not, we read about him. Now Stevenson wrote many stories and essays that are interesting to older people as well as to younger, although many of them were written especially for boys and girls. More than this, his remarkable life is as interesting as his stories.

A sickly boy, he often had to lie in bed while others played, but he had a happy boyhood nevertheless, for he lived in a world created by his imagination. He never tired of listening to the tales told and read to him by his mother and his nurse. He was able to go to school very little and never for very long at a time, yet he was a highly educated man, for he had a quick mind and was untiring in his study of the subjects that he liked. He was born in Scotland and lived in England, France, Switzerland, America, and the Islands of the Pacific, and he died in far-off Samoa. He had an unusual power of making friends and made them freely in every place where he lived. The devotion of native chiefs to him in the islands of the South Seas was beautiful to see. Is it any wonder that a man who had such power for making friends and who had such wonderful experiences of travel should have been able to interest boys and girls and men and women in his wonderful tales?

Robert Louis Stevenson was born in Edinburgh, Scotland, November 13, 1850. His father, Thomas Stevenson, was a lighthouse engineer, as had been his father and his grandfather. His mother was the daughter of a clergyman in Colinton, near Edinburgh. Her health made it necessary to leave much of the care of her son to a nurse, Allison Cunningham, who proved to be an important influence in his life. She was very religious and very superstitious. Moreover, she had a great fund of stories and traditions of Scotland and of the land of the imagination peopled by fairies and spirits. She was also fond of poetry and captivated him by reading and reciting to him many poems that took hold on his imagination. As he grew older and stronger, he paid long visits to his grandfather's manse in Colinton where he played with his cousins and showed such inventive and imaginative power that by common consent he was their leader. Thus, in boyhood, he showed two distinct traits that became decidedly important to his success: his active imagination and his winning personality, which made for him warm friends wherever he went.

His father, a practical Scotchman, had decided ideas about his son's education. Proud of the family record in lighthouse engineering, he could think of no other calling for his only son. It made little difference that the boy cared nothing for mathematics, but only for reading and writing poetry and stories. Not until Robert was half through his course in Edinburgh University did he get his father's consent to give up engineering, a consent granted only on condition that he should study law in order that he might have something surer than literature to depend upon for his daily bread. Hence he studied law, was admitted to the bar, and hung on the door of his father's house the sign, "Robert Louis Stevenson, Advocate."

He had no desire, however, to practise law. But, living on a small allowance from his father, he proceeded to travel in England and France, constantly making friends and gathering material for his writing. His health, never very good, frequently necessitated periods of rest, changes of climate, and careful nursing. He wrote during these early years of young manhood, but he had little income, for there was small market for his writings. Stevenson was getting what was better than money, however, constant practice and wise criticism, for he had made many acquaintances among literary men who read and criticised his work and helped him with the keen interest of friends. One of his favorite haunts was with the artist colony at Gretz where he became acquainted with an American woman, a painter, who was destined to have an important influence on his life.

In 1879, there came a crisis in his affairs and he determined to leave Europe and try his fortunes in America. Mrs. Osbourne, his American painter-friend, had returned to her home in California. Contrary to the unanimous advice of his friends, and without the knowledge of his father, whose approval he knew he could not hope for, he sailed for America, "the land of promise." Traveling second class, he moved freely among the steerage passengers, showed his friendly spirit and learned many facts of their personal history, as well as their hopes and fears in coming to this new land of which they knew little and expected much. On landing in New York he spent one night in a small hotel on West Street, a friendless immigrant, and the next day started on a twelve-day journey to California in an immigrant train. His story of this long journey from England to California he has told in detail in *An Amateur Emigrant* and *Across the Plains.*

He arrived in San Francisco so worn out from travel that he went to the mountains below Monterey to camp by himself and try to regain his health. Here he was found by two kindly goat-herds who befriended him and nursed him back to health. Had it not been for them he would probably have died there, and the world would have never known of Robert Louis Stevenson. Later he found some newspaper work for which he was poorly paid, worked hard with little success, and all the time saw his small store of money growing smaller and smaller. But he kept his courage. He spent nearly a year in California, was married to Mrs. Osbourne, became reconciled to his father, who renewed his allowance of two hundred fifty pounds a year, and urged him to come home. Accordingly, just a year after he had sailed from Liverpool, with his wife he took the steamer in New York, bound for home.

For the next seven years he and his wife went from place to place in Scotland, in England, in Switzerland, and in France, always seeking to find some place where he could win in his fight against disease. All this time he was writing whenever he was not flat on his back, and even then his mind was active. It was during this time that he wrote *Treasure Island, Kidnapped, A Child's Garden of Verses*, and *Dr. Jekyll and Mr. Hyde*. Thus he established his reputation firmly in America as well as in England.

In spite of his long search for health during these seven years, it was evident at the end that he could not live long unless some other change of climate could be found. So it was agreed that he should try America again. It is interesting to compare this second visit with the first, taken eight years before. Then he was alone making his friends among the emigrants in the steerage. Now, with his wife and his mother, he traveled in comfort. Then his arrival was unheralded, and he spent the night in a small hotel near the docks. Now he was met and entertained by writers and publishers and other well-known men of New York. In eight years he had become famous.

He spent the winter rather uncomfortably in the cold climate of Saranac Lake, fighting disease, but always keeping cheerful and working hard. In the spring he conceived the idea of cruising among the islands of the Pacific. Accordingly he purchased a sailing yacht in San Francisco and spent most of the next three years sailing among the islands of the South Seas. Finally, he settled down in the Samoan Islands where he bought four hundred acres of land and built a house. The place he called, Vailima, Samoan for "five waters." Here he lived for the following three years. He so endeared to himself the natives that their love for him was strong and their grief at his death touching to behold. Here he died, December 3, 1894; and here he was buried on a high hill above his house.

Few literary men have left to posterity so many books of high order. Most of them he wrote during the last fourteen years of his life. But when we consider the handicaps under which he wrote during all those years, our wonder and admiration grow. In a letter to George Meredith written a year before his death he says: "For fourteen years I have not had a day's real health; I have wakened sick and gone to bed weary; and I have done my work unflinchingly. I have written in bed and written out of it, written in hemorrhages, written in sickness, written, torn by coughing, written when my head swam for weakness; and for so long, it seems to me I have won my wager and recovered my glove."

On the stone that marks his grave is cut Stevenson's own "Requiem."

> Under the wide and starry sky,
> Dig the grave and let me lie.
> Glad did I live and gladly die,
> And I laid me down with a will.
>
> This be the verse you grave for me:
> *Here he lies where he longed to be,*
> *Home is the sailor, home from the sea,*
> *And the hunter home from the hill.*

A Scale of 3 English Miles

Foremast Hill

North Inlet

Strong tide here

Spye glass hen when South about N.B.

glass going

Spyeglass Hill

Ro Sot Cove

Spring

Swamp

Graves

X Bulk of Treasure Swamp

Cape of ye Woods

White Rock

Mazenmast Hill

Skeleton Island

Hautbowline Head

Foul Ground

Treasure Island
Aug 1750 J.F.

Given G above J.F. & M.r W. Bones Maste of ye Walrus
Savannah this twenty July 1754 W. B.

Facsimile of Chart, latitude and
longitude struck out by J Hawkins

# PART I

## THE OLD BUCCANEER

### CHAPTER I

### THE OLD SEA-DOG AT THE ADMIRAL BENBOW

SQUIRE TRELAWNEY, Doctor Livesey, and the rest of these gentlemen having asked me to write down the whole particulars about Treasure Island, from the beginning to the end, keeping nothing back but the bearings of the island, and that only because there is still treasure not yet lifted, I take up my pen in the year of grace 17—, and go back to the time when my father kept the Admiral Benbow Inn, and the brown old seaman, with the saber-cut, first took up his lodging under our roof.

I remember him as if it were yesterday, as he came plodding to the inn door, his sea-chest following behind him in a hand-barrow; a tall, strong, heavy, nut-brown man; his tarry pig-tail falling over the shoulders of his soiled blue coat; his hands ragged and scarred, with black, broken nails, and the saber-cut across one cheek, a dirty, livid white. I remember him looking round the cove and whistling to himself

3

as he did so, and then breaking out in that old sea-
song that he sung so often afterward,

> "Fifteen men on the dead man's chest,
> Yo-ho-ho and a bottle of rum!"

in the high, old tottering voice that seemed to have
been tuned and broken at the capstan bars.  Then
he rapped on the door with a bit of stick like a handspike that he carried, and when my father appeared,
called roughly for a glass of rum.  This, when it was
brought to him, he drank slowly, like a connoisseur,
lingering on the taste, and still looking about him at
the cliffs and up at our signboard.

"This is a handy cove," said he, at length; "and
a pleasant sittyated grog-shop.  Much company,
mate?"

My father told him no, very little company, the
more was the pity.

"Well, then," said he, "this is the berth for me.
Here you, matey," he cried to the man who trundled
the barrow; "bring up alongside and help up my
chest.  I'll stay here a bit," he continued.  "I'm a
plain man; rum and bacon and eggs is what I want,
and that head up there for to watch ships off.  What
you mought call me?  You mought call me captain.
Oh, I see what you're at—there"; and he threw down
three or four gold pieces on the threshold.  "You
can tell me when I've worked through that," said he,
looking as fierce as a commander.

**All Day He Hung Round the Cove, or Upon the Cliffs, With a Brass Telescope.**

5

And, indeed, bad as his clothes were, and coarsely as he spoke, he had none of the appearance of a man who sailed before the mast, but seemed like a mate or skipper, accustomed to be obeyed or to strike. The man who came with the barrow told us the mail had set him down the morning before at the Royal George; that he had inquired what inns there were along the coast, and hearing ours well spoken of, I suppose, and described as lonely, had chosen it from the others for his place of residence. And that was all we could learn of our guest.

He was a very silent man by custom. All day he hung round the cove, or upon the cliffs, with a brass telescope; all evening he sat in a corner of the parlor next the fire, and drank rum and water very strong. Mostly he would not speak when spoken to; only look up sudden and fierce, and blow through his nose like a fog-horn; and we and the people who came about our house soon learned to let him be. Every day, when he came back from his stroll, he would ask if any seafaring men had gone by along the road. At first we thought it was the want of company of his own kind that made him ask this question; but at last we began to see he was desirous to avoid them. When a seaman put up at the Admiral Benbow (as now and then some did, making by the coast road for Bristol) he would look in at him through the curtained door before he entered the parlor; and he was always sure to be as silent as a mouse when any such was present. For me, at least, there was no secret about the matter: for I was, in a way, a sharer in his alarms.

He had taken me aside one day and promised me a silver fourpenny on the first of every month if I would only keep my "weather eye open for a seafaring man with one leg," and let him know the moment he appeared. Often enough, when the first of the month came round, and I applied to him for my wage, he would only blow through his nose at me, and stare me down, but before the week was out he was sure to think better of it, bring me my fourpenny piece, and repeat his orders to look out for "the seafaring man with one leg."

How that personage haunted my dreams, I need scarcely tell you. On stormy nights, when the wind shook the four corners of the house, and the surf roared along the cove and up the cliffs, I would see him in a thousand forms, and with a thousand diabolical expressions. Now the leg would be cut off at the knee, now at the hip; now he was a monstrous kind of a creature who had never had but the one leg, and that in the middle of his body. To see him leap and run and pursue me over hedge and ditch, was the worst of nightmares. And altogether I paid pretty dear for my monthly fourpenny piece in the shape of these abominable fancies.

But though I was so terrified by the idea of the seafaring man with one leg, I was far less afraid of the

captain himself than anybody else who knew him.
There were nights when he took a deal more rum
and water than his head would carry; and then he
would sometimes sit and sing his wicked, old, wild
sea-songs, minding nobody; but sometimes he would
call for glasses round, and force all the trembling
company to listen to his stories or bear a chorus to
his singing.  Often I have heard the house shaking
with "Yo-ho-ho and a bottle of rum," all the neighbors joining in for dear life, with the fear of death
upon them, and each singing louder than the other
to avoid remark.  For in these fits he was the most
overriding companion ever known; he would slap
his hand on the table for silence all round; he would
fly up in a passion of anger at a question, or sometimes because none was put, and so he judged the
company was not following his story.  Nor would
he allow anyone to leave the inn till he had drunk
himself sleepy and reeled off to bed.

His stories were what frightened people worst of
all.  Dreadful stories they were; about hanging, and
walking the plank, and storms at sea, and the Dry
Tortugas, and wild deeds and places on the Spanish
Main.  By his own account, he must have lived his
life among some of the wickedest men that God ever
allowed upon the sea; and the language in which he
told these stories shocked our plain country people
almost as much as the crimes that he described.
My father was always saying the inn would be ruined,

for people would soon cease coming there to be tyrannized over and put down, and sent shivering to their beds; but I really believe his presence did us good. People were frightened at the time, but on looking back they rather liked it; it was a fine excitement in a quiet country life; and there was even a party of the younger men who pretended to admire him, calling him a "true sea-dog," and a "real old salt," and such like names, and saying there was the sort of man that made England terrible at sea.

In one way, indeed, he bade fair to ruin us; for he kept on staying week after week, and at last month after month, so that all the money had been long exhausted, and still my father never plucked up the heart to insist on having more. If ever he mentioned it, the captain blew through his nose so loudly that you might say he roared, and stared my poor father out of the room. I have seen him wringing his hands after such a rebuff, and I am sure the annoyance and the terror he lived in must have greatly hastened his early and unhappy death.

All the time he lived with us the captain made no change whatever in his dress but to buy some stockings from a hawker. One of the cocks of his hat having fallen down, he let it hang from that day forth, though it was a great annoyance when it blew. I remember the appearance of his coat, which he patched himself upstairs in his room, and which, before the end, was nothing but patches. He never wrote or received a letter, and he never spoke with any but the neighbors, and with these, for the most part, only when drunk on rum. The great sea-chest none of us had ever seen open.

He was only once crossed, and that was toward the end, when my poor father was far gone in a decline that took him off. Doctor Livesey came late one afternoon to see the patient, took a bit of dinner from my mother, and went into the parlor to smoke a pipe until his horse should come down from the hamlet, for we had no stabling at the old Benbow. I followed him in, and I remember observing the contrast the neat, bright doctor, with his powder as white as snow, and his bright, black eyes and pleasant manners, made with the coltish country folk, and above all, with that filthy, heavy, bleared scarecrow of a pirate of ours, sitting far gone in rum, with his arms on the table. Suddenly he—the captain, that is—began to pipe up his eternal song:

"Fifteen men on the dead man's chest—
  Yo-ho-ho and a bottle of rum!
Drink and the devil had done for the rest—
  Yo-ho-ho and a bottle of rum!"

At first I had supposed "the dead man's chest" to be that identical big box of his upstairs in the front room, and the thought had been mingled in my nightmares with that of the one-legged seafaring man. But by this time we had all long ceased to pay any particular notice to the song; it was new, that night, to nobody but Doctor Livesey, and on him I observed it did not produce an agreeable effect, for he looked up for a moment quite angrily before he went on with his talk to old Taylor the gardener, on a new cure for rheumatics. In the meantime the captain gradually brightened up at his own music, and at last flapped his hand upon the table before him in a way we all knew to mean—silence. The voices stopped at once, all but Doctor Livesey's; he went on as before, speaking clear and kind, and drawing briskly at his pipe between every word or two. The captain glared at him for awhile, flapped his hand again, glared still harder, and at last broke out with a villainous low oath: "Silence, there, between decks!"

"Were you addressing me, sir?" said the doctor; and when the ruffian had told him, with another oath, that this was so, replied, "I have only one thing to say to you, sir, that if you keep on drinking rum, the world will soon be quit of a very dirty scoundrel!"

The old fellow's fury was awful. He sprang to his feet, drew and opened a sailor's clasp-knife, and balancing it open on the palm of his hand, threatened to pin the doctor to the wall.

The doctor never so much as moved. He spoke to him, as before, over his shoulder, and in the same tone of voice, rather high, so that all the room might hear, but perfectly calm and steady:

"If you do not put that knife this instant into

your pocket, I promise, upon my honor, you shall hang at the next assizes."

Then followed a battle of looks between them; but the captain soon knuckled under, put up his weapon, and resumed his seat, grumbling like a beaten dog.

"And now, sir," continued the doctor, "since I now know there's such a fellow in my district, you may count I'll have an eye upon you day and night. I'm not a doctor only, I'm a magistrate; and if I catch a breath of complaint against you, if it's only for a piece of incivility like to-night's, I'll take effectual means to have you hunted down and routed out of this. Let that suffice."

Soon after Doctor Livesey's horse came to the door and he rode away, but the captain held his peace that evening, and for many evenings to come.

## CHAPTER II

## BLACK DOG APPEARS AND DISAPPEARS

IT was not very long after this that there occurred the first of the mysterious events that rid us at last of the captain, though not, as you will see, of his affairs. It was a bitter cold winter, with long, hard frosts and heavy gales; and it was plain from the first that my poor father was little likely to see the spring. He sunk daily, and my mother and I had all the inn upon our hands, and were kept busy enough without paying much regard to our unpleasant guest.

It was one January morning, very early—a pinching, frosty morning—the cove all gray with hoarfrost, the ripple lapping softly on the stones, the sun still low, and only touching the hill-tops and shining far to seaward. The captain had risen earlier than usual, and set out down the beach, his cutlass swinging under the broad skirts of the old blue coat, his brass telescope under his arm, his hat tilted back upon his head. I remember his breath hanging like smoke in his wake as he strode off, and the last sound I heard of him, as he turned the big rock, was a loud snort of indignation, as though his mind was still running upon Doctor Livesey.

13

Well, mother was upstairs with father, and I was laying the breakfast table against the captain's return, when the parlor door opened and a man stepped in on whom I had never set my eyes before. He was a pale, tallowy creature, wanting two fingers of the left hand; and, though he wore a cutlass, he did not look much like a fighter. I had always my eyes open for seafaring men, with one leg or two, and I remember this one puzzled me. He was not sailorly, and yet he had a smack of the sea about him too.

I asked him what was for his service, and he said he would take rum, but as I was going out of the room to fetch it he sat down upon a table and motioned to me to draw near. I paused where I was with my napkin in my hand.

"Come here, sonny," said he. "Come nearer here."

I took a step nearer.

"Is this here table for my mate Bill?" he asked, with a kind of leer.

I told him I did not know his mate Bill, and this was for a person who stayed at our house, whom we called the captain.

"Well," said he, "my mate Bill would be called the captain, as like as not. He has a cut on one cheek, and a mighty pleasant way with him, particularly in drink, has my mate Bill. We'll put it, for argument like, that your captain has a cut on one cheek—and we'll put it, if you like, that that cheek's the right one. Ah, well! I told you. Now, is my mate Bill in this here house?"

I told him he was out walking.

"Which way, sonny? Which way is he gone?"

And when I had pointed out the rock and told him how the captain was likely to return, and how soon, and answered a few other questions, "Ah," said he, "this'll be as good as drink to my mate Bill."

The expression of his face as he said these words was not at all pleasant, and I had my own reasons for thinking that the stranger was mistaken, even supposing he meant what he said. But it was no affair of mine, I thought; and, besides, it was difficult to know what to do. The stranger kept hanging about just inside the inn door, peering round the corner like a cat waiting for a mouse. Once I stepped out myself into the road, but he immediately called me back, and, as I did not obey quick enough for his fancy, a most horrible change came over his tallowy face, and he ordered me in with an oath that made me jump.

As soon as I was back again he returned to his former manner, half-fawning, half-sneering, patted me on the shoulder, told me I was a good boy, and he had taken quite a fancy to me. "I have a son of my own," said he, "as like you as two blocks, and he's all the pride of my 'art. But the great thing for boys is discipline, sonny—discipline. Now, if you had sailed along of Bill, you wouldn't have stood there to be spoke to twice—not you.  That was never Bill's way, nor the way of sich as sailed with him.  And here, sure enough, is my mate Bill, with a spy-glass under his arm, bless his old 'art, to be sure.  You and me'll just go back into the parlor, sonny, and get behind the door, and we'll give Bill a little surprise—bless his 'art, I say again."

So saying, the stranger backed along with me into the parlor, and put me behind him in the corner, so that we were both hidden by the open door.  I was very uneasy and alarmed, as you may fancy, and it rather added to my fears to observe that the stranger was certainly frightened himself.  He cleared the hilt of his cutlass and loosened the blade in the sheath, and all the time we were waiting there he kept swallowing as if he felt what we used to call a lump in the throat.

At last in strode the captain, slammed the door behind him, without looking to the right or left, and marched straight across the room to where his breakfast awaited him.

"Bill," said the stranger, in a voice that I thought he had tried to make bold and big.

The captain spun round on his heel and fronted us; all the brown had gone out of his face, and even his nose was blue; he had the look of a man who sees a ghost, or the Evil One, or something worse, if anything can be; and, upon my word, I felt sorry to see him, all in a moment, turn so old and sick.

"Come, Bill, you know me; you know an old ship-mate, Bill, surely," said the stranger.

The captain made a sort of gasp.

"Black Dog!" said he.

"And who else?" returned the other, getting more at his ease. "Black Dog as ever was, come for to see his old shipmate, Billy, at the Admiral Benbow Inn. Ah, Bill, Bill, we have seen a sight of times, us two, since I lost them two talons," holding up his mutilated hand.

"Now, look here," said the captain; "you've run me down; here I am; well, then, speak up; what is it?"

"That's you, Bill," returned Black Dog; "you're in the right of it, Billy. I'll have a glass of rum from this dear child here, as I've took such a liking to; and we'll sit down, if you please, and talk square, like old shipmates."

When I returned with the rum they were already seated on either side of the captain's breakfast table—Black Dog next to the door, and sitting sideways, so as to have one eye on his old shipmate and one, as I thought, on his retreat.

He bade me go and leave the door wide open. "None of your key-holes for me, sonny," he said, and I left them together and retired into the bar.

For a long time, though I certainly did my best to listen, I could hear nothing but a low gabbling; but at last the voices began to grow higher, and I could pick up a word or two, mostly oaths, from the captain.

"No, no, no, no; and an end of it!" he cried once. And again, "If it comes to swinging, swing all, say I."

Then all of a sudden there was a tremendous explosion of oaths and other noises; the chair and table went over in a lump, a clash of steel followed, and then a cry of pain, and the next instant I saw Black Dog in full flight, and the captain hotly pursuing, both with drawn cutlasses, and the former streaming blood from the left shoulder. Just at the door the captain aimed at the fugitive one last tremendous cut, which would certainly have split him to the chine had it not been intercepted by our big signboard of Admiral Benbow. You may see the notch on the lower side of the frame to this day.

That blow was the last of the battle. Once out upon the road, Black Dog, in spite of his wound, showed a wonderful clean pair of heels, and disappeared over the edge of the hill in half a minute. The captain, for his part, stood staring at the signboard like a bewildered man. Then he passed his hand over his eyes several times, and at last turned back into the house.

"Jim," says he, "rum"; and as he spoke he reeled a little, and caught himself with one hand against the wall.

"Are you hurt?" cried I.

"Rum," he repeated. "I must get away from here. Rum! rum!"

I ran to fetch it, but I was quite unsteadied by all that had fallen out, and I broke one glass and fouled the tap, and while I was still getting in my own way, I heard a loud fall in the parlor, and, running in, beheld the captain lying full length upon the floor. At the same instant my mother, alarmed by the cries and fighting, came running downstairs to help me. Between us we raised his head. He was breathing very loud and hard, but his eyes were closed and his face was a horrible color.

"Dear, deary me!" cried my mother, "what a disgrace upon the house! And your poor father sick!"

In the meantime we had no idea what to do to help the captain, nor any other thought but that he had got his death-hurt in the scuffle with the stranger. I got the rum, to be sure, and tried to put it down his throat, but his teeth were tightly shut, and his jaws as strong as iron. It was a happy relief for us when the door opened and Doctor Livesey came in, on his visit to my father.

"Oh, doctor," we cried, "what shall we do? Where is he wounded?"

"Wounded? A fiddle-stick's end!" said the doctor. "No more wounded than you or I. The man has had a stroke, as I warned him. Now, Mrs. Hawkins, just you run upstairs to your husband and tell him, if possible, nothing about it. For my part, I must do my best to save this fellow's trebly worth-less life; and Jim here will get me a basin."

When I got back with the basin the doctor had already ripped up the captain's sleeve and exposed his great sinewy arm. It was tattooed in several places. "Here's luck," "A fair wind," and "Billy Bones, his fancy," were very neatly and clearly exe-cuted on the forearm; and up near the shoulder there was a sketch of a gallows and a man hanging from it—done, as I thought, with great spirit.

"Prophetic," said the doctor, touching this picture with his finger. "And now, Master Billy Bones, if that be your name, we'll have a look at the color of your blood. Jim," he said, "are you afraid of blood?"

"No, sir," said I.

"Well, then," said he, "you hold the basin," and with that he took his lancet and opened a vein.

A great deal of blood was taken before the captain opened his eyes and looked mistily about him. First he recognized the doctor with an unmistakable frown; then his glance fell upon me, and he looked relieved. But suddenly his color changed, and he tried to raise himself, crying:

"Where's Black Dog?"

"There is no Black Dog here," said the doctor, "except what you have on your own back. You have been drinking rum; you have had a stroke precisely as I told you; and I have just, very much against my own will, dragged you headforemost out of the grave. Now, Mr. Bones——"

"That's not my name," he interrupted.

"Much I care," returned the doctor. "It's the name of a buccaneer of my acquaintance, and I call you by it for the sake of shortness, and what I have to say to you is this: One glass of rum won't kill you, but if you take one you'll take another and another, and I stake my wig if you don't break off short, you'll die; do you understand that? die, and go to your own place, like the man in the Bible. Come, now, make an effort. I'll help you to your bed for once."

Between us, with much trouble, we managed to hoist him upstairs, and laid him on his bed, where his head fell back on the pillow, as if he were almost fainting.

"Now, mind you," said the doctor, "I clear my conscience—the name of rum for you is death."

And with that he went off to see my father, taking me with him by the arm.

"This is nothing," he said, as soon as he had closed the door. "I have drawn blood enough to keep him quiet awhile; he should lie for a week where he is—that is the best thing for him and you, but another stroke would settle him."

## CHAPTER III

## THE BLACK SPOT

ABOUT noon I stopped at the captain's door with some cooling drinks and medicines. He was lying very much as we had left him, only a little higher, and he seemed both weak and excited.

"Jim," he said, "you're the only one here that's worth anything; and you know I've always been good to you. Never a month but I've given you a silver fourpenny for yourself. And now you see, mate, I'm pretty low, and deserted by all; and Jim, you'll bring me one noggin of rum, now won't you, matey?"

"The doctor——" I began.

But he broke in cursing the doctor, in a feeble voice, but heartily. "Doctors is all swabs," he said; "and that doctor there, why, what do he know about seafaring men? I been in places hot as pitch, and mates dropping round with Yellow Jack, and the blessed land a-heaving like the sea with earthquakes —what do the doctor know of lands like that?—and I lived on rum, I tell you. It's been meat and drink, and man and wife, to me; and if I am not to have my rum now I'm a poor old hulk on a lee shore. My blood'll be on you, Jim, and that doctor swab," and he ran on again for awhile with curses. "Look, Jim,

22

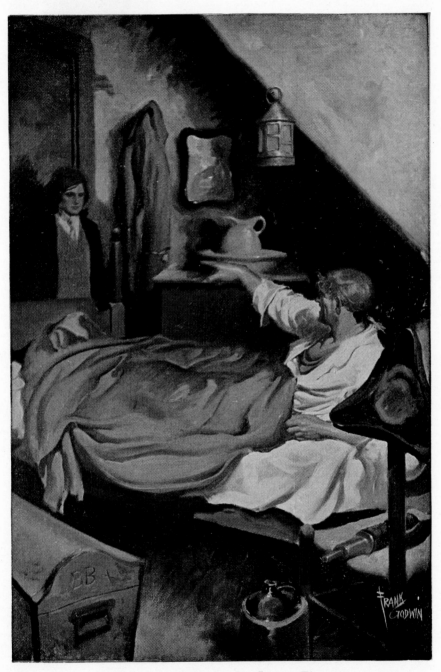

"I Seen Old Flint in the Corner There."

how my fingers fidges," he continued in the pleading tone. "I can't keep 'em still, not I. I haven't had a drop this blessed day. That doctor's a fool, I tell you. If I don't have a drain o' rum, Jim, I'll have the horrors; I seen some on 'em already. I seen old Flint in the corner there, behind you; as plain as print, I seen him; and if I get the horrors, I'm a man that has lived rough, and I'll raise Cain. Your doctor hisself said one glass wouldn't hurt me. I'll give you a golden guinea for a noggin, Jim."

He was growing more and more excited, and this alarmed me, for my father, who was very low that day, needed quiet; besides, I was reassured by the doctor's words, now quoted to me, and rather offended by the offer of a bribe.

"I want none of your money," said I, "but what you owe my father. I'll get you one glass and no more."

When I brought it to him he seized it greedily and drank it out.

"Aye, aye," said he, "that's some better, sure enough. And now, matey, did the doctor say how long I was to lie here in this old berth?"

"A week at least," said I.

"Thunder!" he cried. "A week! I can't do that; they'd have a black spot on me by then. The lubbers is going about to get the wind of me this blessed moment; lubbers as couldn't keep what they got, and want to nail what is another's. Is that seamanly behavior, now, I want to know? But I'm a saving soul. I never wasted good money of mine, nor lost it neither; and I'll trick 'em again. I'm not afraid on 'em. I'll shake out another reef, matey, and daddle 'em again."

As he was thus speaking, he had risen from bed with great difficulty, holding to my shoulder with a grip that almost made me cry out, and moving his legs like so much dead weight. His words, spirited as they were in meaning, contrasted sadly with the weakness of the voice in which they were uttered. He paused when he had got into a sitting position on the edge.

"That doctor's done me," he murmured. "My ears is singing. Lay me back."

Before I could do much to help him he had fallen back again to his former place, where he lay for awhile silent.

"Jim," he said, at length, "you saw that seafaring man to-day?"

"Black Dog?" I asked.

"Ah! Black Dog," said he. "*He's* a bad 'un; but there's worse that put him on. Now, if I can't get away nohow, and they tip me the black spot, mind you, it's my old sea-chest they're after; you get on a horse—you can, can't you? Well, then, you get on a horse and go to—well, yes, I will!—to that eternal doctor swab, and tell him to pipe all hands—magistrates and sich—and he'll lay 'em aboard at the Admiral Benbow—all old Flint's crew, man and boy, all on 'em that's left. I was first mate, I was, old Flint's first mate, and I'm the on'y one as knows the place. He gave it me to Savannah, when he lay a-dying, like as if I was to now, you see. But you won't peach unless they get the black spot on me, or unless you see that Black Dog again, or a seafaring man with one leg, Jim—him above all."

"But what is the black spot, captain?" I asked.

"That's a summons, mate. I'll tell you if they get that. But you keep your weather-eye open, Jim, and I'll share with you equals, upon my honor."

He wandered a little longer, his voice growing weaker; but soon after I had given him his medicine, which he took like a child, with the remark, "If ever a seaman wanted drugs, it's me," he fell at last into a heavy swoon-like sleep, in which I left him. What I should have done had all gone well I do not know. Probably I should have told the whole story to the doctor; for I was in mortal fear lest the captain should repent of his confessions and make an end of me. But as things fell out, my poor father died quite suddenly that evening, which put all other matters on one side. Our natural distress, the visits of the neighbors, the arranging of the funeral, and all the work of the inn to be carried on in the meanwhile, kept me so busy that I had scarcely time to think of the captain, far less to be afraid of him.

He got downstairs next morning, to be sure, and had his meals as usual, though he eat little, and had

more, I am afraid, than his usual supply of rum, for
he helped himself out of the bar, scowling and blowing through his nose, and no one dared to cross him.
On the night before the funeral he was as drunk as
ever; and it was shocking, in that house of mourning,
to hear him singing away his ugly old sea-song; but
weak as he was, we were all in fear of death for him,
and the doctor was suddenly taken up with a case
many miles away, and was never near the house after
my father's death.  I have said the captain was
weak, and indeed he seemed rather to grow weaker
than to regain his strength.  He clambered up and
down stairs, and went from the parlor to the bar and
back again, and sometimes put his nose out-of-doors
to smell the sea, holding on to the walls as he went
for support, and breathing hard and fast, like a man
on a steep mountain.  He never particularly addressed me, and it is my belief he had as good as forgotten his confidences; but his temper was more
flighty, and, allowing for his bodily weakness, more
violent than ever.  He had an alarming way now
when he was drunk of drawing his cutlass and laying
it bare before him on the table.  But with all that,
he minded people less, and seemed shut up in his
own thoughts and rather wandering.  Once, for instance, to our extreme wonder, he piped up to a
different air, a kind of country love-song, that he must
have learned in his youth before he had begun to
follow the sea.

So things passed until the day after the funeral and about three o'clock of a bitter, foggy, frosty afternoon, I was standing at the door for a moment, full of sad thoughts about my father, when I saw someone drawing slowly near along the road. He was plainly blind, for he tapped before him with a stick, and wore a great green shade over his eyes and nose; and he was hunched, as if with age or weakness, and wore a huge old tattered sea-cloak with a hood that made him appear positively deformed. I never saw in my life a more dreadful-looking figure. He stopped a little from the inn and, raising his voice in an old sing-song, addressed the air in front of him:

"Will any kind friend inform a poor blind man, who has lost the precious sight of his eyes in the gracious defense of his native country, England, and God bless King George!—where or in what part of this country he may now be?"

"You are at the Admiral Benbow, Black Hill Cove, my good man," said I.

"I hear a voice," said he, "a young voice. Will you give me your hand, my kind young friend, and lead me in?"

I held out my hand, and the horrible, soft-spoken, eyeless creature gripped it in a moment like a vise. I was so much startled that I struggled to withdraw, but the blind man pulled me close up to him with a single action of his arm.

"Now, boy," he said, "take me in to the captain."

"Sir," said I, "upon my word I dare not."

"Oh," he sneered, "that's it! Take me in straight, or I'll break your arm."

He gave it, as he spoke, a wrench that made me cry out.

"Sir," said I, "it is for yourself I mean. The captain is not what he used to be. He sits with a drawn cutlass. Another gentleman——"

"Come, now, march," interrupted he, and I never heard a voice so cruel, and cold, and ugly as that blind man's. It cowed me more than the pain, and I began to obey him at once, walking straight in at the door and toward the parlor, where the sick old buccaneer was sitting, dazed with rum. The blind man clung close to me, holding me in one iron fist, and leaning almost more of his weight on me than I could carry. "Lead me straight up to him, and when I'm in view, cry out, 'Here's a friend for you, Bill.' If you don't, I'll do this," and with that he gave me a twitch that I thought would have made me faint. Between this and that, I was so utterly terrified by the blind beggar that I forgot my terror of the captain, and as I opened the parlor door, cried out the words he had ordered in a trembling voice.

The poor captain raised his eyes, and at one look the rum went out of him and left him staring sober. The expression of his face was not so much of terror as of mortal sickness. He made a movement to rise,

"Now, Boy," He Said, "Take Me in to the Captain."

but I do not believe he had enough force left in his body.

"Now, Bill, sit where you are," said the beggar. "If I can't see, I can hear a finger stirring. Business is business. Hold out your left hand. Boy, take his left hand by the wrist and bring it near to my right."

We both obeyed him to the letter, and I saw him pass something from the hollow of the hand that held his stick into the palm of the captain's, which closed upon it instantly.

"And now that's done," said the blind man, and at the words he suddenly left hold of me, and with incredible accuracy and nimbleness, skipped out of the parlor and into the road, where, as I stood motionless, I could hear his stick go tap-tap-tapping into the distance.

It was some time before either I or the captain seemed to gather our senses; but at length, and about the same moment, I released his wrist, which I was still holding, and he drew in his hand, and looked sharply into the palm.

"Ten o'clock!" he cried. "Six hours! We'll do them yet!" and he sprung to his feet.

Even as he did so, he reeled, put his hand to his throat, stood swaying for a moment, and then, with a peculiar sound, fell from his whole height face foremost to the floor.

I ran to him at once, calling to my mother. But

haste was all in vain. The captain had been struck dead by thundering apoplexy. It is a curious thing to understand, for I had certainly never liked the man, though of late I had begun to pity him, but as soon as I saw that he was dead I burst into a flood of tears. It was the second death I had known, and the sorrow of the first was still fresh in my heart.

## CHAPTER IV

## THE SEA-CHEST

I LOST no time, of course, in telling my mother all that I knew, and perhaps should have told her long before, and we saw ourselves at once in a difficult and dangerous position. Some of the man's money—if he had any—was certainly due to us, but it was not likely that our captain's shipmates, above all, the two specimens seen by me—Black Dog and the blind beggar—would be inclined to give up their booty in payment of the dead man's debts. The captain's order to mount at once and ride for Doctor Livesey would have left my mother alone and unprotected, which was not to be thought of. Indeed, it seemed impossible for either of us to remain much longer in the house; the fall of coals in the kitchen grate, the very ticking of the clock, filled us with alarm.

The neighborhood, to our ears, seemed haunted by approaching footsteps; and what between the dead body of the captain on the parlor floor and the thought of that detestable blind beggar hovering near at hand and ready to return, there were moments when, as the saying goes, I jumped in my skin for terror. Something must speedily be resolved upon, and it occurred to us at last to go forth together and seek help in the neighboring hamlet. No sooner said than done. Bare-headed as we were, we ran out at once in the gathering evening and the frosty fog.

The hamlet lay not many hundred yards away, though out of view, on the other side of the next cove; and what greatly encouraged me, it was in an opposite direction from that whence the blind man had made his appearance, and whither he had presumably returned. We were not many minutes on the road, though we sometimes stopped to lay hold of each other and hearken. But there was no unusual sound—nothing but the low wash of the ripple and the croaking of the crows in the wood.

It was already candle-light when we reached the hamlet, and I shall never forget how much I was cheered to see the yellow shine in doors and windows; but that, as it proved, was the best of the help we were likely to get in that quarter. For—you would have thought men would have been ashamed of themselves—no soul would consent to return with us to the Admiral Benbow. The more we told of our troubles, the more—man, woman, and child—they clung to the shelter of their houses. The name of Captain Flint, though it was strange to me, was well enough known to some there, and carried a great weight of terror. Some of the men who had been to field-work on the far side of the Admiral Benbow remembered, besides, to have seen several strangers on the road, and, taking them to be smugglers, to have bolted away; and one at least had seen a little lugger in what we called Kitt's Hole. For that matter, anyone who was a comrade of the captain's was enough to frighten them to death. And the short and the long of the matter was, that while we could get several who were willing enough to ride to Doctor Livesey's, which lay in another direction, not one would help us to defend the inn.

They say cowardice is infectious; but then argument is, on the other hand, a great emboldener; and so when each had his say, my mother made them a speech. She would not, she declared, lose money that belonged to her fatherless boy. "If none of the rest of you dare," she said, "Jim and I dare. Back we will go, the way we came, and small thanks to you big, hulking, chicken-hearted men! We'll have that chest open, if we die for it. And I'll thank you for that bag, Mrs. Crossley, to bring back our lawful money in."

Of course I said I would go with my mother; and of course they all cried out at our foolhardiness; but even then not a man would go along with us. All they would do was to give me a loaded pistol, lest we were attacked; and to promise to have horses ready saddled, in case we were pursued on our return; while one lad was to ride forward to the doctor's in search of armed assistance.

My heart was beating fiercely when we two set forth in the cold night upon this dangerous venture. A full moon was beginning to rise and peered redly

through the upper edges of the fog, and this increased
our haste, for it was plain, before we came forth again,
that all would be bright as day, and our departure
exposed to the eyes of any watchers. We slipped
along the hedges, noiseless and swift, nor did we see
or hear anything to increase our terrors till, to our
huge relief, the door of the Admiral Benbow had closed
behind us.

I slipped the bolt at once, and we stood and panted
for a moment in the dark, alone in the house with the
dead captain's body. Then my mother got a candle
in the bar, and, holding each other's hands, we advanced into the parlor. He lay as we had left him,
on his back, with his eyes open, and one arm stretched
out.

"Draw down the blind, Jim," whispered my
mother; "they might come and watch outside. And
now," said she, when I had done so, "we have to
get the key off *that*; and who's to touch it, I should
like to know?" and she gave a kind of sob as she said
the words.

I went down on my knees at once. On the floor
close to his hand there was a little round of paper,
blackened on one side. I could not doubt that this
was the *black spot*; and, taking it up, I found written
on the other side, in a very good, clear hand, this
short message, "You have till ten to-night."

"He had till ten, mother," said I; and, just as I
said it, our old clock began striking. This sudden

noise startled us shockingly; but the news was good, for it was only six.

"Now, Jim," she said, "that key!"

I felt in his pockets, one after another. A few small coins, a thimble, and some thread and big needles, a piece of pigtail tobacco bitten away at the end, his gully with the crooked handle, a pocket compass, and a tinder-box, were all that they contained, and I began to despair.

"Perhaps it's round his neck," suggested my mother.

Overcoming a strong repugnance, I tore open his shirt at the neck, and there, sure enough, hanging to a bit of tarry string, which I cut with his own gully, we found the key. At this triumph we were filled with hope, and hurried upstairs, without delay, to the little room where he had slept so long, and where his box had stood since the day of his arrival.

It was like any other seaman's chest on the outside, the initial "B" burned on the top of it with a hot iron, and the corners somewhat smashed and broken as by long, rough usage.

"Give me the key," said my mother, and though the lock was very stiff, she had turned it and thrown back the lid in a twinkling.

A strong smell of tobacco and tar arose from the interior, but nothing was to be seen on the top except a suit of very good clothes, carefully brushed and folded. They had never been worn, my mother said.

Under that the miscellany began—a quadrant, a tin canikin, several sticks of tobacco, two brace of very handsome pistols, a piece of bar silver, an old Spanish watch, and some other trinkets of little value and mostly of foreign make, a pair of compasses mounted with brass, and five or six curious West Indian shells. It has often set me thinking since that he should have carried about these shells with him in his wandering, guilty, haunted life.

In the meantime we found nothing of any value but the silver and the trinkets, and neither of these were in our way. Underneath there was an old boat-cloak, whitened with sea-salt on many a harbor-bar. My mother pulled it up with impatience, and there lay before us, the last things in the chest, a bundle tied up in oil-cloth, and looking like papers, and a canvas bag that gave forth, at a touch, the jingle of gold.

"I'll show those rogues that I'm an honest woman," said my mother. "I'll have my dues and not a farthing over. Hold Mrs. Crossley's bag." And she began to count over the amount of the captain's score from the sailor's bag into the one that I was holding.

It was a long, difficult business, for the coins were of all countries and sizes—doubloons, and louis-d'ors, and guineas, and pieces of eight, and I know not what besides, all shaken together at random. The guineas, too, were about the scarcest, and it was with these only that my mother knew how to make her count.

When we were about halfway through, I suddenly put my hands upon her arm, for I had heard in the silent, frosty air, a sound that brought my heart into my mouth—the tap-tapping of the blind man's stick upon the frozen road. It drew nearer and nearer, while we sat holding our breath. Then it struck sharp on the inn door, and then we could hear the handle being turned, and the bolt rattling as the wretched being tried to enter; and then there was a long time of silence both within and without. At last the tapping recommenced, and to our indescribable joy and gratitude, died slowly away again until it ceased to be heard.

"Mother," said I, "take the whole and let's be going," for I was sure the bolted door must have seemed suspicious, and would bring the whole hornet's nest about our ears, though how thankful I was that I had bolted it, none could tell who had never met that terrible blind man.

But my mother, frightened as she was, would not consent to take a fraction more than was due to her, and was obstinately unwilling to be content with less. It was not yet seven, she said, by a long way; she knew her rights and she would have them; and she was still arguing with me, when a little low whistle sounded a good way off upon the hill. That was enough, and more than enough, for both of us.

**"And I'll Take This to Square the Count," Said I.**

"I'll take what I have," she said, jumping to her feet.

"And I'll take this to square the count," said I, picking up the oilskin packet.

Next moment we were both groping downstairs, leaving the candle by the empty chest; and the next we had opened the door and were in full retreat. We had not started a moment too soon. The fog was rapidly dispersing; already the moon shone quite clear on the high ground on either side, and it was only in the exact bottom of the dell and round the tavern door that a thin veil still hung unbroken to conceal the first steps of our escape. Far less than halfway to the hamlet, very little beyond the bottom of the hill, we must come forth into the moonlight. Nor was this all; for the sound of several footsteps running came already to our ears, and as we looked back in their direction, a light, tossing to and fro, and still rapidly advancing, showed that one of the newcomers carried a lantern.

"My dear," said my mother, suddenly, "take the money and run on. I am going to faint."

This was certainly the end for both of us, I thought. How I cursed the cowardice of the neighbors! how I blamed my poor mother for her honesty and her greed; for her past foolhardiness and present weakness! We were just at the little bridge, by good fortune, and I helped her, tottering as she was, to the edge of the bank, where, sure enough, she gave a sigh and fell on my shoulder. I do not know how I found the strength to do it all, and I am afraid it was roughly done, but I managed to drag her down the bank and a little way under the arch. Farther I could not move her, for the bridge was too low to let me do more than crawl below it. So there we had to stay—my mother almost entirely exposed, and both of us within ear-shot of the inn.

## CHAPTER V

## THE LAST OF THE BLIND MAN

**M**Y curiosity, in a sense, was stronger than my fear; for I could not remain where I was, but crept back to the bank again, whence, sheltering my head behind a bush of broom, I might command the road before our door. I was scarcely in position ere my enemies began to arrive, seven or eight of them, running hard, their feet beating out of time along the road, and the man with the lantern some paces in front. Three men ran together, hand in hand, and I made out, even through the mist, that the middle man of this trio was the blind beggar. The next moment his voice showed me that I was right.

"Down with the door!" he cried.

"Aye, aye, sir!" answered two or three; and a rush was made upon the Admiral Benbow, the lantern-bearer following; and then I could see them pause, and hear speeches passed in a lower key, as if they were surprised to find the door open. But the pause was brief, for the blind man again issued his commands. His voice sounded louder and higher, as if he were afire with eagerness and rage.

"In, in, in!" he shouted, and cursed them for their delay.

42

Four or five of them obeyed at once, two remaining on the road with the formidable beggar. There was a pause, then a cry of surprise, and then a voice shouting from the house:

"Bill's dead!"

But the blind man swore at them again for their delay.

"Search him, some of you shirking lubbers, and the rest of you aloft and get the chest," he cried.

I could hear their feet rattling up our old stairs, so that the house must have shook with it. Promptly afterward fresh sounds of astonishment arose; the window of the captain's room was thrown open with a slam and a jingle of broken glass, and a man leaned out into the moonlight, head and shoulders, and addressed the blind beggar on the road below him.

"Pew!" he cried, "they've been before us. Someone's turned the chest out alow and aloft."

"Is it there?" roared Pew.

"The money's there."

The blind man cursed the money.

"Flint's fist, I mean," he cried.

"We don't see it here, nohow," returned the man.

"Here, you below here, is it on Bill?" cried the blind man again.

At that another fellow, probably him who had remained below to search the captain's body, came to the door of the inn. "Bill's been overhauled a'ready," said he, "nothin' left."

"It's these people of the inn—it's that boy. I wish I had put his eyes out!" cried the blind man, Pew. "They were here no time ago—they had the door bolted when I tried it. Scatter, lads, and find 'em."

"Sure enough, they left their glim here," said the fellow from the window.

"Scatter and find 'em! Rout the house out!" reiterated Pew, striking with his stick upon the road.

Then there followed a great to-do through all our old inn, heavy feet pounding to and fro, furniture all thrown over, doors kicked in, until the very rocks re-echoed, and the men came out again, one after another, on the road, and declared that we were nowhere to be found. And just then the same whistle that had alarmed my mother and myself over the dead captain's money was once more clearly audible through the night, but this time twice repeated. I had thought it to be the blind man's trumpet, so to speak, summoning his crew to the assault; but I now found that it was a signal from the hillside toward the hamlet, and from its effect upon the buccaneers, a signal to warn them of approaching danger.

"There's Dirk again," said one. "Twice! We'll have to budge, mates."

"Budge, you skulk!" cried Pew. "Dirk was a fool and a coward from the first—you wouldn't mind him. They must be close by; they can't be far; you have your hands on it. Scatter and look for them, dogs. Oh, shiver my soul," he cried, "if I had eyes!"

This appeal seemed to produce some effect, for two of the fellows began to look here and there among the lumber, but half-heartedly, I thought, and with half an eye to their own danger all the time, while the rest stood irresolute on the road.

"You have your hands on thousands, you fools, and you hang a leg! You'd be as rich as kings if you could find it, and you know it's here, and you stand there malingering. There wasn't one of you dared face Bill, and I did it—a blind man! And I'm to lose my chance for you! I'm to be a poor, crawling beggar, sponging for rum, when I might be rolling in a coach! If you had the pluck of a weevil in a biscuit, you would catch them still."

"Hang it, Pew, we've got the doubloons!" grumbled one.

"They might have hid the blessed thing," said another. "Take the Georges, Pew, and don't stand here squalling."

Squalling was the word for it; Pew's anger rose so high at these objections, till at last, his passion completely taking the upper hand, he struck at them right and left in his blindness, and his stick sounded heavily on more than one.

These, in their turn, cursed back at the blind miscreant, threatened him in horrid terms, and tried in vain to catch the stick and wrest it from his grasp.

This quarrel was the saving of us; for while it was still raging, another sound came from the top of the hill on the side of the hamlet—the tramp of horses galloping. Almost at the same time a pistol-shot, flash, and report came from the hedge-side. And that was plainly the last signal of danger, for the buccaneers turned at once and ran, separating in every direction, one seaward along the cove, one slant across the hill, and so on, so that in half a minute not a sign of them remained but Pew. Him they had deserted, whether in sheer panic or out of revenge for his ill words and blows, I know not; but there he remained behind, tapping up and down the road in a frenzy, and groping and calling for his comrades. Finally he took the wrong turn, and ran a few steps past me, toward the hamlet, crying:

"Johnny, Black Dog, Dirk," and other names, "you won't leave old Pew, mates—not old Pew?"

Just then the noise of horses topped the rise, and four or five riders came in sight in the moonlight, and swept at full gallop down the slope.

At this Pew saw his error, turned with a scream, and ran straight for the ditch, into which he rolled. But he was on his feet again in a second, and made another dash, now utterly bewildered, right under the nearest of the coming horses.

The rider tried to save him, but in vain. Down went Pew with a cry that rang high into the night, and the four hoofs trampled and spurned him and passed by. He fell on his side, then gently collapsed upon his face, and moved no more.

I leaped to my feet and hailed the riders. They were pulling up, at any rate, horrified at the accident, and I soon saw what they were. One, tailing out behind the rest, was a lad that had gone from the hamlet to Doctor Livesey's; the rest were revenue officers, whom he had met by the way, and with whom he had had the intelligence to return at once. Some news of the lugger in Kitt's Hole had found its way to Supervisor Dance, and sent him forth that night in our direction, and to that circumstance my mother and I owed our preservation from death.

Pew was dead, stone dead. As for my mother, when we had carried her up to the hamlet, a little cold water and salts very soon brought her back again, and she was none the worse for her terror, though she still continued to deplore the balance of the money.

In the meantime the supervisor rode on, as fast as he could, to Kitt's Hole; but his men had to dismount and grope down the dingle, leading, and sometimes supporting, their horses, and in continual fear of ambushers; so it was no great matter for surprise that when we got down to the Hole the lugger was already under way, though still close in. He hailed her. A voice replied, telling him to keep out of the moonlight, or he would get some lead in him, and at the same time a bullet whistled close by his arm.

Soon after, the lugger doubled the point and disappeared. Mr. Dance stood there, as he said, "like a fish out of water," and all he could do was to dispatch a man to B—— to warn the cutter. "And that," said he, "is just about as good as nothing. They've got off clean, and there's an end. Only," he added, "I'm glad I trod on Master Pew's corns," for by this time he had heard my story.

I went back with him to the Admiral Benbow, and you cannot imagine a house in such a state of smash; the very clock had been thrown down by these fellows in their furious hunt after my mother and myself; and though nothing had actually been taken away except the captain's money-bag and a little silver from the till, I could see at once that we were ruined. Mr. Dance could make nothing of the scene.

"They got the money, you say? Well, then, Hawkins, what in fortune were they after? More money, I suppose?"

"No sir; not money, I think," replied I. "In fact, sir, I believe I have the thing in my breast-pocket; and, to tell you the truth, I should like to get it put in safety."

"To be sure, boy; quite right," said he. "I'll take it, if you like."

"I thought, perhaps, Doctor Livesey——" I began.

"Perfectly right," he interrupted, very cheerily, "perfectly right—a gentleman and a magistrate.

And, now I come to think of it, I might as well ride round there myself and report to him or squire. Master Pew's dead, when all's done; not that I regret it, but he's dead, you see, and people will make it out against an officer of his majesty's revenue, if make it out they can.  Now, I'll tell you, Hawkins, if you like, I'll take you along."

I thanked him heartily for the offer, and we walked back to the hamlet where the horses were.  By the time I had told mother of my purpose they were all in the saddle.

"Dogger," said Mr. Dance, "you have a good horse; take up this lad behind you."

As soon as I was mounted, holding on to Dogger's belt, the supervisor gave the word, and the party struck out at a bouncing trot on the road to Doctor Livesey's house.

## Chapter VI

## THE CAPTAIN'S PAPERS

WE rode hard all the way, till we drew up before Doctor Livesey's door. The house was all dark in front.

Mr. Dance told me to jump down and knock, and Dogger gave me a stirrup to descend by. The door was opened almost at once by the maid.

"Is Doctor Livesey in?" I asked.

"No," she said. He had come home in the afternoon, but had gone up to the Hall to dine and pass the evening with the squire.

"So there we go, boys," said Mr. Dance.

This time, as the distance was short, I did not mount, but ran with Dogger's stirrup-leather to the lodge gates, and up the long, leafless, moonlit avenue to where the white line of the Hall buildings looked on either hand on great old gardens. Here Mr. Dance dismounted, and taking me along with him, was admitted at a word into the house.

The servant led us down a matted passage, and showed us at the end into a great library, all lined with bookcases and busts upon top of them, where the squire and Doctor Livesey sat, pipe in hand, on either side of the bright fire.

I had never seen the squire so near at hand. He was a tall man, over six feet high, and broad in proportion, and he had a bluff, rough-and-ready face, all roughened and reddened and lined in his long travels. His eyebrows were very black, and moved readily, and this gave him a look of some temper, not bad, you would say, but quick and high.

"Come in, Mr. Dance," said he, very stately and condescending.

"Good-evening, Dance," said the Doctor, with a nod. "And good-evening to you, friend Jim. What good wind brings you here?"

The supervisor stood up straight and stiff, and told his story like a lesson; and you should have seen how the two gentlemen leaned forward and looked at each other, and forgot to smoke in their surprise and interest. When they heard how my mother went back to the inn, Doctor Livesey fairly slapped his thigh, and the squire cried "Bravo!" and broke his long pipe against the grate. Long before it was done Mr. Trelawney (that, you will remember, was the squire's name) had got up from his seat, and was striding about the room, and the doctor, as if to hear the better, had taken off his powdered wig, and sat there, looking very strange indeed with his own close-cropped, black poll.

At last Mr. Dance finished the story.

"Mr. Dance," said the squire, "you are a very noble fellow. And as for riding down that black,

atrocious miscreant, I regard it as an act of virtue, sir,
like stamping on a cockroach. This lad Hawkins is
a trump, I perceive. Hawkins, will you ring that
bell? Mr. Dance must have some ale."

"And so, Jim," said the doctor, "you have the
thing that they were after, have you?"

"Here it is, sir," said I, and gave him the oilskin
packet.

The doctor looked it all over, as if his fingers were
itching to open it; but, instead of doing that, he put it
quietly in the pocket of his coat.

"Squire," said he, "when Dance has had his ale he
must, of course, be off on his majesty's service; but I
mean to keep Jim Hawkins here to sleep at my house,
and, with your permission, I propose we should have
up the cold pie, and let him sup."

"As you will, Livesey," said the squire; "Hawkins
has earned better than cold pie."

So a big pigeon pie was brought in and put on a
side-table, and I made a hearty supper, for I was as
hungry as a hawk, while Mr. Dance was further complimented, and at last dismissed.

"And now, squire," said the doctor.

"And now, Livesey," said the squire, in the same
breath.

"One at a time, one at a time," laughed Doctor
Livesey. "You have heard of this Flint, I suppose?"

"Heard of him!" cried the squire. "Heard of him,

"And so, Jim," Said the Doctor, "You Have the Thing That They
Were After, Have You?"

you say! He was the blood-thirstiest buccaneer that
sailed. Blackbeard was a child to Flint. The Span-
iards were so prodigiously afraid of him that, I tell
you, sir, I was sometimes proud I was an English-
man. I've seen his topsails with these eyes, off Trini-
dad, and the cowardly son of a rum-puncheon that I
sailed with put back—put back, sir, into Port of
Spain."

"Well, I've heard of him myself, in England,"
said the doctor. "But the point is, had he money?"

"Money!" cried the squire. "Have you heard the
story? What were these villains after but money?
What do they care for but money? For what would
they risk their rascal carcasses but money?"

"That we shall soon know," replied the doctor.
"But you are so confoundedly hot-headed and ex-
clamatory that I cannot get a word in. What I want
to know is this: Supposing that I have here in my
pocket some clew to where Flint buried his treasure,
will that treasure amount to much?"

"Amount, sir!" cried the squire. "It will amount
to this: If we have the clew you talk about, I fit out
a ship in Bristol dock, and take you and Hawkins
here along, and I'll have that treasure if I search a
year."

"Very well," said the doctor. "Now, then, if
Jim is agreeable, we'll open the packet," and he laid
it before him on the table.

The bundle was sewn together, and the doctor had

to get out his instrument case and cut the stitches with his medical scissors. It contained two things— a book and a sealed paper.

"First of all we'll try the book," observed the doctor.

The squire and I were both peering over his shoulder as he opened it, for Doctor Livesey had kindly motioned me to come round from the side-table, where I had been eating, to enjoy the sport of the search. On the first page there were only some scraps of writing, such as a man with a pen in his hand might make for idleness or practice. One was the same as the tattoo mark, "Billy Bones his fancy"; then there was "Mr. W. Bones, mate," "No more rum," "Off Palm Key he got itt," and some other snatches, mostly single words and unintelligible. I could not help wondering who it was that had "got itt," and what "itt" was that he got. A knife in his back as like as not.

"Not much instruction there," said Doctor Livesey, as he passed on.

The next ten or twelve pages were filled with a curious series of entries. There was a date at one end of the line and at the other was a sum of money, as in common account-books; but instead of explanatory writing, only a varying number of crosses between the two. On the 12th of June, 1745, for instance, a sum of seventy pounds had plainly become due to someone, and there was nothing but six crosses to ex-plain the cause. In a few cases, to be sure, the name of a place would be added, as "Offe Caraccas"; or a mere entry of latitude and longitude, as "62 deg. 17 min. 20 sec., 19 deg. 2 min. 40 sec."

The record lasted over nearly twenty years, the amount of the separate entries growing larger as time went on, and at the end a grand total had been made out, after five or six wrong additions, and these words appended, "Bones his pile."

"I can't make head or tail of this," said Doctor Livesey.

"The thing is as clear as noonday," cried the squire. "This is the black-hearted hound's account-book. These crosses stand for the names of ships or towns that they sunk or plundered. The sums are the scoundrel's share, and where he feared an ambiguity, you see he added something clearer. 'Offe Caraccas,' now you see here was some unhappy vessel boarded off that coast. God help the poor souls that manned her—coral long ago."

"Right!" said the doctor. "See what it is to be a traveler. Right! And the amounts increase, you see, as he rose in rank."

There was little else in the volume but a few bearings of places noted in the blank leaves toward the end, and a table for reducing French, English, and Spanish moneys to a common value.

"Thrifty man!" cried the doctor. "He wasn't the one to be cheated."

"And now," said the squire, "for the other."

The paper had been sealed in several places with a thimble by way of seal; the very thimble, perhaps, that I had found in the captain's pocket. The doctor opened the seals with great care, and there fell out the map of an island, with latitude and longitude, soundings, names of hills and bays and inlets, and every particular that would be needed to bring a ship to a safe anchorage upon its shores. It was about nine miles long and five across, shaped, you might say, like a fat dragon standing up, and had two fine land-locked harbors, and a hill in the center part marked "The Spy-glass." There were several additions of a later date; but, above all, three crosses of red ink— two on the north part of the island, one in the south-west, and, beside this last, in the same red ink, and in a small, neat hand, very different from the captain's tottery characters, these words: "Bulk of treasure here."

Over on the back the same hand had written this further information:

"Tall tree, Spy-glass shoulder, bearing a point to the N. of N. N. E.

"Skeleton Island E. S. E. and by E.

"Ten feet.

"The bar silver is in the north cache; you can find it by the trend of the east hummock, ten fathoms south of the black crag with the face on it.

"The arms are easy found, in the sandhill, N. point of north inlet cape, bearing E. and a quarter N.

"**J. F.**"

That was all, but brief as it was, and, to me, in-
comprehensible, it filled the squire and Doctor Livesey
with delight.

"Livesey," said the squire, "you will give up this
wretched practice at once. To-morrow I start for
Bristol. In three weeks' time—three weeks!—two
weeks—ten days—we'll have the best ship, sir, and
the choicest crew in England. Hawkins shall come
as cabin-boy. You'll make a famous cabin-boy, Hawkins. You, Livesey, are ship's doctor; I am admiral.
We'll take Redruth, Joyce, and Hunter. We'll have
favorable winds and a quick passage, and not the
least difficulty in finding the spot, and money to
eat—to roll in—to play duck and drake with ever
after."

"Trelawney," said the doctor, "I'll go with you;
and, I'll go bail for it, so will Jim, and be a credit to
the undertaking. There's only one man I'm afraid
of."

"And who is that?" cried the squire. "Name the
dog, sir!"

"You," replied the doctor, "for you cannot hold
your tongue. We are not the only men who know
of this paper. These fellows who attacked the inn
to-night—bold, desperate blades, for sure—and the
rest who stayed aboard that lugger, and more, I dare
say, not far off, are, one and all, through thick and
thin, bound that they'll get that money. We must
none of us go alone till we get to sea. Jim and I shall

stick together in the meanwhile; you'll take Joyce and Hunter when you ride to Bristol, and, from first to last, not one of us must breathe a word of what we've found."

"Livesey," returned the squire, "you are always in the right of it. I'll be as silent as the grave."

# PART II

## THE SEA COOK

### CHAPTER VII

### I GO TO BRISTOL

IT was longer than the squire imagined ere we were ready for the sea, and none of our first plans—not even Doctor Livesey's, of keeping me beside him —could be carried out as we intended. The doctor had to go to London for a physician to take charge of his practice; the squire was hard at work at Bristol; and I lived on at the Hall under the charge of old Redruth, the gamekeeper, almost a prisoner, but full of sea-dreams and the most charming anticipations of strange islands and adventures. I brooded by the hour together over the map, all the details of which I well remembered. Sitting by the fire in the house-keeper's room, I approached that island, in my fancy, from every possible direction; I explored every acre of its surface; I climbed a thousand times to that tall hill they call the Spy-glass, and from the top enjoyed the most wonderful and changing prospects. Sometimes the isle was thick with savages, with whom we fought; sometimes full of dangerous animals that hunted us; but in all my fancies nothing occurred to me so strange and tragic as our actual adventures.

So the weeks passed on, till one fine day there came a letter addressed to Doctor Livesey, with this addition, "To be opened in the case of his absence, by Tom Redruth or Young Hawkins." Obeying this order, we found, or rather I found—for the game-keeper was a poor hand at reading anything but print—the following important news:

"OLD ANCHOR INN, BRISTOL, March 1, 17—.

"DEAR LIVESEY: As I do not know whether you are at the Hall or still in London, I send this in double to both places.

"The ship is bought and fitted. She lies at anchor, ready for sea. You never imagined a sweeter schooner—a child might sail her—two hundred tons; name, *Hispaniola*.

"I got her through my old friend, Blandly, who has proved himself throughout the most surprising trump. The admirable fellow literally slaved in my interest, and so, I may say, did everyone in Bristol, as soon as they got wind of the port we sailed for—treasure, I mean——

"Redruth," said I, interrupting the letter, "Doctor Livesey will not like that. The squire has been talking, after all."

"Well, who's got a better right?" growled the gamekeeper. "A pretty rum go if squire ain't to talk for Doctor Livesey, I should think."

At that I gave up all attempt at commentary, and read straight on:

"Blandly himself found the *Hispaniola*, and by the most admirable management got her for the merest trifle. There is a class of men in Bristol monstrously prejudiced against Blandly.

They go the length of declaring that this honest creature would do anything for money; that the *Hispaniola* belonged to him, and that he sold it to me absurdly high—the most transparent calumnies. None of them dare, however, to deny the merits of the ship.

"So far there was not a hitch. The workpeople, to be sure —riggers and what not—were most annoyingly slow, but time cured that. It was the crew that troubled me.

"I wished a round score of men—in case of natives, buccaneers, or the odious French—and I had the worry of the deuce itself to find so much as half a dozen, till the most remarkable stroke of fortune brought me the very man that I required.

"I was standing on the dock, when, by the merest accident, I fell in talk with him. I found he was an old sailor, kept a public house, knew all the seafaring men in Bristol, had lost his health ashore, and wanted a good berth as cook to get to sea again. He had hobbled down there that morning, he said, to get a smell of the salt.

"I was monstrously touched—so would you have been— and, out of pure pity, I engaged him on the spot to be ship's cook. Long John Silver, he is called, and has lost a leg; but that I regarded as a recommendation, since he lost it in his country's service, under the immortal Hawke. He has no pension, Livesey. Imagine the abominable age we live in!

"Well, sir, I thought I had only found a cook, but it was a crew I had discovered. Between Silver and myself we got together in a few days a company of the toughest old salts imaginable—not pretty to look at, but fellows, by their faces, of the most indomitable spirit. I declare we could fight a frigate.

"Long John even got rid of two out of the six or seven I had already engaged. He showed me in a moment that they were just the sort of fresh-water swabs we had to fear in an adventure of importance.

"I am in the most magnificent health and spirits, eating like a bull, sleeping like a tree, yet I shall not enjoy a moment till I hear my old tarpaulins tramping around the capstan. Seaward ho! Hang the treasure! It's the glory of the sea that has turned my head. So now, Livesey, come post: do not lose an hour, if you respect me.

"Let young Hawkins go at once to see his mother, with Redruth for a guard, and then both come full speed to Bristol.

JOHN TRELAWNEY.

"P. S.—I did not tell you that Blandly, who, by the way, is to send a consort after us if we don't turn up by the end of August, had found an admirable fellow for sailing-master—a stiff man, which I regret, but, in all other respects, a treasure. Long John Silver unearthed a very competent man for a mate, a man named Arrow. I have a boatswain who pipes, Livesey; so things shall go man-o'-war fashion on board the good ship *Hispaniola*.

"I forgot to tell you that Silver is a man of substance; I know of my own knowledge that he has a banker's account, which has never been overdrawn. He leaves his wife to manage the inn; and as she is a woman of color, a pair of old bachelors like you and I may be excused for guessing that it is the wife, quite as much as the health, that sends him back to roving.

J. T.

"P. P. S.—Hawkins may stay one night with his mother.

J. T."

You can fancy the excitement into which that letter put me. I was half beside myself with glee, and if ever I despied a man, it was old Tom Redruth, who could do nothing but grumble and lament. Any of the under-gamekeepers would gladly have changed places with him; but such was not the squire's pleasure, and the squire's pleasure was like law among them all. Nobody but old Redruth would have dared so much as even to grumble.

The next morning he and I sat out on foot for the Admiral Benbow, and there I found my mother in good health and spirits. The captain, who had so long been a cause of so much discomfort, was gone

where the wicked cease from troubling. The squire
had had everything repaired, and the public rooms
and the sign repainted, and had added some furniture—above all a beautiful armchair for mother in
the bar. He had found her a boy as an apprentice
also, so that she should not want help while I was
gone.

It was on seeing that boy that I understood, for
the first time, my situation. I had thought up to
that moment of the adventures before me, not at all
of the home that I was leaving; and now at sight of
this clumsy stranger, who was to stay here in my
place beside my mother, I had my first attack of tears.
I am afraid I led that boy a dog's life; for as he was
new to the work, I had a hundred opportunities of
setting him right and putting him down, and I was
not slow to profit by them.

The night passed, and the next day, after dinner,
Redruth and I were afoot again and on the road. I
said good-by to mother and the cove where I had
lived since I was born, and the dear old Admiral Benbow—since he was repainted, no longer quite so dear.
One of my last thoughts was of the captain, who had
so often strode along the beach with his cocked hat,
his saber-cut cheek, and his old brass telescope. Next
moment we had turned the corner, and my home was
out of sight.

The mail picked us up about dusk at the Royal
George on the heath. I was wedged in between

Redruth and a stout old gentleman, and in spite of the swift motion and the cold night air, I must have dozed a great deal from the very first, and then slept like a log up hill and down dale, through stage after stage; for when I was awakened at last, it was by a punch in the ribs, and I opened my eyes to find that we were standing still before a large building in a city street, and that the day had already broken a long time.

"Where are we?" I asked.

"Bristol," said Tom. "Get down."

Mr. Trelawney had taken up his residence at an inn far down the docks, to superintend the work upon the schooner. Thither we had now to walk, and our way, to my great delight, lay along the quays and beside the great multitude of ships of all sizes and rigs and nations. In one, sailors were singing at their work; in another, there were men aloft, high over my head, hanging to threads that seemed no thicker than a spider's. Though I had lived by the shore all my life, I seemed never to have been near the sea till then. The smell of tar and salt was something new. I saw the most wonderful figureheads, that had all been far over the ocean. I saw, besides, many old sailors, with rings in their ears, and whiskers curled in ringlets, and tarry pig-tails, and their swaggering, clumsy sea-walk; and if I had seen as many kings or archbishops I could not have been more delighted.

And I was going to sea myself; to sea in a schooner, with a piping boatswain, and pig-tailed singing seamen; to sea, bound for an unknown island, and to seek for buried treasure.

While I was still in this delightful dream, we came suddenly in front of a large inn, and met Squire Trelawney, all dressed out like a sea officer, in stout blue cloth, coming out of the door with a smile on his face, and a capital imitation of a sailor's walk.

"Here you are!" he cried; "and the doctor came last night from London. Bravo!—the ship's company complete."

"Oh, sir," cried I, "when do we sail?"

"Sail!" says he. "We sail to-morrow."

## Chapter VIII

## AT THE SIGN OF THE "SPY-GLASS"

WHEN I had done breakfasting, the squire gave me a note addressed to John Silver, at the sign of the "Spy-glass," and told me I should easily find the place by following the line of the docks, and keeping a bright lookout for a little tavern with a large brass telescope for a sign. I set off, overjoyed at this opportunity to see some more of the ships and seamen, and picked my way among a great crowd of people and carts and bales, for the dock was now at its busiest, until I found the tavern in question.

It was a bright enough little place of entertainment. The sign was newly painted; the windows had neat red curtains; the floor was cleanly sanded. There was a street on either side, and an open door on both, which made the large, low room pretty clear to see in, in spite of clouds of tobacco smoke.

The customers were mostly seafaring men, and they talked so loudly that I hung at the door, almost afraid to enter.

As I was waiting, a man came out of a side room, and at a glance I was sure he must be Long John. His left leg was cut off close by the hip, and under the left shoulder he carried a crutch, which he managed with wonderful dexterity, hopping about upon it like a bird. He was very tall and strong, with a face as big as a ham—plain and pale, but intelligent and smiling. Indeed, he seemed in the most cheerful spirits, whistling as he moved about among the tables, with a merry word or a slap on the shoulder for the more favored of his guests.

Now, to tell you the truth, from the very first mention of Long John in Squire Trelawney's letter, I had taken a fear in my mind that he might prove to be the very one-legged sailor whom I had watched for so long at the old Benbow. But one look at the man before me was enough. I had seen the captain, and Black Dog, and the blind man Pew, and I thought I knew what a buccaneer was like—a very different creature, according to me, from this clean and pleasant-tempered landlord.

I plucked up courage at once, crossed the threshold, and walked right up to the man where he stood, propped on his crutch, talking to a customer.

"Mr. Silver, sir?" I asked, holding out the note.

"Yes, my lad," said he; "such is my name, to be sure. And who may you be?" And when he saw the squire's letter he seemed to me to give something almost like a start.

"Oh!" said he, quite aloud, and offering his hand, "I see. You are our new cabin-boy; pleased I am to see you."

And he took my hand in his large firm grasp.

**At a Glance I Was Sure He Must Be Long John.**

Just then one of the customers at the far side rose suddenly and made for the door. It was close by him, and he was out in the street in a moment. But his hurry had attracted my notice, and I recognized him at a glance. It was the tallow-faced man, wanting two fingers, who had come first to the Admiral Benbow.

"Oh," I cried, "stop him! it's Black Dog!"

"I don't care two coppers who he is," cried Silver, "but he hasn't paid his score. Harry, run and catch him."

One of the others who was nearest the door leaped up and started in pursuit.

"If he were Admiral Hawke he shall pay his score," cried Silver; and then, relinquishing my hand, "Who did you say he was?" he asked. "Black what?"

"Dog, sir," said I. "Has Mr. Trelawney not told you of the buccaneers? He was one of them."

"So?" cried Silver. "In my house! Ben, run and help Harry. One of those swabs, was he? Was that you drinking with him, Morgan? Step up here."

The man whom he called Morgan—an old, gray-haired, mahogany-faced sailor—came forward pretty sheepishly, rolling his quid.

"Now, Morgan," said Long John, very sternly, "you never clapped your eyes on that Black—Black Dog before, did you, now?"

"Not I, sir," said Morgan, with a salute.

"You didn't know his name, did you?"

"No, sir."

"By the powers, Tom Morgan, it's as good for you!" exclaimed the landlord. "If you had been mixed up with the like of that, you would never have put another foot in my house, you may lay to that. And what was he saying to you?"

"I don't rightly know, sir," answered Morgan.

"Do you call that a head on your shoulders, or a blessed dead-eye?" cried Long John. "Don't rightly know, don't you? Perhaps you don't happen to rightly know who you was speaking to, perhaps? Come now, what was he jawing—v'yges, cap'ns, ships? Pipe up. What was it?"

"We was a-talkin' of keel-hauling," answered Morgan.

"Keel-hauling, was you? and a mighty suitable thing, too, and you may lay to that. Get back to your place for a lubber, Tom."

And then, as Morgan rolled back to his seat, Silver added to me, in a confidential whisper, that was very flattering, as I thought:

"He's quite an honest man, Tom Morgan, on'y stupid. And now," he ran on again, aloud, "let's see—Black Dog? No, I don't know the name, not I. Yet I kind of think I've—yes, I've seen the swab. He used to come here with a blind beggar, he used."

"That he did, you may be sure," said I. "I knew that blind man, too. His name was Pew."

"It was!" cried Silver, now quite excited. "Pew!

That were his name for certain.  Ah, he looked a
shark, he did!  If we run down this Black Dog now,
there'll be news for Cap'n Trelawney!  Ben's a good
runner; few seamen run better than Ben.  He should
run him down, hand over hand, by the powers!  He
talked o' keel-hauling, did he?  *I'll* keel-haul him!"

All the time he was jerking out these phrases he
was stumping up and down the tavern on his crutch,
slapping tables with his hand, and giving such a show
of excitement as would have convinced an Old Bailey
judge or a Bow Street runner.  My suspicions had
been thoroughly reawakened on finding Black Dog
at the "Spy-glass," and I watched the cook narrowly.
But he was too deep, and too ready, and too clever
for me, and by the time the two men had come back
out of breath, and confessed that they had lost the
track in a crowd, and been scolded like thieves, I
would have gone bail for the innocence of Long John
Silver.

"See here, now, Hawkins," said he, "here's a
blessed hard thing on a man like me, now, ain't it?
There's Cap'n Trelawney—what's he to think?  Here
I have this confounded son of a Dutchman sitting
in my own house, drinking of my own rum!  Here
you comes and tells me of it plain; and here I let him
give us all the slip before my blessed deadlights!  Now,
Hawkins, you do me justice with the cap'n.  You're
a lad, you are, but you're as smart as paint.  I see
that when you first came in.  Now, here it is: What

could I do, with this old timber I hobble on? When I was an A B master mariner I'd have come up along-side of him, hand over hand, and broached him to in a brace of old shakes, I would; and now——"

And then, all of a sudden, he stopped, and his jaw dropped as though he had remembered something.

"The score!" he burst out. "Three goes o' rum! Why, shiver my timbers, if I hadn't forgotten my score!"

And, falling on a bench, he laughed until the tears ran down his cheeks. I could not help joining, and we laughed together, peal after peal, until the tavern rang again.

"Why, what a precious old sea-calf I am!" he said, at last, wiping his cheeks. "You and me should get on well, Hawkins, for I'll take my davy I should be rated ship's boy. But, come, now, stand by to go about. This won't do. Dooty is dooty, messmates. I'll put on my old cocked hat and step along of you to Cap'n Trelawney, and report this here affair. For, mind you, it's serious, young Hawkins; and neither you nor me's come out of it with what I should make so bold as to call credit. Nor you neither, says you; not smart—none of the pair of us smart. But dash my buttons! that was a good 'un about my score."

And he began to laugh again, and that so heartily, that though I did not see the joke as he did, I was again obliged to join him in his mirth.

On our little walk along the quays he made himself the most interesting companion, telling me about the different ships that we passed by, their rig, tonnage, and nationality, explaining the work that was going forward—how one was discharging, another taking in cargo, and a third making ready for sea; and every now and then telling me some little anecdote of ships or seamen, or repeating a nautical phrase till I had learned it perfectly.   I began to see that here was one of the best of possible shipmates.

When we got to the inn, the squire and Doctor Livesey were seated together, finishing a quart of ale with a toast in it, before they should go aboard the schooner on a visit of inspection.

Long John told the story from first to last, with a great deal of spirit and the most perfect truth. "That was how it were, now, weren't it, Hawkins?" he would say, now and again, and I could always bear him entirely out.

The two gentlemen regretted that Black Dog had got away, but we all agreed there was nothing to be done, and after he had been complimented, Long John took up his crutch and departed.

"All hands aboard by four this afternoon!" shouted the squire after him.

"Aye, aye, sir," cried the cook in the passage.

"Well, squire," said Doctor Livesey, "I don't put much faith in your discoveries, as a general thing, but I will say this—John Silver suits me."

"That man's a perfect trump," declared the squire.

"And now," added the doctor, "Jim may come on board with us, may he not?"

"To be sure he may," said the squire. "Take your hat, Hawkins, and we'll see the ship."

"That man's a perfect trump," declared the squire.
"And now," added the doctor, "Jim may come on
board with us, may he not?"
"To be sure he may," said the squire. "Take
your hat, Hawkins, and we'll see the ship."

## Chapter IX

## POWDER AND ARMS

THE *Hispaniola* lay some way out, and we went under the figureheads and around the sterns of many other ships, and their cables sometimes grated beneath our keel, and sometimes swung above us. At last, however, we swung alongside, and were met and saluted as we stepped aboard by the mate, Mr. Arrow, a brown old sailor, with earrings in his ears and a squint. He and the squire were very thick and friendly, but I soon observed that things were not the same between Mr. Trelawney and the captain.

This last was a sharp-looking man, who seemed angry with everything on board, and was soon to tell us why, for we hardly got down into the cabin when a sailor followed us.

"Captain Smollett, sir, axing to speak with you," said he.

"I am always at the captain's orders. Show him in," said the squire.

The captain, who was close behind his messenger, entered at once, and shut the door behind him.

"Well, sir," said the captain, "better speak plain, I believe, at the risk of offense. I don't like this cruise;

I don't like the men; and I don't like my officer. That's short and sweet."

"Perhaps, sir, you don't like the ship?" inquired the squire, very angry, as I could see.

"I can't speak as to that, sir, not having seen her tried," said the captain. "She seems a clever craft; more I can't say."

"Possibly, sir, you may not like your employer, either?" said the squire.

But here Doctor Livesey cut in.

"Stay a bit," said he, "stay a bit. No use of such questions as that but to produce ill-feeling. The captain has said too much or he has said too little, and I'm bound to say that I require an explanation of his words. You don't, you say, like this cruise. Now, why?"

"I was engaged, sir, on what we call sealed orders, to sail this ship for that gentleman where he should bid me," said the captain. "So far so good. But now I find that every man before the mast knows more than I do. I don't call that fair, now, do you?"

"No," said Doctor Livesey, "I don't."

"Next," said the captain, "I learn we are going after treasure—hear it from my own hands, mind you. Now, treasure is ticklish work; I don't like treasure voyages on any account; and I don't like them, above all, when they are secret, and when (begging your pardon, Mr. Trelawney) the secret has been told to the parrot."

"Silver's parrot?" asked the squire.

"It's a way of speaking," said the captain.
"Blabbed, I mean. It's my belief neither of you
gentlemen know what you are about; but I'll tell
you my way of it—life or death, and a close run."

"That is all clear, and, I dare say, true enough,"
replied Doctor Livesey. "We take the risk, but we
are not so ignorant as you believe us. Next, you say
you don't like the crew. Are they not good seamen?"

I don't like them, sir," returned Captain Smollett. "And I think I should have had the choosing
of my own hands, if you go to that."

"Perhaps you should," replied the doctor. "My
friend should, perhaps, have taken you along with
him; but the slight, if there be one, was unintentional.
And you don't like Mr. Arrow?"

"I don't sir. I believe he's a good seaman, but
he's too free with the crew to be a good officer. A
mate should keep himself to himself—shouldn't drink
with the men before the mast."

"Do you mean he drinks?" cried the squire.

"No, sir," replied the captain; "only that he's too
familiar."

"Well, now, and the short and long of it, captain?" asked the doctor. "Tell us what you want."

"Well, gentlemen, are you determined to go on
this cruise?"

"Like iron," answered the squire.

"Very good," said the captain. "Then, as you've

heard me very patiently, saying things that I could not prove, hear me a few words more. They are putting the powder and the arms in the fore-hold. Now, you have a good place under the cabin; why not put them there?—first point. Then you are bringing four of your own people with you, and they tell me some of them are to be berthed forward. Why not give them the berths here beside the cabin? —second point."

"Any more?" asked Mr. Trelawney.

"One more," said the captain. "There's been too much blabbing already."

"Far too much," agreed the doctor.

"I'll tell you what I've heard myself," continued Captain Smollett; "that you have a map of an island; that there's crosses on the map to show where treasure is; and that the island lies——" And then he named the latitude and longitude exactly.

"I never told that," cried the squire, "to a soul."

"The hands know it, sir," returned the captain. "Livesey, that must have been you or Hawkins," cried the squire.

"It doesn't much matter who it was," replied the doctor. And I could see that neither he nor the captain paid much regard to Mr. Trelawney's protestations. Neither did I, to be sure, he was so loose a talker; yet in this case I believe he was really right, and that nobody had told the situation of the island.

"Well, gentlemen," continued the captain, "I don't know who has this map, but I make it a point it should be kept secret even from me and Mr. Arrow. Otherwise I would ask you to let me resign."

"I see," said the doctor. "You wish to keep this matter dark, and to make a garrison of the stern part of the ship manned with my friend's own people, and provided with all the arms and powder on board. In other words, you fear a mutiny."

"Sir," said Captain Smollett, "with no intention to take offense, I deny your right to put words into my mouth. No captain, sir, would be justified in going to sea at all if he had ground enough for that. As for Mr. Arrow, I believe him thoroughly honest; some of the men are the same; all may be for what I know. But I am responsible for the ship's safety and the life of every man Jack aboard of her. I see things going, as I think, not quite right; and I ask you to take certain precautions, or let me resign my berth. And that's all."

"Captain Smollett," began the doctor, with a smile, "did ever you hear the fable of the mountain and the mouse? You'll excuse me, I dare say, but you remind me of that fable. When you came in here I'll stake my wig you meant more than this."

"Doctor," said the captain, "you are smart. When I came in here I meant to get discharged. I had no thought that Mr. Trelawney would hear a word."

"No more I would," cried the squire. "Had Livesey not been here I should have seen you to the deuce. As it is, I have heard you. I will do as you desire, but I think the worse of you."

"That's as you please, sir," said the captain. "You'll find I do my duty."

And with that he took his leave.

"Trelawney," said the doctor; "contrary to all my notions, I believe you have managed to get two honest men on board with you—that man and John Silver."

"Silver, if you like," cried the squire, "but as for that intolerable humbug, I declare I think his conduct unmanly, unsailorly, and downright un-English."

"Well," said the doctor, "we shall see."

When we came on deck the men had begun already to take out the arms and powder, yoho-ing at their work, while the captain and Mr. Arrow stood by superintending.

The new arrangement was quite to my liking. The whole schooner had been overhauled; six berths had been made astern, out of what had been the after-part of the main hold, and this set of cabins was only joined to the galley and forecastle by a sparred passage on the port side. It had been originally meant that the captain, Mr. Arrow, Hunter, Joyce, the doctor, and the squire were to occupy these six berths. Now Redruth and I were to get two of them, and Mr. Arrow and the captain were to sleep on deck in the companion, which had been enlarged on each side till you might almost have called it a round-house. Very low it was still, of course, but there was room to swing two hammocks, and even the mate seemed pleased with the arrangement. Even he, per-haps, had been doubtful as to the crew, but that is only guess, for, as you shall hear, we had not long the benefit of his opinion.

We were all hard at work changing the powder and the berths, when the last man or two, and Long John along with them, came off in a shore-boat.

The cook came up the side like a monkey for cleverness, and, as soon as he saw what was doing, "So ho, mates!" said he, "what's this!"

"We're a-changing the powder, Jack," answered one.

"Why, by the powers, " cried Long John, "if we do, we'll miss the morning tide!"

"My orders!" cried the captain, shortly. "You may go below, my man. Hands will want supper."

"Aye, aye, sir," answered the cook; and, touching his forelock, he disappeared at once in the direction of his galley.

"That's a good man, captain," said the doctor.

"Very likely, sir," replied Captain Smollett. "Easy with that, men—easy," he ran on, to the fellows who were shifting the powder; and then sud-denly observing me examining the swivel we carried amidships, a long brass nine—"Here, you ship's boy," he cried, "out o' that! Off with you to the cook and get some work."

And then as I was hurrying off I heard him say, quite loudly, to the doctor:

"I'll have no favorites on my ship."

I assure you I was quite of the squire's way of thinking, and hated the captain deeply.

CHAPTER X

# THE VOYAGE

ALL that night we were in a great bustle getting things stowed in their place, and boatfuls of the squire's friends, Mr. Blandly and the like, coming off to wish him a good voyage and a safe return. We never had a night at the Admiral Benbow when I had half the work; and I was dog-tired when, a little before dawn, the boatswain sounded his pipe, and the crew began to man the capstan bars. I might have been twice as weary, yet I would not have left the deck, all was so new and interesting to me—the brief commands, the shrill notes of the whistle, the men bustling to their places in the glimmer of the ship's lanterns.

"Now, Barbecue, tip us a stave," cried one voice.

"The old one," cried another.

"Aye, aye, mates," said Long John, who was standing by, with his crutch under his arm, and at once broke out in the air and words I knew so well:

"Fifteen men on the dead man's chest"—

And then the whole crew bore chorus:

"Yo-ho-ho and a bottle of rum!"

And at the third "ho!" drove the bars before them with a will.

84

Even at that exciting moment it carried me back to the old Admiral Benbow in a second, and I seemed to hear the voice of the captain piping in the chorus. But soon the anchor was short up; soon it was hanging dripping at the bows; soon the sails began to draw, and the land and shipping to flit by on either side, and before I could lie down to snatch an hour of slumber the *Hispaniola* had begun her voyage to the Isle of Treasure.

I am not going to relate the voyage in detail. It was fairly prosperous. The ship proved to be a good ship, the crew were capable seamen, and the captain thoroughly understood his business. But before we came the length of Treasure Island, two or three things had happened which require to be known.

Mr. Arrow, first of all, turned out even worse than the captain had feared. He had no command among the men, and people did what they pleased with him. But that was by no means the worst of it; for after a day or two at sea he began to appear on deck with hazy eye, red cheeks, stuttering tongue, and other marks of drunkenness. Time after time he was ordered below in disgrace. Sometimes he fell and cut himself; sometimes he lay all day long in his little bunk at one side of the companion; sometimes for a day or two he would be almost sober and attend to his work at least passably.

In the meantime we could never make out where he got the drink. That was the ship's mystery. Watch him as we pleased, we could do nothing to solve it, and when we asked him to his face, he would only laugh, if he were drunk, and if he were sober, deny solemnly that he ever tasted anything but water.

He was not only useless as an officer, and had a bad influence among the men, but it was plain that at this rate he must soon kill himself outright, so nobody was much surprised, nor very sorry, when one dark night, with a head sea, he disappeared entirely and was seen no more.

"Overboard!" said the captain. "Well, gentlemen, that saves the trouble of putting him in irons."

But there we were, without a mate, and it was necessary, of course, to advance one of the men. The boatswain, Job Anderson, was the likeliest man aboard, and though he kept his old title, he served in a way as mate. Mr. Trelawney had followed the sea, and his knowledge made him very useful, for he often took a watch himself in easy weather. And the cockswain, Israel Hands, was a careful, wily, old, experienced seaman, who could be trusted at a pinch with almost anything.

He was a great confidant of Long John Silver, and so the mention of his name leads me on to speak of our ship's cook, Barbecue, as the men called him.

Aboard ship he carried his crutch by a lanyard round his neck, to have both hands as free as possible. It was something to see him wedge the foot of the crutch against a bulkhead, and, propped against it,

yielding to every movement of the ship, get on with
his cooking like someone safe ashore. Still more
strange was it to see him in the heaviest of weather
cross the deck. He had a line or two rigged up to
help him across the widest spaces—Long John's earrings, they were called—and he would hand himself
from one place to another, now using the crutch, now
trailing it alongside by the lanyard, as quickly as
another man could walk. Yet some of the men who
had sailed with him before expressed their pity to
see him so reduced.

"He's no common man, Barbecue," said the cockswain to me. "He had good schooling in his young
days, and can speak like a book when so minded; and
brave—a lion's nothing alongside of Long John! I
see him grapple four and knock their heads together
—him unarmed."

All the crew respected and even obeyed him. He
had a way of talking to each and doing everybody
some particular service. To me he was unweariedly
kind, and always glad to see me in the galley, which
he kept as clean as a new pin; the dishes hanging up
burnished and his parrot in a cage in the corner.

"Come away, Hawkins," he would say; "come and
have a yarn with John. Nobody more welcome than
yourself, my son. Sit you down and hear the news.
Here's Cap'n Flint—I calls my parrot Cap'n Flint,
after the famous buccaneer—here's Cap'n Flint pre-
dicting success to our v'yage. Wasn't you, cap'n?"

And the parrot would say, with great rapidity: "Pieces of eight! pieces of eight! pieces of eight!" till you wondered that it was not out of breath or till John threw his handerchief over the cage.

"Now, that bird," he would say, "is, may be, two hundred years old, Hawkins—they live forever mostly, and if anybody's seen more wickedness it must be the devil himself. She's sailed with England— the great Cap'n England, the pirate. She's been at Madagascar, and at Malabar, and Surinam, and Providence, and Portobello. She was at the fishing up of the wrecked plate ships. It's there she learned 'Pieces of eight,' and little wonder; three hundred and fifty thousand of 'em, Hawkins! She was at the boarding of the 'Viceroy of the Indies' out of Goa, she was, and to look at her you would think she was a babby. But you smelled powder—didn't you, cap'n?"

"Stand by to go about," the parrot would scream. "Ah, she's a handsome craft, she is," the cook would say, and give her sugar from his pocket, and then the bird would peck at the bars and swear straight on, passing belief for wickedness. "There," John would add, "you can't touch pitch and not be mucked, lad. Here's this poor old innocent bird of mine swearing blue fire and none the wiser, you may lay to that. She would swear the same, in a manner of speaking, before the chaplain." And John would touch his forelock with a solemn way he had, that made me think he was the best of men.

In the meantime squire and Captain Smollett were
still on pretty distant terms with one another.  The
squire made no bones about the matter; he despised
the captain.  The captain, on his part, never spoke
but when he was spoken to, and then sharp and short
and dry, and not a word wasted.  He owned, when
driven into a corner, that he seemed to have been
wrong about the crew; that some of them were as
brisk as he wanted to see, and all had behaved fairly
well.  As for the ship, he had taken a downright fancy
to her.  "She'll lie a point nearer the wind than a
man has a right to expect of his own married wife,
sir.  But," he would add, "all I say is, we're not home
again and I don't like the cruise."

The squire, at this, would turn away and march
up and down the deck, chin in air.

"A trifle more of that man," he would say, "and
I should explode."

We had some heavy weather, which only proved
the qualities of the *Hispaniola*.  Every man on
board seemed well content and they must have been
hard to please if they had been otherwise, for it is
my belief there was never a ship's company so spoiled
since Noah put to sea.  Double grog was going on
the least excuse; there was duff on odd days, as for
instance, if the squire heard it was any man's birthday,
and always a barrel of apples standing broached in
the waist, for anyone to help himself that had a fancy.

"Never knew good to come of it yet," the captain

said to Doctor Livesey. "Spoil fok's'le hands, make devils. That's my belief."

But good did come of the apple barrel, as you shall hear, for if it had not been for that we should have had no note of warning and might all have perished by the hand of treachery.

This is how it came about.

We had run up the trades to get the wind of the island we were after—I am not allowed to be more plain—and now we were running down for it with a bright lookout day and night. It was about the last day of our outward voyage, by the largest computation; some time that night, or, at least, before noon of the morrow, we should sight the Treasure Island. We were heading south-southwest, and had a steady breeze abeam and a quiet sea. The *Hispaniola* rolled steadily, dipping her bowsprit now and then with a whiff of spray. All was drawing alow and aloft; everyone was in the bravest spirits, because we were now so near an end of the first part of our adventure.

Now, just after sundown, when all my work was over and I was on my way to my berth, it occurred to me that I should like an apple. I ran on deck. The watch was all forward looking out for the island. The man at the helm was watching the luff of the sail and whistling away gently to himself, and that was the only sound excepting the swish of the sea against the bows and around the sides of the ship.

In I got bodily into the apple barrel, and found

there was scarce an apple left; but, sitting down there in the dark, what with the sound of the waters and the rocking movement of the ship, I had either fallen asleep, or was on the point of doing so when a heavy man sat down with rather a clash close by. The barrel shook as he leaned his shoulders against it, and I was just about to jump up when the man began to speak. It was Silver's voice, and, before I had heard a dozen words, I would not have shown myself for all the world, but lay there, trembling and listening, in the extreme of fear and curiosity; for from these dozen words I understood that the lives of all the honest men aboard depended upon me alone.

## Chapter XI

# WHAT I HEARD IN THE APPLE BARREL

"NO, not I," said Silver. "Flint was cap'n; I was quartermaster, along of my timber leg. The same broadside I lost my leg, old Pew lost his deadlights. It was a master surgeon, him that ampytated me—out of college and all—Latin by the bucket, and what not; but he was hanged like a dog, and sun-dried like the rest, at Corso Castle. That was Roberts' men, that was, and comed of changing names to their ships—Royal Fortune and so on. Now, what a ship was christened, so let her stay, I says. So it was with the Cassandra, as brought us all safe home from Malabar, after England took the Viceroy of the Indies; so it was with the old Walrus, Flint's old ship, as I've seen a-muck with the red blood and fit to sink with gold."

"Ah!" cried another voice, that of the youngest hand on board, and evidently full of admiration, "he was the flower of the flock, was Flint!"

"Davis was a man, too, by all accounts," said Silver. "I never sailed along of him; first with England, then with Flint, that's my story; and now here on my own account, in a manner of speaking. I laid my nine hundred safe, from England, and two

thousand after Flint. That ain't bad for a man
before the mast—all safe in bank. 'Tain't earning
now; it's saving does it, you may lay to that.
Where's all England's men now? I dunno.
Where's Flint's? Why, most on' em aboard here,
and glad to get the duff—been begging before that,
some on 'em. Old Pew, as had lost his sight, and
might have thought shame, spends twelve hundred
pounds in a year, like a lord in Parliament. Where
is he now? Well, he's dead now and under the hatches;
but for two years before that, shiver my timbers!
that man was starving. He begged, and he stole,
and he cut throats, and starved at that, by the powers!"

"Well, it ain't much use, after all," said the young
seaman.

"'Tain't much use for fools, you may lay to it—
that, nor nothing," cried Silver. "But now, you
look here; you're young, you are, but you're as smart
as paint. I see that when I set my eyes on you. and
I'll talk to you like a man."

You can imagine how I felt when I heard this
abominable old rogue addressing another in the very
same words of flattery as he had used to myself. I
think, if I had been able, that I would have killed
him through the barrel. Meantime he ran on, little
supposing he was overheard.

"Here it is about gentlemen of fortune. They
lives rough, and they risk swinging, but they eat and
drink like fighting-cocks, and when a cruise is done,

why, it's hundreds of pounds instead of hundreds of
farthings in their pockets. Now, the most goes for
rum and a good fling, and to sea again in their shirts.
But that's not the course I lay. I puts it all away,
some here, some there, and none too much any-
wheres, by reason of suspicion. I'm fifty, mark you;
once back from this cruise I set up gentleman in
earnest. Time enough, too, says you. Ah, but I've
lived easy in the meantime; never denied myself o'
nothing heart desires, and slept soft and eat dainty
all my days, but when at sea. And how did I begin?
Before the mast, like you!"

"Well," said the other, "but all the other money's
gone now, ain't it? You daren't show face in Bristol
after this."

"Why, where might you suppose it was?" asked
Silver, derisively.

"At Bristol, in banks and places," answered his
companion.

"It were," said the cook; "it were when we
weighed anchor. But my old missis has it all by
now. And the "Spy-glass" is sold, lease and good will
and rigging; and the old girl's off to meet me. I would
tell you where, for I trust you; but it 'ud make jealousy
among the mates."

"And you can trust your missis?" asked the
other.

"Gentlemen of fortune," returned the cook,
"usually trust little among themselves, and right they

are, you may lay to it. But I have a way with me,
I have. When a mate brings a slip on his cable—
one as knows me, I mean—it won't be in the same
world with old John. There was some that was
feared of Pew, and some that was feared of Flint;
but Flint his own self was feared of me. Feared he
was, and proud. They was the roughest crew afloat,
was Flint's; the devil himself would have been feared
to go to sea with them. Well, now, I tell you, I'm
not a boasting man, and you seen yourself how easy
I keep company; but when I was quartermaster, *lambs*
wasn't the word for Flint's old buccaneers. Ah, you
may be sure of yourself in old John's ship."

"Well, I tell you now," replied the lad, "I didn't
half a quarter like the job till I had this talk with
you, John, but there's my hand on it now."

"And a brave lad you were, and smart, too,"
answered Silver, shaking hands so heartily that all
the barrel shook, "and a finer figurehead for a gentleman of fortune I never clapped my eyes on."

By this time I had begun to understand the meaning of their terms. By a "gentleman of fortune"
they plainly meant neither more nor less than a
common pirate, and the little scene that I had overheard was the last act in the corruption of one of the
honest hands—perhaps of the last one left aboard.
But on this point I was soon to be relieved, for Silver
giving a little whistle, a third man strolled up and
sat down by the party.

"Dick's square," said Silver.

"Oh, I know'd Dick was square," returned the voice of the cockswain, Israel Hands. "He's no fool, is Dick." And he turned his quid and spat. "But, look here," he went on, "here's what I want to know, Barbecue—how long are we a-going to stand off and on like a blessed bum-boat? I've had a'most enough o' Cap'n Smollett; he's hazed me long enough, by thunder! I want to go into that cabin, I do. I want their pickles and wines, and that."

"Israel," said Silver, "your head ain't much account, nor never was. But you're able to hear, I reckon; leastways your ears is big enough. Now, here's what I say—you'll berth forward, and you'll live hard, and you'll speak soft, and you'll keep sober, till I give the word; and you may lay to that, my son."

"Well, I don't say no, do I?" growled the cockswain. "What I say is, when? That's what I say."

"When! by the powers!" cried Silver. "Well, now, if you want to know, I'll tell you when. The last moment I can manage; and that's when. Here's a first-rate seaman, Cap'n Smollett, sails the blessed ship for us. Here's this squire and doctor with a map and such—I don't know where it is, do I? No more do you, says you. Well, then, I mean this squire and doctor shall find the stuff, and help us to get it aboard, by the powers. Then we'll see. If I was sure of you all, sons of double Dutchmen, I'd have

Cap'n Smollett navigate us halfway back again before I struck."

"Why, we're all seamen aboard here, I should think," said the lad Dick.

"We're all fok's'le hands, you mean," snapped Silver. "We can steer a course, but who's to set one? That's what all you gentlemen split on, first and last. If I had my way, I'd have Cap'n Smollett work us back into the trades at least; then we'd have no blessed miscalculations and a spoonful of water a day. But I know the sort you are. I'll finish with 'em at the island, as soon's the blunt's on board, and a pity it is. But you're never happy till you're drunk. Split my sides, I've sick heart to sail with the likes of you!"

"Easy all, Long John," cried Israel. "Who's a-crossin' of you?"

"Why, how many tall ships, think ye, now, have I seen laid aboard? and how many brisk lads drying in the sun at Execution Dock?" cried Silver; "and all for this same hurry and hurry and hurry. You hear me? I seen a thing or two at sea, I have. If you would on'y lay your course, and a p'int to windward, you would ride in carriages, you would. But not you! I know you. You'll have your mouthful of rum to-morrow, and go hang."

"Everybody know'd you was a kind of a chapling, John; but there's others as could hand and steer as well as you," said Israel. "They liked a bit o' fun, they did. They wasn't so high and dry, nohow, but took their fling, like jolly companions, every one."

"So?" said Silver. "Well, and where are they now? Pew was that sort, and he died a beggarman. Flint was, and he died of rum at Savannah. Ah, they was a sweet crew, they was! on'y, where are they?"

"But," asked Dick, "when we do lay 'em athwart, what are we to do with 'em, anyhow?"

"There's the man for me!" cried the cook, admiringly. "That's what I call business. Well, what would you think? Put 'em ashore like maroons? That would have been England's way. Or cut 'em down like that much pork? That would have been Flint's or Billy Bones'."

"Billy was the man for that," said Israel. "'Dead men don't bite,' says he. Well, he's dead now, hisself; he knows the long and short on it now; and if ever a rough hand come to port, it was Billy."

"Right you are," said Silver, "rough and ready. But mark you here; I'm an easy man—I'm quite the gentleman, says you; but this time it's serious. Dooty is dooty, mates. I give my vote death. When I'm in Parlyment, and riding in my coach, I don't want none of these sea-lawyers in the cabin a-coming home, unlooked for, like the devil at prayers. Wait is what I say; but when the time comes, why, let her rip!"

"John," cried the cockswain, "you're a man!"

"You'll say so, Israel, when you see," said Silver. "Only one thing I claim—I claim Trelawney. I'll

wring his calf's head off his body with these hands.
Dick!" he added, breaking off, "you must jump up,
like a sweet lad, and get me an apple, to wet my pipe
like."

You may fancy the terror I was in! I should
have leaped out and run for it, if I had found the
strength; but my limbs and heart alike misgave me.
I heard Dick begin to rise, and then someone
seemingly stopped him, and the voice of Hands
exclaimed:

"Oh, stow that! Don't you get sucking of that
bilge, John. Let's have a go of the rum."

"Dick," said Silver, "I trust you. I've a gauge
on the keg, mind. There's the key; you fill a pannikin and bring it up."

Terrified as I was, I could not help thinking to
myself that this must have been how Mr. Arrow got
the strong waters that destroyed him.

Dick was gone but a little while, and during his
absence Israel spoke straight on in the cook's ear.
It was but a word or two that I could catch, and yet
I gathered some important news; for, besides other
scraps that tended to the same purpose, this whole
clause was audible: "Not another man of them'll
jine." Hence there were still faithful men on board.

When Dick returned, one after another of the trio
took the pannikin and drank—one "To luck"; another with a "Here's to old Flint," and Silver himself saying, in a kind of song, "Here's to ourselves,

and hold your luff, plenty of prizes and plenty of duff."

Just then a sort of brightness fell upon me in the barrel, and, looking up, I found the moon had risen, and was silvering the mizzen-top and shining white on the luff of the foresail, and almost at the same time the voice on the lookout shouted, "Land ho!"

## CHAPTER XII

## COUNCIL OF WAR

THERE was a great rush of feet across the deck. I could hear people tumbling up from the cabin and the fok's'le, and, slipping in an instant outside my barrel, I dived behind the foresail, made a double toward the stern, and came out upon the open deck in time to join Hunter and Doctor Livesey in the rush for the weather bow.

There all hands were already congregated. A belt of fog had lifted almost simultaneously with the appearance of the moon. Away to the southwest of us we saw two low hills, about a couple of miles apart, and rising behind one of them a third and higher hill, whose peak was still buried in the fog. All three seemed sharp and conical in figure.

So much I saw almost in a dream, for I had not yet recovered from my horrid fear of a minute or two before. And then I heard the voice of Cap'n Smollett issuing orders. The *Hispaniola* was laid a couple of points nearer the wind, and now sailed a course that would just clear the island on the east.

"And now, men," said the captain, when all was sheeted home, "has any one of you ever seen that land ahead?"

"I have, sir," said Silver. "I've watered there with a trader I was cook in."

"The anchorage is on the south, behind an islet, I fancy?" asked the captain.

"Yes, sir, Skeleton Island they calls it. It were a main place for pirates once, and a hand we had on board knowed all their names for it. That hill to the nor'ard they calls the Foremast Hill; there are three hills in a row running south'ard—fore, main, and mizzen, sir. But the main—that's the big 'un, with the cloud on it—they usually calls the Spy-glass, by reason of a lookout they kept when they was in the anchorage cleaning; for it's there they cleaned their ships, sir, asking your pardon."

"I have a chart here," said Captain Smollett. "See if that's the place."

Long John's eyes burned in his head as he took the chart, but, by the fresh look of the paper, I knew he was doomed to disappointment. This was not the map we found in Billy Bones' chest, but an accurate copy, complete in all things—names, and heights, and soundings—with the single exception of the red crosses and the written notes. Sharp as must have been his annoyance, Silver had the strength of mind to hide it.

"Yes, sir," said he, "this is the spot, to be sure, and very prettily drawed out. Who might have done that, I wonder? The pirates were too ignorant, I reckon. Aye, here it is: 'Captain Kidd's anchor-

Away to the Southwest of Us We Saw Two Low Hills.

age'—just the name my shipmate called it. There's a strong current runs along the south, and then away nor'ard up the west coast. Right you was, sir," said he, "to haul your wind and keep the weather of the island. Leastways, if such was your intention as to enter and careen, and there ain't no better place for that in these waters."

"Thank you, my man," said Captain Smollett. "I'll ask you, later on, to give us a help. You may go."

I was surprised at the coolness with which John avowed his knowledge of the island, and I own I was half-frightened when I saw him drawing nearer to myself. He did not know, to be sure, that I had overheard his council from the apple barrel, and yet I had, by this time, taken such a horror of his cruelty, duplicity, and power, that I could scarce conceal a shudder when he laid his hand upon my arm.

"Ah," said he, "this here is a sweet spot, this island—a sweet spot for a lad to get ashore on. You'll bathe, and you'll climb trees, and you'll hunt goats, you will, and you'll get aloft on them hills like a goat yourself. Why, it makes me young again. I was going to forget my timber leg, I was. It's a pleasant thing to be young, and have ten toes, and you may lay to that. When you want to go a bit of exploring, you just ask old John and he'll put up a snack for you to take along."

And clapping me in the friendliest way upon the shoulder, he hobbled off forward and went below.

Captain Smollett, the squire, and Doctor Livesey were talking together on the quarter-deck, and anxious as I was to tell them my story, I durst not interrupt them openly. While I was still casting about in my thoughts to find some probable excuse, Doctor Livesey called me to his side. He had left his pipe below, and being a slave to tobacco, had meant that I should fetch it; but as soon as I was near enough to speak and not be overheard, I broke out immediately: "Doctor, let me speak. Get the captain and squire down to the cabin, and then make some pretense to send for me. I have terrible news."

The doctor changed countenance a little, but next moment he was master if himself.

"Thank you, Jim," said he, quite loudly; "that was all I wanted to know," as if he had asked me a question.

And with that he turned on his heel and rejoined the other two. They spoke together for a little, and though none of them started, or raised his voice, or so much as whistled, it was plain enough that Doctor Livesey had communicated my request, for the next thing that I heard was the captain giving an order to Job Anderson, and all hands were piped on deck.

"My lads," said Captain Smollett, "I've a word to say to you. This land that we have sighted is the place we have been sailing to. Mr. Trelawney, being a very open-handed gentleman, as we all know, has just asked me a word or two, and as I was able to tell him that every man on board had done his duty, alow and aloft, as I never ask to see it done better, why, he and I and the doctor are going below to the cabin to drink your health and luck, and you'll have grog served out for you to drink *our* health and luck. I'll tell you what I think of this: I think it handsome. And if you think as I do, you'll give a good sea-cheer for the gentleman that does it."

The cheer followed—that was a matter of course —but it rang out so full and hearty, that I confess I could hardly believe these same men were plotting for our blood.

"One more cheer for Cap'n Smollett!" cried Long John, when the first had subsided.

And this also was given with a will.

On the top of that the three gentlemen went below, and not long after word was sent forward that Jim Hawkins was wanted in the cabin.

I found them all three seated round the table, a bottle of Spanish wine and some raisins before them, and the doctor smoking away, with his wig on his lap, and that, I knew, was a sign that he was agitated. The stern window was open, for it was a warm night, and you could see the moon shining behind on the ship's wake.

"Now, Hawkins," said the squire, "you have something to say. Speak up."

I did as I was bid, and, as short as I could make it, told the whole details of Silver's conversation. Nobody interrupted me till I was done, nor did any one of the three of them make so much as a movement, but they kept their eyes upon my face from first to last.

"Jim," said Doctor Livesey, "take a seat."

And they made me sit down at a table beside them, poured me out a glass of wine, filled my hands with raisins, and all three, one after the other, and each with a bow, drank my good health, and their service to me, for my luck and courage.

"Now, captain," said the squire, "you were right and I was wrong. I own myself an ass, and I await your orders."

"No more an ass than I, sir," returned the captain. "I never heard of a crew that meant to mutiny but what showed signs before, for any man that had an eye in his head to see the mischief and take steps according. But this crew," he added, "beats me."

"Captain," said the doctor, "with your permission, that's Silver. A very remarkable man."

"He'd look remarkably well from a yard-arm, sir," returned the captain. "But this is talk; this don't lead to anything. I see three or four points, and with Mr. Trelawney's permission I'll name them."

"You, sir, are the captain. It is for you to speak," said Mr. Trelawney, grandly.

"First point," began Mr. Smollett, "we must go on because we can't turn back. If I gave the word to turn about they would rise at once. Second point, we have time before us—at least until this treasure's found. Third point, there are faithful hands. Now, sir, it's got to come to blows sooner or later, and what I propose is to take time by the forelock, as the saying is, and come to blows some fine day when they least expect it. We can count, I take it, on your own home servants, Mr. Trelawney?"

"As upon myself," declared the squire.

"Three," reckoned the captain; "ourselves make seven, counting Hawkins here. Now about the honest hands?"

"Most likely Trelawney's own men," said the doctor; "those he picked up for himself before he lit on Silver."

"Nay," replied the squire, "Hands was one of mine."

"I did think I could have trusted Hands," added the captain.

"And to think that they're all Englishmen!" broke out the squire. "Sir, I could find it in my heart to blow the ship up."

"Well, gentlemen," said the captain, "the best that I can say is not much. We must lay to, if you please, and keep a bright lookout. It's trying on a man, I know. It would be pleasanter to come to blows. But there's no help for it till we know our men. Lay to and whistle for a wind; that's my view."

"Jim here," said the doctor, "can help us more than anyone. The men are not shy with him and Jim is a noticing lad."

"Hawkins, I put prodigious faith in you," added the squire.

I began to feel pretty desperate at this, for I felt altogether helpless; and yet, by an odd train of circumstances, it was indeed through me that safety came. In the meantime, talk as we pleased, there were only seven out of the twenty-six on whom we knew we could rely, and out of these seven one was a boy, so that the grown men on our side were six to their nineteen.

# PART III

# MY SHORE ADVENTURE

## CHAPTER XIII

## HOW I BEGAN MY SHORE ADVENTURE

THE appearance of the island when I came on deck next morning was altogether changed. Although the breeze had now utterly failed we had made a great deal of way during the night and were now lying becalmed about half a mile to the southeast of the low eastern coast. Gray-colored woods covered a large part of the surface. This even tint was indeed broken up by streaks of yellow sandbreak in the lower lands and by many tall trees of the pine family, out-topping the others—some singly, some in clumps; but the general coloring was uniform and sad. The hills ran up clear above the vegetation in spires of naked rock. All were strangely shaped, and the Spy-glass, which was by three or four hundred feet the tallest on the island, was likewise the strangest in configuration, running up sheer from almost every side and then suddenly cut off at the top like a pedestal to put a statue on.

The *Hispaniola* was rolling scuppers under in the ocean swell. The booms were tearing at the blocks, the rudder was banging to and fro and the whole ship creaking, groaning, and jumping like a manufactory. I had to cling tight to the backstay and the world turned giddily before my eyes, for though I was a good enough sailor when there was way on, this standing still and being rolled about like a bottle was a thing I never learned to stand without a qualm or so, above all in the morning, on an empty stomach.

Perhaps it was this—perhaps it was the look of the island, with its gray, melancholy woods, and wild stone spires, and the surf that we could both see and hear foaming and thundering on the steep beach—at least, although the sun shone bright and hot, and the shore birds were fishing and crying all around us, and you would have thought anyone would have been glad to get to land after being so long at sea, my heart sunk, as the saying is, into my boots, and from that first look onward I hated the very thought of Treasure Island.

We had a dreary morning's work before us, for there was no sign of any wind and the boats had to be got out and manned and the ship warped three or four miles round the corner of the island and up the narrow passage to the haven behind Skeleton Island. I volunteered for one of the boats, where I had of course no business. The heat was sweltering and the men grumbled fiercely over their work. Anderson was in command of my boat, and instead of keeping the crew in order he grumbled as loud as the worst.

"Well," he said, with an oath, "it's not forever."

I thought this was a very bad sign, for, up to that day, the men had gone briskly and willingly about their business, but the very sight of the island had relaxed the cords of discipline.

All the way in, Long John stood by the steersman and conned the ship. He knew the passage like the palm of his hand; and though the man in the chains got everywhere more water than was down in the chart, John never hesitated once.

"There's a strong scour with the ebb," he said, "and this here passage has been dug out, in a manner of speaking, with a spade."

We brought up just where the anchor was in the chart, about a third of a mile from either shore, the mainland on one side and Skeleton Island on the other. The bottom was clean sand. The plunge of our anchor sent up clouds of birds wheeling and crying over the woods, but in less than a minute they were all down again, and all was once more silent.

The place was entirely land-locked, buried in woods, the trees coming right down to high-water mark, the shores mostly flat, and the hill-tops standing round at a distance in a sort of amphitheater, one here, one there. Two little rivers, or rather two swamps, emptied out into this pond, as you might call it; and the foliage round that part of the shore had a kind of poisonous brightness. From the ship we could see nothing of the house or stockade, for they were quite buried among trees; and if it had not been for the chart on the companion, we might have been the first that had ever anchored there since the islands arose out of the seas.

There was not a breath of air moving, nor a sound but that of the surf booming half a mile away along the beaches and against the rocks outside. A peculiar stagnant smell hung over the anchorage—a smell of sodden leaves and rotten tree-trunks. I observed the doctor sniffing and sniffing, like someone tasting a bad egg.

"I don't know about treasure," he said, "but I'll stake my wig there's fever here."

If the conduct of the men had been alarming in the boat, it became truly threatening when they had come aboard. They lay about the deck, growling together in talk. The slightest order was received with a black look, and grudgingly and carelessly obeyed. Even the honest hands must have caught the infection, for there was not one man aboard to mend another. Mutiny, it was plain, hung over us like a thunder-cloud.

And it was not only we of the cabin party who perceived the danger. Long John was hard at work going from group to group, spending himself in good

advice, and as for example no man could have shown
a better. He fairly outstripped himself in willing-
ness and civility; he was all smiles to everyone. If
an order was given, John would be on his crutch
in an instant, with the cheeriest, "Aye, aye, sir!" in
the world; and when there was nothing else to do,
he kept up one song after another, as if to conceal the
discontent of the rest.

Of all the gloomy features of that gloomy afternoon, this obvious anxiety on the part of Long John,
appeared the worst.

We held a council in the cabin.

"Sir," said the captain, "if I risk another order,
the whole ship'll come about our ears by the run.
You see, sir, here it is. I get a rough answer, do I not?
Well, if I speak back, pikes will be going in two shakes;
if I don't, Silver will see there's something under that,
and the game's up. Now, we've only one man to
rely on."

"And who is that?" asked the squire.

"Silver, sir," returned the captain; "he's as
anxious as you and I to smother things up. This is
a tiff; he'd soon talk 'em out of it if he had the chance,
and what I propose to do is to give him the chance.
Let's allow the men an afternoon ashore. If they all
go, why, we'll fight the ship. If they none of them
go, well, then, we hold the cabin, and God defend the
right. If some go, you mark my words, sir, Silver'll
bring 'em aboard again as mild as lambs."

It was so decided; loaded pistols were served out to all the sure men. Hunter, Joyce, and Redruth were taken into our confidence, and received the news with less surprise and better spirit than we had looked for, and then the captain went on deck and addressed the crew.

"My lads," said he, "we've had a hot day, and are all tired and out of sorts. A turn ashore'll hurt nobody; the boats are still in the water; you can take the gigs, and as many as please can go ashore for the afternoon. I'll fire a gun half an hour before sun-down."

I believe the silly fellows must have thought they would break their shins over the treasure as soon as they were landed; for they all came out of their sulks in a moment, and gave a cheer that started the echo in a far-away hill, and sent the birds once more flying and squalling round the anchorage.

The captain was too bright to be in the way. He whipped out of sight in a moment, leaving Silver to arrange the party, and I fancy it was well he did so. Had he been on deck, he could no longer so much as have pretended not to understand the situation. It was as plain as day. Silver was the captain, and a mighty rebellious crew he had of it. The honest hands—and I was soon to see it proved that there were such on board—must have been very stupid fellows. Or, rather, I suppose the truth was this: that all hands were disaffected by the example of the ringleaders—only some more, some less; and a few, being good fellows in the main, could neither be led nor driven any farther. It is one thing to be idle and skulk, and quite another to take a ship and murder a number of innocent men.

At last, however, the party was made up. Six fellows were to stay on board, and the remaining thirteen, including Silver, began to embark.

Then it was that there came into my head the first of the mad notions that contributed so much to save our lives. If six men were left by Silver, it was plain our party could not take and fight the ship; and since only six were left, it was equally plain that the cabin party had no present need of my assistance. It occurred to me at once to go ashore. In a jiffy I had slipped over the side and curled up in the fore-sheets of the nearest boat, and almost at the same moment she shoved off.

No one took notice of me, only the bow oar saying, "Is that you, Jim? Keep your head down." But Silver, from the other boat, looked sharply over and called out to know if that were me; and from that moment I began to regret what I had done.

The crews raced for the beach, but the boat I was in, having some start, and being at once the lighter and the better manned, shot far ahead of her consort, and the bow had struck among the shore-side trees, and I had caught a branch and swung myself out, and plunged into the nearest thicket, while

Silver and the rest were still a hundred yards behind.

"Jim, Jim!" I heard him shouting.

But you may suppose I paid no heed; jumping,
ducking, and breaking through, I ran straight before
my nose, till I could run no longer.

## Chapter XIV

## THE FIRST BLOW

I WAS so pleased at having given the slip to Long John, that I began to enjoy myself and look around me with some interest on the strange land that I was in. I had crossed a marshy tract full of willows, bulrushes, and odd, outlandish, swampish trees; and I had now come out upon the skirts of an open piece of undulating, sandy country, about a mile long, dotted with a few pines, and a great number of contorted trees, not unlike the oak in growth, but pale in the foliage, like willows. On the far side of the open stood one of the hills, with two quaint, craggy peaks, shining vividly in the sun.

I now felt for the first time the joy of exploration. The isle was uninhabited; my shipmates I had left behind, and nothing lived in front of me but dumb brutes and fowls. I turned hither and thither among the trees. Here and there were flowering plants, unknown to me; here and there I saw snakes, and one raised his head from a ledge of rock and hissed at me with a noise not unlike the spinning of a top. Little did I suppose that he was a deadly enemy, and that the noise was the famous rattle.

117

Then I came to a long thicket of these oak-like trees—live, or evergreen, oaks, I heard afterward they should be called—which grew low along the sand-like brambles, the boughs curiously twisted, the foliage compact, like thatch. The thicket stretched down from the top of one of the sandy knolls, spreading and growing taller as it went, until it reached the margin of the broad, reedy fen, through which the nearest of the little rivers soaked its way into the anchorage. The marsh was steaming in the strong sun, and the outline of the Spy-glass trembled through the haze.

All at once there began to go a sort of bustle among the bulrushes; a wild duck flew up with a quack, another followed, and soon over the whole surface of the marsh a great cloud of birds hung screaming and circling in the air. I judged at once that some of my shipmates must be drawing near along the borders of the fen. Nor was I deceived, for soon I heard the very distant and low tones of a human voice, which, as I continued to give ear, grew steadily louder and nearer.

This put me in great fear, and I crawled under cover of the nearest live-oak, and squatted there, hearkening, as silent as a mouse.

Another voice answered; and then the first voice, which I now recognized to be Silver's, once more took up the story, and ran on for a long while in a stream, only now and again interrupted by the other. By the sound they must have been talking earnestly, and almost fiercely, but no distinct word came to my hearing.

At last the speakers seemed to have paused, and perhaps to have sat down, for not only did they cease to draw any nearer, but the birds themselves began to grow more quiet, and to settle again to their places in the swamp.

And now I began to feel that I was neglecting my business; that since I had been so foolhardy as to come ashore with these desperadoes, the least I could do was to overhear them at their councils, and that my plain and obvious duty was to draw as close as I could manage, under the favorable ambush of the crouching trees.

I could tell the direction of the speakers pretty exactly, not only by the sound of their voices, but by the behavior of the few birds that still hung in alarm above the heads of the intruders.

Crawling on all-fours I made steadily but slowly toward them, till at last, raising my head to an aperture among the leaves, I could see clear down into a little green dell beside the marsh, and closely set about with trees, where Long John Silver and another of the crew stood face to face in conversation.

The sun beat full upon them. Silver had thrown his hat beside him on the ground, and his great, smooth, blonde face, all shining with heat, was lifted to the other man's in a kind of appeal.

"Mate," he was saying, "it's because I thinks gold-dust of you—gold-dust, and you may lay to that! If I hadn't took to you like pitch, do you think I'd have been here a-warning of you? All's up— you can't make nor mend; it's to save your neck that I'm a-speaking, and if one of the wild 'uns knew it, where 'ud I be, Tom—now tell me, where 'ud I be?"

"Silver," said the other man—and I observed he was not only red in the face, but spoke as hoarse as a crow, and his voice shook, too, like a taut rope— "Silver," says he, "you're old, and you're honest, or has the name for it; and you've money, too, which lots of poor sailors hasn't; and you're brave, or I'm mistook. And will you tell me you'll let yourself be led away with that kind of a mess of swabs? Not you! As sure as God sees me, I'd sooner lose my hand. If I turn agin my dooty——"

And then all of a sudden he was interrupted by a noise. I had found one of the honest hands—well, here, at that same moment, came news of another. Far away out in the marsh there arose, all of a sudden, a sound like the cry of anger, then another on the back of it, and then one horrid, long-drawn scream. The rocks of the Spy-glass re-echoed it a score of times; the whole troop of marsh-birds rose again, darkening heaven with a simultaneous whir; and long after that death-yell was still ringing in my brain, silence had re-established its empire, and only the rustle of the redescending birds and the boom

of the distant surges disturbed the languor of the
afternoon.

Tom had leaped at the sound, like a horse at the
spur; but Silver had not winked an eye. He stood
where he was, resting lightly on his crutch, watching
his companion like a snake about to spring.

"John!" said the sailor, stretching out his hand.
"Hands off!" cried Silver, leaping back a yard, as
it seemed to me, with the speed and security of a trained
gymnast.

"Hands off, if you like, John Silver," said the
other. "It's a black conscience that can make you
feared of me. But, in heaven's name, tell me what
was that?"

"That?" returned Silver, smiling away, but
warier than ever, his eye a mere pin-point in his big
face, but gleaming like a crumb of glass. "That?
Oh, I reckon that'll be Alan."

And at this poor Tom flashed out like a hero.

"Alan!" he cried. "Then rest his soul for a true
seaman! And as for you, John Silver, long you've
been a mate of mine, but you're mate of mine no
more. If I die like a dog I'll die in my dooty. You've
killed Alan, have you? Kill me, too, if you can. But
I defies you."

And with that this brave fellow turned his back
directly on the cook and set off walking for the
beach. But he was not destined to go far. With a
cry John seized the branch of a tree, whipped the

crutch out of his armpit, and sent that uncouth missile hurling through the air. It struck poor Tom, point foremost, and with stunning violence, right between the shoulders in the middle of his back. His hands flew up, he gave a sort of gasp and fell.

Whether he was injured much or little, none could ever tell. Like enough, to judge from the sound, his back was broken on the spot. But he had no time given him to recover. Silver, agile as a monkey, even without leg or crutch, was on the top of him next moment, and had twice buried his knife up to the hilt in that defenseless body. From my place of ambush I could hear him pant aloud as he struck the blows.

I do not know what it rightly is to faint, but I do know that for the next little while the whole world swam away from before me in a whirling mist; Silver and the birds and the tall Spy-glass hill-top going round and round and topsy-turvy before my eyes, and all manner of bells ringing, and distant voices shouting in my ear.

When I came again to myself the monster had pulled himself together, his crutch under his arm, his hat upon his head. Just before him Tom lay motionless upon the sward; but the murderer minded him not a whit, cleansing his blood-stained knife the while upon a whisp of grass. Everything else was unchanged, the sun still shining mercilessly upon the steaming marsh and the tall pinnacle of the moun-

**It Struck Poor Tom, Point Foremost.**

123

tain, and I could scarce persuade myself that murder
had actually been done and a human life cruelly cut
short a moment since, before my eyes.

But now John put his hand into his pocket, brought
out a whistle, and blew upon it several modulated
blasts, that rang far across the heated air. I could
not tell, of course, the meaning of the signal, but it
instantly awoke my fears. More men would be coming. I might be discovered. They had already slain
two of the honest people; after Tom and Alan, might
not I come next?

Instantly I began to extricate myself and crawl
back again, with what speed and silence I could
manage, to the more open portion of the wood. As
I did so I could hear hails coming and going between
the old buccaneer and his comrades, and this sound
of danger lent me wings. As soon as I was clear
of the thicket, I ran as I never ran before, scarce
minding the direction of my flight, so long as it led
me from the murderers, and as I ran, fear grew and
grew upon me, until it turned into a kind of frenzy.

Indeed, could anyone be more entirely lost than I?
When the gun fired, how should I dare to go down
to the boats among the fiends, still smoking from
their crime? Would not the first of them who saw
me wring my neck like a snipe's? Would not my
absence itself be an evidence to them of my alarm,
and therefore of my fatal knowledge? It was all over,
I thought. Good-by to the *Hispaniola*, good-by to

the squire, the doctor, and the captain.  There was nothing left for me but death by starvation, or death by the hands of the mutineers.

All this while, as I say, I was still running, and, without taking notice, I had drawn near to the foot of the little hill with the two peaks, and had got into a part of the island where the wild oaks grew more widely apart, and seemed more like forest trees in their bearing and dimensions.  Mingled with these were a few scattered pines, some fifty, some nearer seventy, feet high.  The air, too, smelled more freshly than down beside the marsh.

And here a fresh alarm brought me to a stand-still with a thumping heart.

## CHAPTER XV

## THE MAN OF THE ISLAND

FROM the side of the hill, which was here steep and stony, a spout of gravel was dislodged, and fell rattling and bounding through the trees. My eyes turned instinctively in that direction, and I saw a figure leap with great rapidity behind the trunk of a pine. What it was, whether bear, or man, or monkey, I could in nowise tell. It seemed dark and shaggy; more I knew not. But the terror of this new apparition brought me to a stand.

I was now, it seemed, cut off upon both sides; behind me the murderers, before me this lurking nondescript. And immediately I began to prefer the dangers that I knew to those I knew not. Silver himself appeared less terrible in contrast with this creature of the woods, and I turned on my heel, and, looking sharply behind me over my shoulder, began to retrace my steps in the direction of the boats.

Instantly the figure reappeared, and, making a wide circuit, began to head me off. I was tired, at any rate, but had I been as fresh as when I rose, I could see it was in vain for me to contend in speed with such an adversary. From trunk to trunk the creature

flitted like a deer, running man-like on two legs, but
unlike any man that I had ever seen, stooping almost
double as it ran. Yet a man it was; I could no longer
be in doubt about that.

I began to recall what I had heard of cannibals.
I was within an ace of calling for help. But the mere
fact that he was a man, however wild, had somewhat
reassured me, and my fear of Silver began to revive
in proportion. I stood still, therefore, and cast about
for some method of escape, and as I was so thinking,
the recollection of my pistol flashed into my mind.
As soon as I remembered I was not defenseless, courage
glowed again in my heart, and I set my face resolutely
for this man of the island, and walked briskly toward
him.

He was concealed by this time, behind another
tree-trunk, but he must have been watching me
closely, for as soon as I began to move in his direction he reappeared and took a step to meet me. Then
he hesitated, drew back, came forward again, and
at last, to my wonder and confusion, threw himself
on his knees and held out his clasped hands in supplication.

At that I once more stopped.

"Who are you?" I asked.

"Ben Gunn," he answered, and his voice sounded
hoarse and awkward, like a rusty lock. "I'm poor
Ben Gunn, I am; and I haven't spoke with a Christian these three years."

I could now see that he was a white man like
myself, and that his features were even pleasing.
His skin, wherever it was exposed, was burned by the
sun; even his lips were black, and his fair eyes looked
quite startling in so dark a face. Of all the beggar-
men that I had seen or fancied, he was the chief for
raggedness. He was clothed with tatters of old ship's
canvas and old sea-cloth, and this extraordinary patch-
work was all held together by a system of the most
various and incongruous fastenings, brass buttons,
bits of stick, and loops of tarry gaskin. About his
waist he wore an old brass-buckled leather belt, which
was the one thing solid in his whole accouterment.

"Three years!" I cried. "Were you ship-
wrecked?"

"Nay, mate," said he, "marooned."

I had heard the word and I knew it stood for a
horrible kind of punishment common enough among
the buccaneers, in which the offender is put ashore
with a little powder and shot and left behind on some
desolate and distant island.

"Marooned three years agone," he continued,
"and lived on goats since then, and berries and
oysters. Wherever a man is, says I, a man can do
for himself. But, mate, my heart is sore for Christian diet. You mightn't happen to have a piece of
cheese about you, now? No? Well, many's the long
night I've dreamed of cheese—toasted, mostly—and
woke up again, and here I were."

"Ben Gunn," He Answered.

129

"If ever I can get aboard again," said I, "you shall have cheese by the stone."

All this time he had been feeling the stuff of my jacket, smoothing my hands, looking at my boots, and generally, in the intervals of his speech, showing a childish pleasure in the presence of a fellow creature. But at my last words he perked up into a kind of startled slyness.

"If ever you get aboard again, says you?" he repeated. "Why, now, who's to hinder you?"

"Not you, I know," was my reply.

"And right you was," he cried. "Now you—what do you call yourself, mate?"

"Jim," I told him.

"Jim, Jim," says he, quite pleased, apparently. "Well, now, Jim, I've lived that rough as you'd be ashamed to hear of. Now, for instance, you wouldn't think I had a pious mother—to look at me?" he asked.

"Why, no, not in particular," I answered.

"Ah, well," said he, "but I had—remarkable pious. And I was a civil, pious boy, and could rattle off my catechism that fast as you couldn't tell one word from another. And here's what it come to, Jim, and it begun with chuck-farthen on the blessed gravestones! That's what it begun with, but it went further'n that, and so my mother told me, and predicked the whole, she did, the pious woman. But it were Providence that put me here. I've thought it all out in this here lonely island and I'm back on piety. You can't catch me tasting rum so much, but just a thimbleful for luck, of course, the first chance I have. I'm bound I'll be good, and I see the way to. And, Jim"—looking all round him and lowering his voice to a whisper—"I'm rich."

I now felt sure that the poor fellow had gone crazy in his solitude, and I suppose I must have shown the feeling in my face, for he repeated the statement hotly:

"Rich! rich! I says. And I'll tell you what, I'll make a man of you, Jim. Ah, Jim, you'll bless your stars, you will, you was the first that found me!"

And at this there came suddenly a lowering shadow over his face and he tightened his grasp upon my hand and raised a forefinger threateningly before my eyes.

"Now, Jim, you tell me true; that ain't Flint's ship?" he asked.

At this I had a happy inspiration. I began to believe that I had found an ally and I answered him at once.

"It's not Flint's ship and Flint is dead, but I'll tell you true, as you ask me—there are some of Flint's hands aboard; worse luck for the rest of us."

"Not a man—with one—leg?" he gasped.

"Silver?" I asked.

"Ah, Silver!" says he, "that were his name."

"He's the cook and the ringleader, too."

He was still holding me by the wrist and at that he gave it quite a wring.

"If you was sent by Long John," he said, "I'm as good as pork and I know it. But where was you, do you suppose?"

I had made my mind up in a moment, and by way of answer told him the whole story of our voyage and the predicament in which we found ourselves. He heard me with the keenest interest, and when I had done he patted me on the head.

"You're a good lad, Jim," he said, "and you're all in a clove hitch, ain't you? Well, you just put your trust in Ben Gunn—Ben Gunn's the man to do it. Would you think it likely, now, that your squire would prove a liberal-minded one in case of help—him being in a clove hitch, as you remark?"

I told him the squire was the most liberal of men.

"Aye, but you see," returned Ben Gunn, "I didn't mean giving me a gate to keep and a suit of livery clothes, and such; that's not my mark, Jim. What I mean is, would he be likely to come down to the toon of, say one thousand pounds out of money that's as good as a man's own already?"

"I am sure he would," said I. "As it was, all hands were to share."

"*And* a passage home?" he added, with a look of great shrewdness.

"Why," I cried, "the squire's a gentleman. And, besides, if we got rid of the others, we should want you to help work the vessel home."

"Ah," said he, "so you would." And he seemed very much relieved.

"Now, I'll tell you what," he went on. "So much I'll tell you, and no more. I were in Flint's ship when he buried the treasure; he and six along— six strong seamen. They was ashore nigh on a week, and us standing off and on in the old Walrus. One fine day up went the signal, and here come Flint by himself in a little boat, and his head done up in a blue scarf. The sun was getting up, and mortal white he looked about the cutwater. But, there he was, you mind, and the six all dead—dead and buried. How had he done it, not a man aboard us could make out. It was battle, murder, and sudden death—least-ways, him against six. Billy Bones was the mate; Long John, he was quartermaster; and they asked him where the treasure was. 'Ah,' says he, 'you can go ashore, if you like and stay,' he says; 'but as for the ship, she'll beat up for more, by thunder!' That's what he said.

"Well, I was in another ship three years back, and we sighted this island. 'Boys,' said I, 'here's Flint's treasure; let's land and find it.' The cap'n was dis-pleased at that; but my messmates were all of a mind, and landed. Twelve days they looked for it, and every day they had the worse words for

me, until one fine morning all hands went aboard.
'As for you, Benjamin Gunn,' says they, 'here's a
musket,' they says, 'and a spade, and pick-ax. You
can stay here and find Flint's money for yourself,'
they says.

"Well, Jim, three years have I been here, and not
a bite of Christian diet from that day to this. But
now, look you here; look at me. Do I look like a
man before the mast? No, says you. Nor I weren't
neither, I says."

And with that he winked and pinched me hard.

"Just you mention them words to your squire,
Jim," he went on. "Nor he weren't, neither—that's
the words. Three years he were the man of this island, light and dark, fair and rain; and sometimes
he would, may be, think upon a prayer (says you),
and sometimes he would, may be, think of his old
mother, so be as she's alive (you'll say); but the
most part of Gunn's time (this is what you'll say)
—the most part of his time was took up with another matter. And then you'll give him a nip, like
I do."

And he pinched me again, in the most confidential
manner.

"Then," he continued, "then you'll up, and you'll
say this: Gunn is a good man (you'll say), and he
puts a precious sight more confidence—a precious
sight, mind that—in gen'leman born than in these
gen'lemen of fortune, having been one hisself."

"Well," I said, "I don't understand one word
that you've been saying. But that's neither here nor
there; for how am I to get on board?"

"Ah," said he," "that's the hitch for sure. Well,
there's my boat that I made with my two hands. I
keep her under the white rock. If the worst come
to the worst, we might try that after dark. Hi!"
he broke out, "what's that?"

For just then, although the sun had still an hour or
two to run, all the echoes of the island awoke and
bellowed to the thunder of a cannon.

"They have begun to fight!" I cried. "Follow
me!"

And I began to run toward the anchorage, my
terrors all forgotten; while, close at my side, the
marooned man in his goatskins trotted easily and
lightly.

"Left, left," says he; "keep to your left hand, mate
Jim! Under the trees with you! There's where I
killed my first goat. They don't come down here
now; they're all mastheaded on them mountings for
the fear of Benjamin Gunn. Ah! and there's the
cetemery"—cemetery he must have meant. "You
see the mounds? I come here and prayed, nows and
thens, when I thought may be a Sunday would be
about doo. It weren't quite a chapel, but it seemed
more solemn like; and then, says you, Ben Gunn was
shorthanded—no chapling, nor so much as a Bible
and a flag, you says."

So he kept talking as I ran, neither expecting nor receiving any answer.

The cannon-shot was followed, after a considerable interval, by a volley of small arms.

Another pause, and then, not a quarter of a mile in front of me, I beheld the Union Jack flutter in the air above a wood.

## PART IV

## THE STOCKADE

## CHAPTER XVI

## NARRATIVE CONTINUED BY THE DOCTOR— HOW THE SHIP WAS ABANDONED

IT was about half-past one—three bells in the sea phrase—that the two boats went ashore from the *Hispaniola.* The captain, the squire, and I were talking matters over in the cabin. Had there been a breath of wind, we should have fallen on the six mutineers who were left aboard with us, slipped our cable, and away to sea. But the wind was wanting; and, to complete our helplessness, down came Hunter with the news that Jim Hawkins had slipped into a boat and was gone ashore with the rest.

It had never occurred to us to doubt Jim Hawkins, but we were alarmed for his safety. With the men in the temper they were in, it seemed an even chance if we should see the lad again. We ran on deck. The pitch was bubbling in the seams; the nasty stench of the place turned me sick; if ever a man smelled fever and dysentery, it was in that abominable anchorage. The six scoundrels were sitting grumbling under

137

a sail in the forecastle; ashore we could see the gigs made fast, and a man sitting in each, hard by where the river runs in. One of them was whistling "Lillibullero."

Waiting was a strain, and it was decided that Hunter and I should go ashore with the jolly-boat, in quest of information.

The gigs had leaned to their right, but Hunter and I pulled straight in, in the direction of the stockade upon the chart. The two who were left guarding their boats seemed in a bustle at our appearance; "Lillibullero" stopped off, and I could see the pair discussing what they ought to do. Had they gone and told Silver, all might have turned out differently; but they had their orders, I suppose, and decided to sit quietly where they were and hark back again to "Lillibullero."

There was a slight bend in the coast, and I steered so as to put it between us. Even before we landed we had thus lost sight of the gigs; I jumped out and came as near running as I durst, with a big silk handkerchief under my hat for coolness' sake, and a brace of pistols ready primed for safety.

I had not gone a hundred yards when I came on the stockade.

This was how it was: A spring of clear water arose at the top of a knoll. Well on the knoll, and inclosing the spring, they had clapped a stout log house, fit to hold two score people on a pinch, and

loop-holed for musketry on every side. All around
this they had cleared a wide space, and then the
thing was completed by a paling six feet high, without
door or opening, too strong to pull down without time
and labor, and too open to shelter the besiegers.
The people in the log house had them in every
way; they stood quiet in the shelter and shot the
others like partridges. All they wanted was a
good watch and food; for, short of a complete
surprise, they might have held the place against a
regiment.

What particularly took my fancy was the spring.
For, though we had a good enough place of it in the
cabin of the *Hispaniola*, with plenty of arms and
ammunition, and things to eat, and excellent wines,
there had been one thing overlooked—we had no
water. I was thinking this over, when there came
ringing over the island the cry of a man at the point
of death. I was not new to violent death—I have
served his Royal Highness the Duke of Cumberland,
and got a wound myself at Fontenoy—but I know
my pulse went dot and carry one. "Jim Hawkins
is gone," was my first thought.

It is something to have been an old soldier, but
more still to have been a doctor. There is no time
to dilly-dally in our work. And so now I made up
my mind instantly, and with no time lost returned
to the shore and jumped on board the jolly-boat.

By good fortune Hunter pulled a good oar. We

made the water fly, and the boat was soon alongside and I aboard the schooner.

I found them all shaken, as was natural. The squire was sitting down, as white as a sheet, thinking of the harm he had led us to, the good soul! and one of the six forecastle hands was little better.

"There's a man," said Captain Smollett, nodding toward him, "new to this work. He came nigh-hand fainting, doctor, when he heard the cry. Another touch of the rudder and that man would join us."

I told my plan to the captain, and between us we settled on the details of its accomplishment.

We put old Redruth in the gallery between the cabin and the forecastle, with three or four loaded muskets and a mattress for protection. Hunter brought the boat round under the stern port, and Joyce and I set to work loading her with powder, tins, muskets, bags of biscuits, kegs of pork, a cask of cognac, and my invaluable medicine chest.

In the meantime the squire and the captain stayed on deck, and the latter hailed the cockswain, who was the principal man aboard.

"Mr. Hands," he said, "here are two of us with a brace of pistols each. If any one of you six make a signal of any description, that man's dead."

They were a good deal taken aback; and, after a little consultation, one and all tumbled down the fore companion, thinking, no doubt, to take us on the rear. But when they saw Redruth waiting for them in the sparred gallery, they went about ship at once, and a head popped out again on deck.

"Down, dog!" cried the captain.

And the head popped back again, and we heard no more for the time of these six very faint-hearted seamen.

By this time, tumbling things in as they came, we had the jolly-boat loaded as much as we dared. Joyce and I got out through the stern port, and we made for shore again, as fast as oars could take us.

This second trip fairly aroused the watchers along shore. "Lillibullero" was dropped again, and just before we lost sight of them behind the little point, one of them whipped ashore and disappeared. I had half a mind to change my plan and destroy their boats, but I feared that Silver and the others might be close at hand, and all might very well be lost by trying for too much.

We had soon touched land in the same place as before and set to provision the block-house. All three made the first journey, heavily laden, and tossed our stores over the palisade. Then, leaving Joyce to guard them—one man, to be sure, but with half a dozen muskets—Hunter and I returned to the jolly-boat, and loaded ourselves once more. So we proceeded, without pausing to take breath, till the whole cargo was bestowed, when the two servants took up their position in the block-house, and I, with all my power, sculled back to the *Hispaniola*.

That we should have risked a second boat-load seems more daring than it really was. They had the advantage of numbers, of course, but we had the advantage of arms. Not one of the men ashore had a musket, and before they could get within range for pistol shooting, we flattered ourselves we should be able to give a good account of a half-dozen at least.

The squire was waiting for me at the stern window, all his faintness gone from him. He caught the painter and made it fast, and we fell to loading the boat for our very lives. Pork, powder, and biscuit was the cargo, with only a musket and a cutlass apiece for squire and me and Redruth and the captain. The rest of the arms and powder we dropped over-board in two fathoms and a half of water, so that we could see the bright steel shining far below us in the sun on the clean, sandy bottom.

By this time the tide was beginning to ebb, and the ship was swinging round to her anchor. Voices were heard faintly hallooing in the direction of the two gigs; and though this reassured us for Joyce and Hunter, who were well to the eastward, it warned our party to be off.

Redruth retreated from his place in the gallery and dropped into the boat, which we then brought round to the ship's counter, to be handier for Captain Smollett.

"Now, men," said he, "do you hear me?"

There was no answer from the forecastle.

"It's to you, Abraham Gray—it's to you I am speaking."

Still no reply.

"Gray," resumed Mr. Smollett, a little louder, "I am leaving this ship, and I order you to follow your captain. I know you are a good man at bottom, and I dare say not one of the lot of you's as bad as he makes out. I have my watch here in my hand; I give you thirty seconds to join me in."

There was a pause.

"Come, my fine fellow," continued the captain, "don't hang so long in stays. I'm risking my life and the lives of these good gentlemen every second."

There was a sudden scuffle, a sound of blows, and out burst Abraham Gray with a knife-cut on the side of the cheek, and came running to the captain, like a dog to the whistle.

"I'm with you, sir," said he.

And the next moment he and the captain had dropped aboard of us, and we had shoved off and given way.

We were clear out of the ship, but not yet ashore in our stockade.

CHAPTER XVII

# NARRATIVE CONTINUED BY THE DOCTOR— THE JOLLY-BOAT'S LAST TRIP

THIS fifth trip was quite different from any of the others. In the first place, the little gallipot of a boat that we were in was gravely overloaded. Five grown men, and three of them—Trelawney, Redruth, and the captain—over six feet high, was already more than she was meant to carry. Add to that the powder, pork, and the bread-bags. The gunwale was lipping astern. Several times we shipped a little water, and my breeches and the tails of my coat were all soaking wet before we had gone a hundred yards.

The captain made us trim the boat, and we got her to lie a little more evenly. All the same, we were afraid to breathe.

In the second place, the ebb was now making—a strong, rippling current running westward through the basin, and then south'ard and seaward down the straits by which we had entered in the morning. Even the ripples were a danger to our overloaded craft, but the worst of it was that we were swept out of our true course, and away from our landing-place behind the point. If we let the current have its way we should come ashore beside the gigs, where the pirates might appear at any moment.

"I cannot keep her head for the stockade, sir," said I to the captain. I was steering, while he and Redruth, two fresh men, were at the oars. "The tide keeps washing her down. Could you pull a little stronger?"

"Not without swamping the boat," said he. "You must bear up, sir, if you please—bear up until you see you're gaining."

I tried, and found by experiment that the tide kept sweeping us westward until I had laid her head due east, or just about right angles to the way we ought to go.

"We'll never get ashore at this rate," said I.

"If it's the only course that we can lie, sir, we must even lie it," returned the captain. "We must keep up stream. You see, sir," he went on, "if once we dropped to leeward of the landing-place, it's hard to say where we should get ashore, besides the chance of being boarded by the gigs; whereas, the way we go the current must slacken, and then we can dodge back along the shore."

"The current's less a'ready, sir," said the man Gray, who was sitting in the fore-sheets; "you can ease her off a bit."

"Thank you, my man," said I, quite as if nothing had happened, for we had all quietly made up our minds to treat him like one of ourselves.

Suddenly the captain spoke up again, and I thought his voice was a little changed.

"The gun!" said he.

"I have thought of that," said I, for I made sure he was thinking of a bombardment of the fort. "They could never get the gun ashore, and if they did, they could never haul it through the woods."

"Look astern, doctor," replied the captain.

We had entirely forgotten the long nine; and there, to our horror, were the five rogues, busy about her, getting off her jacket, as they called the stout tarpaulin cover under which she sailed. Not only that, but it flashed into my mind at the same moment that the round shot and the powder for the gun had been left behind, and a stroke with an ax would put it all into the possession of the evil ones aboard.

"Israel was Flint's gunner," said Gray, hoarsely.

At any risk, we put the boat's head direct for the landing-place. By this time we had got so far out of the run of the current that we kept steerage-way even at our necessarily gentle rate of rowing, and I could keep her steady for the goal. But the worst of it was, that with the course I now held, we turned our broadside instead of our stern to the *Hispaniola*, and offered a target like a barn door.

I could hear, as well as see, that brandy-faced rascal, Israel Hands, plumping down a round shot on the deck.

"Who's the best shot?" asked the captain.

"Mr. Trelawney, out and away," said I.

"Mr. Trelawney, will you please pick me off one of those men, sir? Hands, if possible," said the captain.

Trelawney was as cold as steel. He looked to the priming of his gun.

"Now," cried the captain, "easy with that gun, sir, or you'll swamp the boat. All hands stand by to trim her when he aims."

The squire raised his gun, the rowing ceased, and we leaned over to the other side to keep the balance, and all was so nicely contrived that we did not ship a drop.

They had the gun, by this time, slewed around upon the swivel, and Hands, who was at the muzzle, with the rammer, was, in consequence, the most exposed. However, we had no luck; for just as Trelawney fired, down he stooped, the ball whistling over him, and it was one of the other four who fell.

The cry he gave was echoed, not only by his companions on board, but by a great number of voices from the shore, and looking in that direction I saw the other pirates trooping out from among the trees and tumbling into their places in the boats.

"Here come the gigs, sir," said I.

"Give way, then," said the captain. "We mustn't mind if we swamp her now. If we can't get ashore, all's up."

"Only one of the gigs is being manned, sir," I added; "the crew of the other is most likely going round by shore to cut us off."

"They'll have a hot run, sir," returned the captain. "Jack ashore, you know. It's not them I mind; it's the round shot. Carpet bowls! My lady's maid couldn't miss. Tell us, squire, when you see the match, and we'll hold water."

In the meantime we had been making headway at a good pace for a boat so overloaded, and we had shipped but little water in the process. We were now close in; thirty or forty strokes and we should beach her, for the ebb had already disclosed a narrow belt of sand below the clustering trees. The gig was no longer to be feared; the little point had already concealed it from our eyes. The ebb-tide, which had so cruelly delayed us, was now making reparation, and delaying our assailants. The one source of danger was the gun.

"If I durst," said the captain, "I'd stop and pick off another man."

But it was plain that they meant nothing should delay their shot. They had never so much as looked at their fallen comrade, though he was not dead, and I could see him trying to crawl away.

"Ready!" cried the squire.

"Hold!" cried the captain, quick as an echo.

And he and Redruth backed with a great heave

that sent her stern bodily under water. The report fell in at the same instant of time. This was the first that Jim heard, the sound of the squire's shot not having reached him. When the ball passed, not one of us precisely knew, but I fancy it must have been over our heads, and that the wind of it may have contributed to our disaster.

At any rate the boat sunk by the stern, quite gently, in three feet of water, leaving the captain and myself, facing each other, on our feet. The other three took complete headers, and came up again, drenched and bubbling.

So far there was no great harm. No lives were lost, and we could wade ashore in safety. But there were all our stores at the bottom, and, to make things worse, only two guns out of five remained in a state for service. Mine I had snatched from my knees, and held over my head, by a sort of instinct. As for the captain, he had carried his over his shoulder by a bandoleer, and, like a wise man, lock uppermost. The other three had gone down with the boat. To add to our concern, we heard voices already drawing near us in the woods along shore; and we had not only the danger of being cut off from the stockade in our half-crippled state, but the fear before us whether, if Hunter and Joyce were attacked by half a dozen, they would have the sense and conduct to stand firm. Hunter was steady, that we knew; Joyce was a doubtful case—a pleasant, polite man for a valet, and to brush one's clothes, but not entirely fitted for a man of war.

With all this in our minds, we waded ashore as fast as we could, leaving behind us the poor jolly-boat, and a good half of all our powder and provisions.

## CHAPTER XVIII

## NARRATIVE CONTINUED BY THE DOCTOR—
## END OF THE FIRST DAY'S FIGHTING

WE made our best speed across the strip of wood that now divided us from the stockade, and at every step we took the voices of the buccaneers rang nearer. Soon we could hear their footfalls as they ran, and the cracking of the branches as they breasted across a bit of thicket.

I began to see we should have a brush for it in earnest, and looked to my priming.

"Captain," said I, "Trelawney is the dead shot. Give him your gun; his own is useless."

They exchanged guns, and Trelawney, silent and cool, as he had been since the beginning of the bustle, hung a moment on his heel to see that all was fit for service. At the same time, observing Gray to be unarmed, I handed him my cutlass. It did all our hearts good to see him spit in his hand, knit his brows, and make the blade sing through the air. It was plain from every line of his body that our new hand was worth his salt.

Forty paces farther we came to the edge of the wood and saw the stockade in front of us. We struck the inclosure about the middle of the south side, and,

151

almost at the same time, seven mutineers—Job Anderson, the boatswain, at their head—appeared in full cry at the southwestern corner.

They paused, as if taken aback, and before they recovered, not only the squire and I, but Hunter and Joyce from the block-house, had time to fire. The four shots came in rather a scattering volley, but they did the business; one of the enemy actually fell, and the rest, without hesitation, turned and plunged into the trees.

After reloading we walked down the outside of the palisade to see to the fallen enemy. He was stone dead—shot through the heart.

We began to rejoice over our good success, when just at that moment a pistol cracked in the bush, a ball whistled close past my ear, and poor Tom Redruth stumbled and fell his length on the ground. Both the squire and I returned the shot, but as we had nothing to aim at, it is probable we only wasted powder. Then we reloaded and turned our attention to poor Tom.

The captain and Gray were already examining him, and I saw with half an eye that all was over.

I believe the readiness of our return volley had scattered the mutineers once more, for we were suffered without further molestation to get the poor old gamekeeper hoisted over the stockade, and carried, groaning and bleeding, into the log house.

Poor old fellow! he had not uttered one word of

surprise, complaint, fear, or even acquiescence, from the very beginning of our troubles till now, when we had laid him down in the log house to die. He had lain like a Trojan behind his mattress in the gallery; he had followed every order silently, doggedly, and well; he was the oldest of our party by a score of years; and now, sullen, old, serviceable servant, it was he that was to die.

The squire dropped down beside him on his knees and kissed his hands, crying like a child.

"Be I going, doctor?" he asked.

"Tom, my man," said I, "you're going home."

"I wish I had had a lick at them with the gun first," he replied.

"Tom," said the squire, "say you forgive me, won't you?"

"Would that be respectful like, from me to you, squire?" was the answer. "Howsoever, so be it, amen!"

After a little while of silence he said he thought somebody might read a prayer. "It's the custom, sir," he added, apologetically. And not long after, without another word, he passed away.

In the meantime the captain, whom I had observed to be wonderfully swollen about the chest and pockets, had turned out a great many various stores—the British colors, a Bible, a coil of stoutish rope, pen, ink, the log-book, and pounds of tobacco. He had found a longish fir-tree lying felled and cleared in the inclosure, and, with the help of Hunter, he had set it up at the corner of the log-house where the trunks crossed and made an angle. Then, climbing on the roof, he had with his own hand bent and run up the colors.

This seemed mightily to relieve him. He re-entered the log-house and set about counting up the stores, as if nothing else existed. But he had an eye on Tom's passage for all that, and as soon as all was over came forward with another flag and reverently spread it on the body.

"Don't you take on, sir," he said, shaking the squire's hand. "All's well with him; no fear for a hand that's been shot down in his duty to captain and owner. It mayn't be good divinity, but it's a fact."

Then he pulled me aside.

"Doctor Livesey," he said, "in how many weeks do you and squire expect the consort?"

I told him it was a question, not of weeks, but of months; that if we were not back by the end of August, Blandly was to send to find us, but neither sooner nor later. "You can calculate for yourself," I said.

"Why, yes," returned the captain, scratching his head, "and making a large allowance, sir, for all the gifts of Providence, I should say we were pretty close hauled."

"How do you mean?" I asked.

"It's a pity, sir, we lost that second load. That's

what I mean," replied the captain. "As for powder and shot, we'll do. But the rations are short, very short—so short, Doctor Livesey, that we're perhaps as well without that extra mouth."

And he pointed to the dead body under the flag.

Just then, with a roar and a whistle, a round shot passed high above the roof of the log house and plumped far beyond us in the wood.

"O-ho!" said the captain. "Blaze away! You've little enough powder already, my lads."

At the second trial the aim was better and the ball descended inside the stockade, scattering a cloud of sand, but doing no further damage.

"Captain," said the squire, "the house is quite invisible from the ship. It must be the flag they are aiming at. Would it not be wiser to take it in?"

"Strike my colors!" cried the captain. "No, sir, not I," and as soon as he had said the words I think we all agreed with him. For it was not only a piece of stout, seamanly good feeling; it was good policy besides, and showed our enemies that we despised their cannonade.

All through the evening they kept thundering away. Ball after ball flew over or fell short, or kicked up the sand in the inclosure; but they had to fire so high that the shot fell dead and buried itself in the soft sand. We had no ricochet to fear; and though one popped in through the roof of the log-house and out again through the floor, we soon got used to that sort of horse-play and minded it no more than cricket.

"There is one thing good about all this," observed the captain; "the wood in front of us is likely clear. The ebb has made a good while; our stores should be uncovered. Volunteers to go and bring in pork."

Gray and Hunter were the first to come forward. Well armed, they stole out of the stockade, but it proved a useless mission. The mutineers were bolder than we fancied, or they put more trust in Israel's gunnery, for four or five of them were busy carrying off our stores and wading out with them to one of the gigs that lay close by, pulling an oar or so to hold her steady against the current. Silver was in the stern-sheets in command, and every man of them was now provided with a musket from some secret magazine of their own.

The captain sat down to his log, and here is the beginning of the entry:

"Alexander Smollett, master; David Livesey, ship's doctor; Abraham Gray, carpenter's mate; John Trelawney, owner; John Hunter and Richard Joyce, owner's servants, landsmen—being all that is left faithful of the ship's company—with stores for ten days at short rations, came ashore this day and flew British colors on the log-house in Treasure Island. Thomas Redruth, owner's servant, landsman, shot by the mutineers; James Hawkins, cabin-boy——"

And at the same time I was wondering over poor Jim Hawkins' fate.

A hail on the land side.

"Somebody hailing us," said Hunter, who was on guard.

"Doctor! squire! captain!  Hallo, Hunter, is that you?" came the cries.

And I ran to the door in time to see Jim Hawkins, safe and sound, come climbing over the stockade.

## Chapter XIX

# NARRATIVE RESUMED BY JIM HAWKINS— THE GARRISON AT THE STOCKADE

A S soon as Ben Gunn saw the colors he came to a halt, stopped me by the arm, and sat down.

"Now," said he, "there's your friends, sure enough."

"Far more likely it's the mutineers," I answered.

"That!" he cried. "Why, in a place like this, where nobody puts in but gen'lemen of fortune, Silver would fly the Jolly Roger, you don't make no doubt of that. No, that's your friends. There's been blows, too, and I reckon your friends has had the best of it; and here they are ashore in the old stockade, as was made years and years ago by Flint. Ah! he was the man to have a headpiece, was Flint. Barring rum, his match was never seen. He were afraid of none, not he; on'y Silver—Silver was that genteel."

"Well," said I, "that may be so, and so be it; all the more reason that I should hurry on and join my friends."

"Nay, mate," returned Ben, "not you. You're a good boy, or I'm mistook; but you're on'y a boy, all told. Now Ben Gunn is fly. Rum wouldn't

158

bring me there, where you're going—not rum
wouldn't, till I see your born gen'leman, and gets it
on his word of honor. And you won't forget my
words: 'A precious sight' (that's what you'll say), 'a
precious sight more confidence'—and then nips him."

And he pinched me the third time with the same
air of cleverness.

"And when Ben Gunn is wanted you know where
to find him, Jim. Just where you found him today.
And him that comes is to have a white thing in his
hand; and he's to come alone. Oh! and you'll say
this: 'Ben Gunn,' says you, 'has reasons of his
own.'"

"Well," said I, "I believe I understand. You
have something to propose, and you wish to see the
squire or the doctor, and you're to be found where I
found you. Is that all?"

"And when? says you," he added. "Why, from
about noon observation to about six bells."

"Good," says I, "and now may I go?"

"You won't forget?" he inquired, anxiously.
"Precious sight, and reasons of his own, says you.
Reasons of his own; that's the mainstay; as between
man and man. Well, then"—still holding me—"I
reckon you can go, Jim. And Jim, if you was to see
Silver, you wouldn't go for to sell Ben Gunn? wild
horses wouldn't draw it from you? No, says you.
And if them pirates came ashore, Jim, what would
you say but there'd be widders in the morning?"

Here he was interrupted by a loud report, and a cannon-ball came tearing through the trees and pitched in the sand, not a hundred yards from where we two were talking. The next moment each of us had taken to our heels in a different direction.

For a good hour to come frequent reports shook the island, and balls kept crashing through the woods. I moved from hiding-place to hiding-place, always pursued, or so it seemed to me, by these terrifying missiles. But toward the end of the bombardment, though still I durst not venture in the direction of the stockade, where the balls fell oftenest, I had begun, in a manner, to pluck up my heart again; and after a long detour to the east, crept down among the shore-side trees.

The sun had just set, the sea breeze was rustling and tumbling in the woods, and ruffling the gray surface of the anchorage; the tide, too, was far out, and great tracts of sand lay uncovered; the air, after the heat of the day, chilled me through my jacket.

The *Hispaniola* still lay where she had anchored; but, sure enough, there was the Jolly Roger—the black flag of piracy—flying from her peak. Even as I looked there came another red flash and another report, that sent the echoes clattering, and one more round shot whistled through the air. It was the last of the cannonade.

I lay for some time watching the bustle which succeeded the attack. Men were demolishing something with axes on the beach near the stockade—the poor jolly-boat, I afterward discovered. Away, near the mouth of the river, a great fire was glowing among the trees, and between that point and the ship one of the gigs kept coming and going, the men, whom I had seen so gloomy, shouting at the oars like children. But there was a sound in their voices which suggested rum.

At length I thought I might return toward the stockade. I was pretty far down on the low, sandy spit that incloses the anchorage to the east, and is joined at half-water to Skeleton Island; and now, as I rose to my feet, I saw, some distance farther down the spit, and rising from among low bushes, an isolated rock pretty high, and peculiarly white in color. It occurred to me that this might be the white rock of which Ben Gunn had spoken, and that some day or other a boat might be wanted, and I should know where to look for one.

Then I skirted among the woods until I had regained the rear, or shoreward side, of the stockade, and was soon warmly welcomed by the faithful party.

I had soon told my story, and began to look about me. The log house was made of unsquared trunks of pine—roof, walls, and floor. The latter stood in several places as much as a foot or a foot and a half above the surface of the sand. There was a porch at the door, and under this porch the little spring welled up into an artificial basin of a rather odd kind—

no other than a great ship's kettle of iron, with the bottom knocked out, and sunk "to her bearings," as the captain said, among the sand.

Little had been left beside the frame-work of the house, but in one corner there was a stone slab laid down by way of hearth, and an old rusty iron basket to contain the fire.

The slopes of the knoll and all the inside of the stockade had been cleared of timber to build the house, and we could see by the stumps what a fine and lofty grove had been destroyed. Most of the soil had been washed away or buried in drift after the removal of the trees; only where the streamlet ran down from the kettle a thick bed of moss and some ferns and little creeping bushes were still green among the sand. Very close around the stockade— too close for defense, they said—the wood still flourished high and dense, all of fir on the land side, but toward the sea with a large admixture of live-oaks.

The cold evening breeze, of which I have spoken, whistled through every chink of the rude building, and sprinkled the floor with a continual rain of fine sand. There was sand in our eyes, sand in our teeth, sand in our suppers, sand dancing in the spring at the bottom of the kettle, for all the world like porridge beginning to boil. Our chimney was a square hole in the roof; it was but a little part of the smoke that found its way out, and the rest eddied about the house, and kept us coughing and wiping the eye.

Add to this that Gray, the new man, had his face tied up in a bandage for a cut he had got in breaking away from the mutineers; and that poor old Tom Redruth, still unburied, lay along the wall, stiff and stark, under the Union Jack.

If we had been allowed to sit idle, we should all have fallen in the blues, but Captain Smollett was never the man for that. All hands were called up before him, and he divided us into watches. The doctor, and Gray, and I, for one; the squire, Hunter, and Joyce upon the other. Tired as we all were, two were sent out for firewood, two more were sent to dig a grave for Redruth, the doctor was named cook, I was put sentry at the door, and the captain himself went from one to another, keeping up our spirits and lending a hand wherever it was wanted.

From time to time the doctor came to the door for a little air and to rest his eyes, which were almost smoked out of his head, and whenever he did so, he had a word for me.

"That man Smollett," he said once, "is a better man than I am. And when I say that it means a deal, Jim."

Another time he came and was silent for awhile. Then he put his head on one side, and looked at me.

"Is this Ben Gunn a man?" he asked.

"I do not know, sir," said I. "I am not very sure whether he's sane."

"If there's any doubt about the matter, he is,"

returned the doctor. "A man who has been three years biting his nails on a desert island, Jim, can't expect to appear as sane as you or me. It doesn't lie in human nature. Was it cheese you said he had a fancy for?"

"Yes, sir, cheese," I answered.

"Well, Jim," says he, "just see the good that comes of being dainty in your food. You've seen my snuff-box, haven't you? And you never saw me take snuff; the reason being that in my snuff-box I carry a piece of Parmesan cheese—a cheese made in Italy, very nutritious. Well, that's for Ben Gunn!"

Before supper was eaten we buried old Tom in the sand, and stood around him for awhile bare-headed in the breeze. A good deal of firewood had been got in, but not enough for the captain's fancy, and he shook his head over it, and told us we "must get back to this to-morrow rather livelier." Then, when we had eaten our pork, and each had a good stiff glass of brandy grog, the three chiefs got together in a corner to discuss our prospects.

It appears they were at their wit's end what to do, the stores being so low that we must have been starved into surrender long before help came. But our best hope, it was decided, was to kill off the buccaneers until they either hauled down their flag or ran away with the *Hispaniola*. From nineteen they were already reduced to fifteen, two others were wounded, and one, at least—the man shot beside the gun—severely wounded, if he were not dead. Every time we had a crack at them, we were to take it, saving our own lives, with the extremest care. And, besides that, we had two able allies—rum and the climate.

As for the first, though we were about half a mile away, we could hear them roaring and singing late into the night; and as for the second, the doctor staked his wig that, camped where they were in the marsh, and unprovided with remedies, the half of them would be on their backs before a week.

"So," he added, "if we are not all shot down first they'll be glad to be packing in the schooner. It's always a ship, and they can get to buccaneering again, I suppose."

"First ship that I ever lost," said Captain Smollett.

I was dead tired, as you may fancy, and when I got to sleep, which was not till after a great deal of tossing, I slept like a log of wood.

The rest had long been up, and had already breakfasted and increased the pile of firewood by about half as much again, when I was awakened by a bustle and the sound of voices.

"Flag of truce!" I heard someone say, and then, immediately after, with a cry of surprise, "Silver himself!"

And, at that, up I jumped, and, rubbing my eyes ran to a loop-hole in the wall.

## Chapter XX

## SILVER'S EMBASSY

SURE enough, there were two men just outside the stockade, one of them waving a white cloth; the other, no less a person than Silver himself, standing placidly by.

It was still quite early, and the coldest morning that I think I ever was abroad in; a chill that pierced into the marrow. The sky was bright and cloudless overhead, and the tops of the trees shone rosily in the sun. But where Silver stood with his lieutenant all was still in shadow, and they waded knee-deep in a low, white vapor, that had crawled during the night out of the morass. The chill and the vapor taken together told a poor tale of the island. It was plainly a damp, feverish, unhealthy spot.

"Keep indoors, men," said the captain. "Ten to one this is a trick."

"Who goes? Stand, or we fire."

"Flag of truce!" cried Silver.

The captain was in the porch keeping himself carefully out of the way of a treacherous shot, should any be intended. He turned and spoke to us.

"Doctor's watch on the lookout. Doctor Livesey, take the north side, if you please; Jim the east;

Gray, west. The watch below, all hands to load
muskets. Lively, men, and careful."

And then he turned again to the mutineers.

"And what do you want with your flag of truce?"
he cried.

This time it was the other man who replied.

"Cap'n Silver, sir, to come on board and make
terms," he shouted.

"Cap'n Silver! Don't know him. Who's he?"
cried the captain. And we could hear him adding to
himself: "Cap'n, is it? My heart, and here's pro-
motion!"

Long John answered for himself.

"Me, sir. These poor lads have chosen me cap'n,
after your desertion, sir"—laying a particular em-
phasis upon the word "desertion." "We're willing
to submit, if we can come to terms, and no bones
about it. All I ask is your word, Cap'n Smollett,
to let me safe and sound out of this here stockade,
and one minute to get out o' shot before a gun is
fired."

"My man," said Captain Smollett, "I have not
the slightest desire to talk to you. If you wish to
talk to me, you can come, that's all. If there's any
treachery, it'll be on your side, and the Lord help
you."

"That's enough, cap'n," shouted Long John,
cheerily. "A word from you's enough. I know a
gentleman, and you may lay to that."

We could see the man who carried the flag of truce attempting to hold Silver back. Nor was that wonderful, seeing how cavalier had been the captain's answer. But Silver laughed at him aloud, and slapped him on the back, as if the idea of alarm had been absurd. Then he advanced to the stockade, threw over his crutch, got a leg up, and with great vigor and skill succeeded in surmounting the fence and dropping safely to the other side.

I will confess that I was far too much taken up with what was going on to be of the slightest use as sentry; indeed, I had already deserted my eastern loop-hole and crept up behind the captain, who had now seated himself on the threshold, with his elbows on his knees, his head in his hands, and his eyes fixed on the water as it bubbled out of the old iron kettle in the sand. He was whistling to himself, "Come, Lasses and Lads."

Silver had terrible hard work getting up the knoll. What with the steepness of the incline, the thick tree-stumps, and the soft sand, he and his crutch were as helpless as a ship in stays. But he stuck to it like a man in silence, and at last arrived before the captain, whom he saluted in the handsomest style. He was tricked out in his best; an immense blue coat, thick with brass buttons, hung as low as to his knees, and a fine laced hat was set on the back of his head.

"Here you are, my man," said the captain, raising his head. "You had better sit down."

"You ain't a-going to let me inside, cap'n?" complained Long John. "It's a main cold morning, to be sure, sir, to sit outside upon the sand."

"Why, Silver," said the captain, "if you had pleased to be an honest man you might have been sitting in your galley. It's your own doing. You're either my ship's cook—and then you were treated handsome—or Cap'n Silver, a common mutineer and pirate, and then you can go hang!"

"Well, well, cap'n," returned the sea-cook, sitting down as he was bidden on the sand, "you'll have to give me a hand up again, that's all. A sweet, pretty place you have of it here. Ah, there's Jim! The top of the morning to you, Jim. Doctor, here's my service. Why, there you all are together like a happy family, in a manner of speaking."

"If you have anything to say, my man, better say it," said the captain.

"Right you are, Cap'n Smollett," replied Silver. "Dooty is dooty, to be sure. Well, now, you look here, that was a good lay of yours last night. I don't deny it was a good lay. Some of you pretty handy with a handspike-end. And I'll not deny neither but what some of my people was shook—may be all was shook; may be I was shook myself; may be that's why I'm here for terms. But you mark me, cap'n, it won't do twice, by thunder! We'll have to do sentry-go, and ease off a point or so on the rum. May be you think we were all a sheet in the wind's eye. But I'll tell you I was sober; I was on'y dog tired; and if I'd awoke a second sooner I'd a caught you at the act, I would. He wasn't dead when I got round to him, not he."

"Well?" says Captain Smollett, as cool as can be.

All that Silver said was a riddle to him, but you would never have guessed it from his tone. As for me, I began to have an inkling. Ben Gunn's last words came back to my mind. I began to suppose that he had paid the buccaneers a visit while they all lay drunk together round their fire, and I reckoned up with glee that we had only fourteen enemies to deal with.

"Well, here it is," said Silver. "We want that treasure, and we'll have it—that's our point! You would just as soon save your lives, I reckon; and that's yours. You have a chart, haven't you?"

"That's as may be," replied the captain.

"Oh, well, you have, I know that," returned Long John. "You needn't be so husky with a man; there ain't a particle of service in that, and you may lay to it. What I mean is, we want your chart. Now, I never meant you no harm, myself."

"That won't do with me, my man," interrupted the captain. "We know exactly what you meant to do, and we don't care; for now, you see, you can't do it."

And the captain looked at him calmly, and proceeded to fill a pipe.

"If Abe Gray——" Silver broke out.

"Avast there!" cried Mr. Smollett. "Gray told me nothing, and I asked him nothing; and what's more I would see you and him and this whole island blown clean out of the water into blazes first. So there's my mind for you, my man, on that."

This little whiff of temper seemed to cool Silver down. [He had been growing nettled before, but now he pulled himself together.

"Like enough," said he. "I would set no limits to what gentlemen might consider ship-shape, or might not, as the case were. And, seein' as how you are about to take a pipe, cap'n, I'll make so free as do likewise."

And he filled a pipe and lighted it; and the two men sat silently smoking for quite awhile, now looking each other in the face, now stopping their tobacco, now leaning forward to spit. It was as good as the play to see them.

"Now," resumed Silver, "here it is. You give us the chart to get the treasure by, and drop shooting poor seamen, and stoving of their heads in while asleep. You do that and we'll offer you a choice. Either you come aboard along with us, once the treasure shipped, and then I'll give you my affy-davy, upon my word of honor, to clap you somewhere safe ashore. Or, if that ain't your fancy, some of my hands, being rough, and having old scores, on account of hazing, then you can stay here, you can.

We'll divide stores with you, man for man; and I'll give my affy-davy, as before, to speak the first ship I sight, and send 'em here to pick you up. Now you'll own that's talking. Handsomer you couldn't look to get, not you. And I hope"—raising his voice—"that all hands in this here block-house will overhaul my words, for what is spoke to one is spoke to all."

Captain Smollett rose from his seat and knocked out the ashes of his pipe in the palm of his left hand.

"Is that all?" he asked.

"Every last word, by thunder!" answered John. "Refuse that and you've seen the last of me but musket-balls."

"Very good," said the captain. "Now you'll hear me. If you'll come up one by one, unarmed, I'll engage to clap you all in irons, and to take you home to a fair trial in England. If you won't, my name is Alexander Smollett, I've flown my sovereign's colors, and I'll see you all to Davy Jones. You can't find the treasure. You can't sail the ship—there's not a man among you fit to sail the ship. You can't fight us—Gray, there, got away from five of you. Your ship's in irons, Master Silver; you're on a lee-shore, and so you'll find. I stand here and tell you so, and they're the last good words you'll get from me; for, in the name of heaven, I'll put a bullet in your back when next I meet you. Tramp, my lad. Bundle out of this, please, hand over hand, and double quick."

Silver's face was a picture; his eyes started in his head with wrath. He shook the fire out of his pipe.

"Give me a hand up!" he cried.

"Not I," returned the captain.

"Who'll give me a hand up?" he roared.

Not a man among us moved. Growling the foulest imprecations, he crawled along the sand till he got hold of the porch and could hoist himself again upon his crutch. Then he spat into the spring.

"There!" he cried, "that's what I think of ye. Before an hour's out, I'll stove in your old blockhouse like a rum puncheon. Laugh, by thunder, laugh! Before an hour's out, ye'll laugh upon the other side. Them that die'll be the lucky ones."

And with a dreadful oath he stumbled off, plowed down the sand, was helped across the stockade, after four or five failures, by the man with a flag of truce, and disappeared in an instant afterward among the trees.

# Chapter XXI

## THE ATTACK

AS SOON as Silver disappeared, the captain, who had been closely watching him, turned toward the interior of the house, and found not a man of us at his post but Gray. It was the first time we had ever seen him angry.

"Quarters!" he roared. And then, as we all slunk back to our places, "Gray," he said, "I'll put your name in the log; you've stood by your duty like a seaman. Mr. Trelawney, I'm surprised at you, sir. Doctor, I thought you had worn the king's coat! If that was how you served at Fontenoy, sir, you'd have been better in your berth."

The doctor's watch were all back at their loop-holes, the rest were busy loading the spare muskets, and everyone with a red face, you may be certain, and a flea in his ear, as the saying is.

The captain looked on for awhile in silence. Then he spoke.

"My lads," he said, "I've given Silver a broad-side. I pitched it in red-hot on purpose; and before the hour's out, as he said, we shall be boarded. We're outnumbered, I needn't tell you that, but we fight in shelter; and, a minute ago, I should have said we fought with discipline. I've no manner of doubt that we can drub them, if you choose."

Then he went the rounds, and saw, as he said, that all was clear.

On the two short sides of the house, east and west, there were only two loop-holes; on the south side where the porch was, two again; and on the north side five. There was a round score of muskets for the seven of us; the firewood had been built into four piles—tables, you might say—one about the middle of each side, and on each of these tables some ammunition and four loaded muskets were laid ready to the hand of the defenders. In the middle, the cutlasses lay ranged.

"Toss out the fire," said the captain; "the chill is past, and we mustn't have smoke in our eyes."

The iron fire-basket was carried bodily out by Mr. Trelawney, and the embers smothered among sand.

"Hawkins hasn't had his breakfast. Hawkins, help yourself, and back to your post to eat it," continued Captain Smollett. "Lively, now, my lad; you'll want it before you've done. Hunter, serve out a round of brandy to all hands."

And while this was going on the captain completed, in his own mind, the plan of the defense.

"Doctor, you will take the door," he resumed. "See and don't expose yourself; keep within, and fire through the porch. Hunter, take the east side, there.

Joyce, you stand by the west, my man. Mr. Trelawney, you are the best shot—you and Gray will take this long north side, with the five loop-holes; it's there the danger is. If they can get up to it, and fire in upon us through our own ports, things would begin to look dirty. Hawkins, neither you nor I are much account at the shooting; we'll stand by to load and bear a hand."

As the captain had said, the chill was past. As soon as the sun had climbed above our girdle of trees, it fell with all its force upon the clearing, and drank up the vapors at a draught. Soon the sand was baking, and the resin melting in the logs of the block-house. Jackets and coats were flung aside; shirts were thrown open at the neck, and rolled up to the shoulders; and we stood there, each at his post, in a fever of heat and anxiety.

An hour passed away.

"Hang them!" said the captain. "This is as dull as the doldrums. Gray, whistle for a wind."

And just at that moment came the first news of the attack.

"If you please, sir," said Joyce, "if I see anyone, am I to fire?"

"I told you so!" cried the captain.

"Thank you, sir," returned Joyce, with the same quiet civility.

Nothing followed for a time, but the remark had set us all on the alert, straining ears and eyes—the musketeers with their pieces balanced in their hands, the captain out in the middle of the block-house, with his mouth very tight and a frown on his face.

So some seconds passed, till suddenly Joyce whipped up his musket and fired. The report had scarcely died away ere it was repeated and repeated from without in a scattering volley, shot behind shot, like a string of geese, from every side of the inclosure. Several bullets struck the log house, but not one entered; and, as the smoke cleared away and vanished, the stockade and the woods around it looked as quiet and empty as before. Not a bough waved, not the gleam of a musket-barrel betrayed the presence of our foes.

"Did you hit your man?" asked the captain.

"No, sir," replied Joyce. "I believe not, sir."

"Next best thing to tell the truth," muttered Captain Smollett. "Load his gun, Hawkins. How many should you say there were on your side, doctor?"

"I know precisely," said Doctor Livesey. "Three shots were fired on this side. I saw the three flashes —two close together—one farther to the west.

"Three!" repeated the captain. "And how many on yours, Mr. Trelawney?"

But this was not so easily answered. There had come many from the north—seven, by the squire's computation; eight or nine, according to Gray. From the east and west only a single shot had been fired. It was plain, therefore, that the attack would be developed from the north, and that on the other three sides we were only to be annoyed by a show of hostilities. But Captain Smollett made no change in his arrangements. If the mutineers succeeded in crossing the stockade, he argued, they would take possession of any unprotected loop-hole, and shoot us down like rats in our own stronghold.

Nor had we much time left to us for thought. Suddenly, with a loud huzza, a little cloud of pirates leaped from the woods on the north side, and ran straight on the stockade. At the same moment, the fire was once more opened from the woods, and a rifle ball sung through the doorway, and knocked the doctor's musket into bits.

The boarders swarmed over the fence like monkeys. Squire and Gray fired again and yet again; three men fell, one forward into the inclosure, two back on the outside. But of these, one was evidently more frightened than hurt, for he was on his feet again in a crack, and instantly disappeared among the trees.

Two had bit the dust, one had fled, four had made good their footing inside our defenses; while from the shelter of the woods seven or eight men, each evidently supplied with several muskets, kept up a hot though useless fire on the log house.

The four who had boarded made straight before them for the building, shouting as they ran, and the men among the trees shouted back to encourage them.

Several shots were fired, but such was the hurry of the marksmen, that not one appeared to have taken effect. In a moment the four pirates had swarmed up the mound and were upon us.

The head of Job Anderson, the boatswain, appeared at the middle loop-hole.

"At 'em, all hands—all hands!" he roared, in a voice of thunder.

At the same moment another pirate grasped Hunter's musket by the muzzle, wrenched it from his hands, plucked it through the loop-hole, and, with one stunning blow, laid the poor fellow senseless on the floor. Meanwhile a third, running unharmed all round the house, appeared suddenly in the doorway, and fell with his cutlass on the doctor.

Our position was utterly reversed. A moment since we were firing, under cover, at an exposed enemy; now it was we who lay uncovered, and could not return a blow.

The log house was full of smoke, to which we owed our comparative safety. Cries of confusion, the flashes and reports of pistol-shots, and one loud groan rang in my ears.

"Out, lads, out! and fight 'em in the open! Cutlasses!" cried the captain.

I snatched a cutlass from the pile, and someone, at the same time snatching another, gave me a cut across the knuckles which I hardly felt. I dashed out of the door into the clear sunlight. Someone was close behind, I knew not whom. Right in front, the doctor was pursuing his assailant down the hill, and, just as my eyes fell upon him, beat down his guard, and sent him sprawling on his back, with a great slash across his face.

"Round the house, lads! round the house!" cried the captain, and even in the hurly-burly I perceived a change in his voice.

Mechanically I obeyed, turned eastward, and, with my cutlass raised, ran round the corner of the house. Next moment I was face to face with Anderson. He roared aloud, and his hanger went up above his head, flashing in the sunlight. I had not time to be afraid, but, as the blow still hung impending, leaped in a trice upon one side, and missing my foot in the soft sand rolled headlong down the slope.

When I had first sallied from the door, the other mutineers had been already swarming up the palisade to make an end of us. One man, in a red night-cap, with his cutlass in his mouth, had even got upon the top and thrown a leg across. Well, so short had been the interval, that when I found my feet again all was in the same posture, the fellow with the red night-cap still halfway over, another still just showing his head above the top of the stockade. And yet, in this breath of time, the fight was over, and the victory ours.

Gray, following close behind me, had cut down the big boatswain ere he had time to recover from his lost blow. Another had been shot at a loop-hole in the very act of firing into the house, and now lay in agony, the pistol still smoking in his hand. A third, as I had seen, the doctor had disposed of at a blow. Of the four who had scaled the palisade, one only remained unaccounted for, and he, having left his cutlass on the field, was now clambering out again with the fear of death upon him.

"Fire—fire from the house!" cried the doctor. "And you, lads, back into cover."

But his words were unheeded, no shot was fired, and the last boarder made good his escape and disappeared with the rest into the wood. In three seconds nothing remained of the attacking party but the five who had fallen, four on the inside and one on the outside of the palisade.

The doctor and Gray and I ran full speed for shelter. The survivors would soon be back where they had left their muskets, and at any moment the fire might recommence.

The house was by this time somewhat cleared of smoke, and we saw at a glance the price we had paid for victory. Hunter lay beside his loop-hole, stunned; Joyce, by his shot through the head, never to move again, while right in the center the squire was supporting the captain, one as pale as the other.

"The captain's wounded," said Mr. Trelawney.

"Have they run?" asked Mr. Smollett.

"All that could, you may be bound," returned the doctor; "but there's five of them will never run again."

"Five!" cried the captain. "Come, that's better. Five against three leaves us four to nine. That's better odds than we had at starting. We were seven to nineteen then, or thought we were, and that's as bad to bear."*

* The mutineers were soon only eight in number, for the man shot by Mr. Trelawney on board the schooner died that same evening of his wound. But this was, of course, not known till after by the faithful party.

# PART V

## MY SEA ADVENTURE

### CHAPTER XXII

## HOW I BEGAN MY SEA ADVENTURE

THERE was no return of the mutineers—not so much as another shot out of the woods. They had "got their rations for that day," as the captain put it, and we had the place to ourselves and a quiet time to overhaul the wounded and get dinner. Squire and I cooked outside, in spite of the danger, and even outside we could hardly tell what we were at, for the horror of the loud groans that reached us from the doctor's patients.

Out of the eight men who had fallen in the action only three still breathed—that one of the pirates who had been shot at the loop-hole, Hunter, and Captain Smollett—and of these the first two were as good as dead; the mutineer, indeed, died under the doctor's knife, and Hunter, do what we could, never recovered consciousness in this world. He lingered all day, breathing loudly like the old buccaneer at home in his apoplectic fit; but the bones of his chest had been crushed by the blow, and his skull fractured in falling, and some time in the following night, without sign or sound, he went to his Maker.

As for the captain, his wounds were grievous indeed, but not dangerous. No organ was fatally injured. Anderson's ball—for it was Job that shot him first—had broken his shoulder-blade and touched the lung, not badly; the second had only torn and displaced some muscles in the calf. He was sure to recover, the doctor said, but in the meantime, and for weeks to come, he must not walk or move his arm, nor so much as speak when he could help it.

My own accidental cut across the knuckles was a flea-bite. Doctor Livesey patched it up with plaster, and pulled my ears for me into the bargain.

After dinner the squire and the doctor sat by the captain's side awhile in consultation; and when they had talked to their heart's content, it being then a little past noon, the doctor took up his hat and pistols, girt on a cutlass, put the chart in his pocket, and with a musket over his shoulder, crossed the palisade on the north side and set off briskly through the trees.

Gray and I were sitting together at the far end of the block-house, to be out of ear-shot of our officers, consulting, and Gray took his pipe out of his mouth and fairly forgot to put it back again, so thunderstruck he was at this occurrence.

"Why, in the name of Davy Jones," said he, "is Doctor Livesey mad?"

"Why, no," says I. "He's about the last of this crew for that, I take it."

"Well, shipmate," said Gray, "mad he may not be, but if *he's* not, mark my words, *I* am."

"I take it," replied I, "the doctor has his idea, and if I am right, he's going now to see Ben Gunn."

I was right, as appeared later; but in the meantime, the house being stifling hot, and the little patch of sand inside the palisade ablaze with midday sun, I began to get another thought into my head, which was not by any means so right. What I began to do was to envy the doctor, walking in the cool shadow of the woods, with the birds about him and the pleasant smell of the pines, while I sat grilling, with my clothes stuck to the hot resin, and so much blood about me, and so many poor dead bodies lying all around, that I took a disgust of the place that was almost as strong as fear.

All the time I was washing out the block-house, and then washing up the things from dinner, this disgust and envy kept growing stronger and stronger, till at last, being near a bread-bag, and no one there observing me, I took the first step toward my escapade and filled both pockets of my coat with biscuit.

I was a fool, if you like, and certainly I was going to do a foolish, overbold act, but I was determined to do it with all the precautions in my power. These biscuits, should anything befall me, would keep me at least from starving till far on in the next day.

The next thing I laid hold of was a brace of pistols, and as I already had a powder-horn and bullets, I felt myself well supplied with arms.

As for the scheme I had in my head, it was not a bad one in itself. It was to go down the sandy spit that divides the anchorage on the east from the open sea, find the white rock I had observed last evening, and ascertain whether it was there or not that Ben Gunn had hidden his boat—a thing quite worth doing, as I still believe. But as I was certain I should not be allowed to leave the inclosure, my only plan was to take French leave and slip out when nobody was watching, and that was so bad a way of doing it as made the thing itself wrong. But I was only a boy and I had made my mind up.

Well, as things at last fell out, I found an admirable opportunity. The squire and Gray were busy helping the captain with his bandages; the coast was clear; I made a bolt for it over the stockade and into the thickest of the trees, and before my absence was observed I was out of cry of my companions.

This was my second folly, far worse than the first, as I left but two sound men to guard the house; but, like the first, it was a help toward saving all of us.

I took my way straight for the east coast of the island, for I was determined to go down the sea side of the spit to avoid all chance of observation from the anchorage. It was already late in the afternoon, although still warm and sunny. As I continued to

thread the tall woods I could hear from far before
me not only the continuous thunder of the surf, but a
certain tossing of foliage and grinding of boughs
which showed me the sea breeze had set in higher
than usual. Soon cool draughts of air began to
reach me, and a few steps farther I came forth into
the open borders of the grove and saw the sea lying
blue and sunny to the horizon and the surf tumbling
and tossing its foam along the beach.

I have never seen the sea quiet round Treasure
Island. The sun might blaze overhead, the air be
without a breath, the surface smooth and blue, but
still these great rollers would be running along all
the external coast, thundering and thundering by day
and night, and I scarce believe there is one spot in the
island where a man would be out of ear-shot of their
noise.

I walked along beside the surf with great enjoy-
ment, till, thinking I was now got far enough to the
south, I took the cover of some thick bushes and
crept warily up to the ridge of the spit.

Behind me was the sea, in front the anchorage.
The sea breeze, as though it had the sooner blown
itself out by its unusual violence, was already at an
end; it had been succeeded by light, variable airs
from the south and southeast, carrying great banks
of fog; and the anchorage, under lee of Skeleton
Island, lay still and leaden as when first we entered
it. The *Hispaniola*, in that unbroken mirror, was

exactly portrayed from the truck to the water-line, the Jolly Roger hanging from her peak.

Alongside lay one of the gigs, Silver in the stern-sheets—him I could always recognize—while a couple of men were leaning over the stern bulwarks, one of them with a red cap—the very rogue that I had seen some hours before stride-legs upon the palisade. Apparently they were talking and laughing, though at that distance—upward of a mile—I could of course hear no word of what was said. All at once there began the most horrid, unearthly screaming, which at first startled me badly; though I had soon remembered the voice of Captain Flint, and even thought I could make out the bird by her bright plumage as she sat perched upon her master's wrist.

Soon after the jolly-boat shoved off and pulled for shore, and the man with the red cap and his comrade went below by the cabin companion.

Just about the same time the sun had gone down behind the Spy-glass and as the fog was collecting rapidly, it began to grow dark in earnest. I saw I must lose no time if I were to find the boat that evening.

The white rock, visible enough above the brush, was still some eighth of a mile farther down the spit, and it took me a goodish while to get up with it, crawling, often on all-fours, among the scrub. Night had almost come when I laid my hand on its rough sides. Right below it there was an exceedingly small hollow of green turf, hidden by banks and a thick under-

wood about knee-deep, that grew there very plenti-
fully; and in the center of the dell, sure enough, a
little tent of goat-skins, like what the gypsies carry
about with them in England.

I dropped into the hollow, lifted the side of the
tent, and there was Ben Gunn's boat—home-made if
ever anything was home-made—a rude, lop-sided
framework of tough wood, and stretched upon that
a covering of goat-skin, with the hair inside. The
thing was extremely small, even for me, and I can
hardly imagine that it could have floated with a full-
sized man. There was one thwart set as low as
possible, a kind of stretcher in the bows, and a double
paddle for propulsion.

I had not then seen a coracle, such as the ancient
Britons made, but I have seen one since, and I can
give you no fairer idea of Ben Gunn's boat than by
saying it was like the first and the worst coracle ever
made by man. But the great advantage of the coracle it certainly possessed, for it was exceedingly
light and portable.

Well, now that I had found the boat, you would
have thought I had had enough of truantry for once;
but in the meantime I had taken another notion, and
become so obstinately fond of it that I would have
carried it out, I believe, in the teeth of Captain
Smollett himself. This was to slip out under cover
of the night, cut the *Hispaniola* adrift, and let her go
ashore where she fancied. I had quite made up my

mind that the mutineers, after their repulse of the
morning, had nothing nearer their hearts than to up
anchor and away to sea; this, I thought, it would be
a fine thing to prevent, and now that I had seen how
they left their watchman unprovided with a boat, I
thought it might be done with little risk.

Down I sat to wait for darkness, and made a hearty
meal of biscuit. It was a night out of ten thousand
for my purpose. The fog had now buried all heaven.
As the last rays of daylight dwindled and disappeared,
absolute blackness settled down on Treasure Island.
And when, at last, I shouldered the coracle, and groped
my way stumblingly out of the hollow where I had
supped, there were but two points visible on the whole
anchorage.

One was the great fire on shore, by which the de-
feated pirates lay carousing in the swamp. The
other, a mere blur of light upon the darkness, in-
dicated the position of the anchored ship. She had
swung around to the ebb—her bow was now toward
me—the only lights on board were in the cabin; and
what I saw was merely a reflection on the fog of the
strong rays that flowed from the stern window.

The ebb had already run some time, and I had to
wade through the long belt of swampy sand, where I
sunk several times above the ankle, before I came to
the edge of the retreating water, and wading a little
way in, with some strength and dexterity, set my
coracle, keel downward, on the surface.

## Chapter XXIII

## THE EBB-TIDE RUNS

THE coracle—as I had ample reason to know before I was done with her—was a very safe boat for a person of my height and weight, both buoyant and clever in a seaway; but she was the most cross-grained, lop-sided craft to manage. Do as you pleased, she always made more leeway than anything else, and turning round and round was the maneuver she was best at. Even Ben Gunn himself has admitted that she was "queer to handle till you knew her way."

Certainly I did not know her way. She turned in every direction but the one I was bound to go; the most part of the time we were broadside on, and I am very sure I never should have made the ship at all but for the tide. By good fortune, paddle as I pleased, the tide was still sweeping me down; and there lay the *Hispaniola* right in the fair way, hardly to be missed.

First she loomed before me like a blot of something yet blacker than darkness, then her spars and hull began to take shape, and the next moment, as it seemed (for the farther I went the brisker grew the current of the ebb), I was alongside of her hawser, and had laid hold.

The hawser was as taut as a bowstring—so strong she pulled upon her anchor. All round the hull, in the blackness, the rippling current bubbled and chattered like a little mountain stream. One cut with my sea gully, and the *Hispaniola* would go humming down the tide.

So far so good; but it next occurred to my recollection that a taut hawser, suddenly cut, is a thing as dangerous as a kicking horse. Ten to one, if I were so foolhardy as to cut the *Hispaniola* from her anchor, I and the coracle would be knocked clean out of the water.

This brought me to a full stop, and if fortune had not again particularly favored me, I should have had to abandon my design. But the light airs which had begun blowing from the southeast and south had hauled round after nightfall into the southwest. Just while I was meditating, a puff came, caught the Hispaniola, and forced her up into the current; and, to my great joy, I felt the hawser slacken in my grasp, and the hand by which I held it dip for a second under water.

With that I made my mind up, took out my gully, opened it with my teeth, and cut one strand after another, till the vessel swung by two. Then I lay quiet, waiting to sever these last when the strain should be once more lightened by a breath of wind.

All this time I had heard the sound of loud voices

from the cabin; but, to say truth, my mind had been so entirely taken up with other thoughts that I had scarcely given ear. Now, however, when I had nothing else to do, I began to pay more heed.

One I recognized for the cockswain's, Israel Hands, that had been Flint's gunner in former days. The other was, of course, my friend of the red nightcap. Both men were plainly the worse of drink, and they were still drinking; for, even while I was listening, one of them, with a drunken cry, opened the stern window and threw out something, which I divined to be an empty bottle. But they were not only tipsy; it was plain that they were furiously angry. Oaths flew like hailstones, and every now and then there came forth such an explosion as I thought was sure to end in blows. But each time the quarrel passed off, and the voices grumbled lower for awhile, until the next crisis came, and, in its turn, passed away without result.

On shore I could see the glow of the great campfire burning warmly through the shore-side trees. Someone was singing a dull, old, droning sailor's song, with a droop and a quaver at the end of every verse, and seemingly no end to it at all but the patience of the singer. I had heard it on the voyage more than once, and remembered these words:

> "But one man of the crew alive,
> What put to sea with seventy-five."

And I thought it was a ditty rather too dolefully appropriate for a company that had met such cruel losses in the morning. But, indeed, from what I saw, all these buccaneers were as callous as the sea they sailed on.

At last the breeze came; the schooner sidled and drew nearer in the dark; I felt the hawser slacken once more, and with a good, tough effort, cut the last fibers through.

The breeze had but little action on the coracle, and I was almost instantly swept against the bows of the *Hispaniola*. At the same time the schooner began to turn upon her heel, spinning slowly, end for end, across the current.

I wrought like a fiend, for I expected every moment to be swamped; and since I found I could not push the coracle directly off, I now shoved straight astern. At length I was clear of my dangerous neighbor, and just as I gave the last impulsion, my hands came across a light cord that was trailing overboard across the stern bulwarks. Instantly I grasped it.

Why I should have done so I can hardly say. It was at first mere instinct, but once I had it in my hands and found it fast, curiosity began to get the upper hand, and I determined I should have one look through the cabin window.

I pulled in hand over hand on the cord, and, when I judged myself near enough, rose at infinite risk to

about half my height, and thus commanded the roof
and a slice of the interior of the cabin.

By this time the schooner and her little consort
were gliding pretty swiftly through the water; indeed, we had already fetched up level with the camp-
fire.  The ship was talking, as sailors say, loudly,
treading the innumerable ripples with an incessant
weltering splash; and until I got my eye above the
window-sill I could not comprehend why the watchmen had taken no alarm.  One glance, however, was
sufficient; and it was only one glance that I durst
take from that unsteady skiff.  It showed me Hands
and his companion locked together in deadly wrestle,
each with a hand upon the other's throat.

I dropped upon the thwart again, none too soon,
for I was near overboard.  I could see nothing for
the moment but these two furious, encrimsoned faces,
swaying together under the smoky lamp; and I shut
my eyes to let them grow once more familiar with
the darkness.

The endless ballad had come to an end at last, and
the whole diminished company about the camp-fire
had broken into the chorus I had heard so often:

> "Fifteen men on the dead man's chest—
>   Yo-ho-ho and a bottle of rum!
> Drink and the devil had done for the rest—
>   Yo-ho-ho and a bottle of rum!"

I was just thinking how busy drink and the devil
were at that very moment in the cabin of the *His-*

*paniola*, when I was surprised by a sudden lurch of the coracle. At the same moment she yawed sharply and seemed to change her course. The speed in the meantime had strangely increased.

I opened my eyes at once. All around me were little ripples, coming over with a sharp bristling sound and slightly phosphorescent. The *Hispaniola* herself, a few yards in whose wake I was still being whirled along, seemed to stagger in her course, and I saw her spars toss a little against the blackness of the night; nay, as I looked longer, I made sure she also was wheeling to the southward.

I glanced over my shoulder and my heart jumped against my ribs. There, right behind me, was the glow of the camp-fire. The current had turned at right angles, sweeping round along with it the tall schooner and the little dancing coracle; ever quickening, ever bubbling higher, ever muttering louder, it went spinning through the narrows for the open sea.

Suddenly the schooner in front of me gave a violent yaw, turning, perhaps, through twenty degrees; and almost at the same moment one shout followed another from on board. I could hear feet pounding on the companion ladder, and I knew that the two drunkards had at last been interrupted in their quarrel and awakened to a sense of their disaster.

I lay down flat in the bottom of that wretched skiff and devoutly recommended my spirit to its

Maker. At the end of the straits I made sure we must fall into some bar of raging breakers, where all my troubles would be ended speedily; and though I could perhaps bear to die, I could not bear to look upon my fate as it approached.

So I must have lain for hours, continually beaten to and fro upon the billows, now and again wetted with flying sprays, and never ceasing to expect death at the next plunge. Gradually weariness grew upon me; a numbness, an occasional stupor, fell upon my mind even in the midst of my terrors, until sleep at last intervened, and in my sea-tossed coracle I lay and dreamed of home and the Old Admiral Benbow.

CHAPTER XXIV

## THE CRUISE OF THE CORACLE

IT was broad day when I awoke and found myself tossing at the southwest end of Treasure Island. The sun was up, but was still hid from me behind the great bulk of the Spy-glass, which on this side descended almost to the sea in formidable cliffs.

Haulbowline Head and Mizzen-mast Hill were at my elbow, the hill bare and dark, the head bound with cliffs forty or fifty feet high and fringed with great masses of fallen rock. I was scarce a quarter of a mile to seaward, and it was my first thought to paddle in and land.

That notion was soon given over. Among the fallen rocks the breakers spouted and bellowed; loud reverberations, heavy sprays flying and falling, succeeded one another from second to second; and I saw myself, if I ventured nearer, dashed to death upon the rough shore or spending my strength in vain to scale the beetling crags.

Nor was that all, for crawling together on flat tables of rock, or letting themselves drop into the sea with loud reports, I beheld huge slimy monsters —soft snails, as it were, of incredible bigness—two

198

or three score of them together, making the rocks to echo with their barkings.

I have understood since that they were sea-lions, and entirely harmless. But the look of them, added to the difficulty of the shore and the high running of the surf, was more than enough to disgust me of that landing-place. I felt willing rather to starve at sea than to confront such perils.

In the meantime I had a better chance, as I supposed, before me. North of Haulbowline Head the land runs in a long way, leaving, at low tide, a long stretch of yellow sand. To the north of that, again, there comes another cape—Cape of the Woods, as it was marked upon the chart—buried in tall green pines, which descended to the margin of the sea.

I remembered what Silver had said about the current that sets northward along the whole west coast of Treasure Island; and seeing from my position that I was already under its influence, I preferred to leave Haulbowline Head behind me, and reserve my strength for an attempt to land upon the kindlier-looking Cape of the Woods.

There was a great, smooth swell upon the sea. The wind blowing steady and gentle from the south, there was no contrariety between that and the current, and the billows rose and fell unbroken.

Had it been otherwise, I must long ago have perished; but as it was, it is surprising how easily and securely my little and light boat could ride. Often, as I still lay at the bottom, and kept no more than an eye above the gunwale, I would see a big blue summit heaving close above me; yet the coracle would but bounce a little, dance as if on springs, and subside on the other side into the trough as lightly as a bird.

I began after a little to grow very bold, and set up to try my skill at paddling. But even a small change in the disposition of the weight will produce violent changes in the behavior of a coracle. And I had hardly moved before the boat, giving up at once her gentle, dancing movement, ran straight down a slope of water so steep that it made me giddy, and struck her nose, with a spout of spray, deep into the side of the next wave.

I was drenched and terrified, and fell instantly back into my old position, whereupon the coracle seemed to find her head again, and led me softly as before among the billows. It was plain she was not to be interfered with, and at that rate, since I could in no way influence her course, what hope had I left of reaching land?

I began to be horribly frightened, but I kept my head, for all that. First, moving with all care, I gradually bailed out the coracle with my sea-cap; then getting my eye once more above the gunwale, I set myself to study how it was she managed to slip so quietly through the rollers.

I found each wave, instead of the big, smooth, glossy mountain it looks from shore, or from a ves-

sel's deck, was for all the world like any range of hills
on the dry land, full of peaks and smooth places and
valleys. The coracle, left to herself, turning from side
to side, threaded, so to speak, her way through these
lower parts, and avoided the steep slopes and higher
toppling summits of the wave.

"Well, now," thought I to myself, "it is plain I
must lie where I am, and not disturb the balance; but
it is plain, also, that I can put the paddle over the
side, and from time to time, in smooth places, give
her a shove or two toward land."

No sooner thought upon than done. There I lay
on my elbows, in the most trying attitude, and every
now and again gave a weak stroke or two to turn her
head to shore.

It was very tiring, and slow work, yet I did visibly
gain ground; and, as we drew near the Cape of the
Woods, though I saw I must infallibly miss that
point, I had still made some hundred yards of easting.
I was, indeed, close in. I could see the cool, green
tree-tops swaying together in the breeze, and I felt
sure I should make the next promontory without
fail.

It was high time, for I now began to be tortured
with thirst. The glow of the sun from above, its
thousandfold reflection from the waves, the sea-water
that fell and dried upon me, caking my very lips with
salt, combined to make my throat burn and my brain
ache. The sight of the trees so near at hand had

almost made me sick with longing; but the current had soon carried me past the point; and, as the next reach of sea opened out, I beheld a sight that changed the nature of my thoughts.

Right in front of me, not half a mile away, I beheld the *Hispaniola* under sail. I made sure, of course, that I should be taken, but I was so distressed for want of water, that I scarce knew whether to be glad or sorry at the thought; and, long before I had come to a conclusion, surprise had taken entire possession of my mind, and I could do nothing but stare and wonder.

The *Hispaniola* was under her mainsail and two jibs, and the beautiful white canvas shone in the sun like snow or silver. When I first sighted her, all her sails were drawing, she was lying a course about northwest, and I presumed the men on board were going round the island on their way back to the anchorage. Presently she began to fetch more and more to the westward, so that I thought they had sighted me and were going about in chase. At last, however, she fell right into the wind's eye, was taken dead aback, and stood there awhile helpless, with her sails shivering.

"Clumsy fellows," said I, "they must still be drunk as owls." And I thought how Captain Smollett would have set them skipping.

Meanwhile the schooner gradually fell off, and filled again upon another tack, sailed swiftly for a minute or so, and brought up once more dead in the wind's eye. Again and again was this repeated. To and fro, up and down, north, south, east, and west, the *Hispaniola* sailed by swoops and dashes, and at each repetition ended as she had begun, with idly flapping canvas. It became plain to me that nobody was steering. And, if so, where were the men? Either they were dead drunk, or had deserted her, I thought, and perhaps if I could get on board, I might return the vessel to her captain.

The current was bearing coracle and schooner southward at an equal rate. As for the latter's sailing, it was so wild and intermittent, and she hung each time so long in irons, that she certainly gained nothing, if she did not even lose. If only I dared to sit up and paddle I made sure that I could overhaul her. The scheme had an air of adventure that inspired me, and the thought of the water-breaker beside the fore-companion doubled my growing courage.

Up I got, was welcomed almost instantly by another cloud of spray, but this time stuck to my purpose and set myself with all my strength and caution to paddle after the unsteered *Hispaniola*. Once I shipped a sea so heavy that I had to stop and bail, with my heart fluttering like a bird, but gradually I got into the way of the thing and guided my coracle among the waves, with only now and then a blow upon her bows and a dash of foam in my face.

I was now gaining rapidly on the schooner. I

could see the brass glisten on the tiller as it banged about, and still no soul appeared upon her decks. I could not choose but suppose she was deserted. If not, the men were lying drunk below, where I might batten them down perhaps, and do what I chose with the ship.

For some time she had been doing the worst thing possible for me—standing still. She headed nearly due south, yawing of course all the time. Each time she fell off her sails partly filled, and these brought her, in a moment, right to the wind again. I have said this was the worst thing possible for me; for, helpless as she looked in this situation, with the canvas crackling like cannon, and the blocks trundling and banging on the deck, she still continued to run away from me, not only with the speed of the current, but by the whole amount of her leeway, which was naturally great.

But now, at last, I had my chance. The breeze fell, for some seconds, very low, and the current gradually turning her, the *Hispaniola* revolved slowly round her center and at last presented me her stern, with the cabin window still gaping open and the lamp over the table still burning on into the day. The mainsail hung drooped like a banner. She was stock-still but for the current.

For the last little while I had even lost, but now, redoubling my efforts, I began once more to overhaul the chase.

I was not a hundred yards from her when the wind came again in a clap; she filled on the port tack and was off again, stooping and skimming like a swallow.

My first impulse was one of despair, but my second was toward joy. Round she came, till she was broadside on to me—round still till she had covered a half, and then two-thirds, and then three-quarters of the distance that separated us. I could see the waves boiling white under her forefoot. Immensely tall she looked to me from my low station in the coracle.

And then, of a sudden, I began to comprehend. I had scarce time to think—scarce time to act and save myself. I was on the summit of one swell when the schooner came stooping over the next. The bowsprit was over my head. I sprung to my feet and leaped, stamping the coracle under water. With one hand I caught the jib-boom, while my foot was lodged between the stay and the brace, and as I still clung there panting, a dull blow told me that the schooner had charged down upon and struck the coracle and that I was left without retreat on the *Hispaniola*.

## CHAPTER XXV

# I STRIKE THE JOLLY ROGER

I HAD scarce gained a position on the bowsprit when the flying jib flapped and filled upon the other tack with a report like a gun. The schooner trembled to her keel under the reverse, but next moment, the other sails still drawing, the jib flapped back again and hung idle.

This had nearly tossed me off into the sea, and now I lost no time, crawled back along the bowsprit and tumbled head-foremost on the deck.

I was on the lee side of the forecastle, and the mainsail, which was still drawing, concealed from me a certain portion of the after-deck. Not a soul was to be seen. The planks, which had not been swabbed since the mutiny, bore the print of many feet, and an empty bottle, broken by the neck, tumbled to and fro like a live thing in the scuppers.

Suddenly the *Hispaniola* came right into the wind. The jibs behind me cracked aloud; the rudder slammed to; the whole ship gave a sickening heave and shudder; and at the same moment the main-boom swung inboard, the sheet groaning in the blocks, and showed me the lee after-deck.

There were the two watchmen, sure enough; Red-cap on his back, as stiff as a handspike, with his arms stretched out like those of a crucifix, and his teeth showing through his open lips; Israel Hands propped against the bulwarks, his chin on his chest, his hands lying open before him on the deck, his face as white, under its tan, as a tallow candle.

For awhile the ship kept bucking and sidling like a vicious horse, the sails filling, now on one tack, now on another, and the boom swinging to and fro till the mast groaned aloud under the strain. Now and again, too, there would come a cloud of light sprays over the bulwarks, and a heavy blow of the ship's bows against the swell—so much heavier weather was made of it by this great rigged ship than by my home-made, lop-sided coracle, now gone to the bottom of the sea.

At every jump of the schooner, Red-cap slipped to and fro; but—what was ghastly to behold—neither his attitude nor his fixed teeth-disclosing grin was any way disturbed by this rough usage. At every jump, too, Hands appeared still more to sink into himself and settle down upon the deck, his feet sliding ever the farther out, and the whole body canting toward the stern, so that his face became, little by little, hid from me; and at last I could see nothing beyond his ear and the frayed ringlet of one whisker.

At the same time I observed, around both of them, splashes of dark blood upon the planks, and began to feel sure that they had killed each other in their drunken state.

While I was thus looking and wondering, in a calm moment when the ship was still, Israel Hands turned partly round, and with a low moan, writhed himself back to the position in which I had seen him first. The moan, which told of pain and deadly weakness, and the way in which his jaw hung open, went right to my heart. But when I remembered the talk I had overheard from the apple barrel, all pity left me.

I walked aft until I reached the mainmast.

"Come aboard, Mr Hands," I said, ironically.

He rolled his eyes round heavily, but he was too far gone to express surprise. All he could do was to utter one word, "brandy."

It occurred to me there was no time to lose, and dodging the boom as it once more lurched across the deck, I slipped aft and down the companion-stairs into the cabin.

It was such a scene of confusion as you can hardly fancy. All the lock-fast places had been broken open in quest of the chart. The floor was thick with mud, where the ruffians had sat down to drink or consult after wading in the marshes round their camp. The bulkheads, all painted in clear white, and beaded round with gilt, bore a pattern of dirty hands. Dozens of empty bottles clinked together in corners to the rolling of the ship. One of the doctor's medical books lay open on the table, half of the leaves gutted out, I suppose, for pipe-lights. In the midst of all this the lamp still cast a smoky glow, obscure and brown as umber.

I went into the cellar; all the barrels were gone, and of the bottles a most surprising number had been drunk out and thrown away. Certainly, since the mutiny began, not a man of them could ever have been sober.

Foraging about I found a bottle with some brandy left, for Hands; and for myself I routed out some biscuit, some pickled fruits, a great bunch of raisins, and a piece of cheese. With these I came on deck, put down my own stock behind the rudder-head, and well out of the cockswain's reach, went forward to the water-breaker, and had a good, deep drink of water, and then, and not until then, gave Hands the brandy.

He must have drunk a gill before he took the bottle from his mouth.

"Aye," said he, "by thunder, but I wanted some o' that!"

I had sat down already in my own corner and began to eat.

"Much hurt?" I asked him.

He grunted, or, rather, I might say, he barked.

"If that doctor was aboard," he said, "I'd be right enough in a couple of turns; but I don't have no manner of luck, you see, and that's what's the matter with me. As for that swab, he's good and

dead, he is," he added, indicating the man with the
red cap. "He warn't no seaman, anyhow. And where
mought you have come from?"

"Well," said I, "I've come aboard to take possession of this ship, Mr. Hands, and you'll please
regard me as your captain until further notice."

He looked at me sourly enough, but said nothing.
Some of the color had come back into his cheeks,
though he still looked very sick and still continued
to slip out and settle down as the ship banged about.

"By the by," I continued, "I can't have these
colors, Mr. Hands; and by your leave I'll strike 'em.
Better none than these."

And, again dodging the boom, I ran to the color
lines, hauled down their cursed black flag, and
chucked it overboard.

"God save the king!" said I, waving my cap;
"and there's an end to Captain Silver."

He watched me keenly and slyly, his chin all the
while on his breast.

"I reckon," he said at last—"I reckon, Cap'n
Hawkins, you'll kind o' want to get ashore, now.
S'pose we talks."

"Why, yes," says I, "with all my heart, Mr.
Hands. Say on." And I went back to my meal
with a good appetite.

"This man," he began, nodding feebly at the
corpse—"O'Brien were his name—a rank Irelander—
this man and me got the canvas on her, meaning

for to sail her back. Well, *he's* dead now, he is—as dead as bilge; and who's to sail this ship, I don't see. Without I give you a hint, you ain't that man, as far's I can tell. Now, look here, you gives me food and drink, and a old scarf or ankecher to tie my wound up, you do; and I'll tell you how to sail her; and that's about square all round, I take it."

"I'll tell you one thing," says I; "I'm not going back to Captain Kidd's anchorage. I mean to get into North Inlet, and beach her quietly there."

"To be sure you did," he cried. "Why, I ain't sich an infernal lubber, after all. I can see, can't I? I've tried my fling, I have, and I've lost, and it's you has the wind of me. North Inlet? Why, I haven't no ch'ice, not I. I'd help you sail her up to Execution Dock, by thunder! so I would."

Well, as it seemed to me, there was some sense in this. We struck our bargain on the spot. In three minutes I had the *Hispaniola* sailing easily before the wind along the coast of Treasure Island, with good hopes of turning the northern point ere noon, and beating down again as far as North Inlet before high water, when we might beach her safely, and wait till the subsiding tide permitted us to land.

Then I lashed the tiller and went below to my own chest, where I got a soft silk handerchief of my mother's. With this, and with my aid, Hands bound up the great bleeding stab he had received in the thigh, and after he had eaten a little and had a swallow or two more of the brandy, he began to pick up visibly, sat straighter up, spoke louder and clearer, and looked in every way another man.

The breeze served us admirably. We skimmed before it like a bird, the coast of the island flashing by, and the view changing every minute. Soon we were past the high lands and bowling beside low, sandy country, sparsely dotted with dwarf pines, and soon we were beyond that again, and had turned the corner of the rocky hill that ends the island on the north.

I was greatly elated with my new command, and pleased with the bright, sunshiny weather and these different prospects of the coast. I had now plenty of water and good things to eat, and my conscience, which had smitten me hard for my desertion, was quieted by the great conquest I had made. I should, I think, have had nothing left me to desire but for the eyes of the cockswain as they followed me derisively about the deck, and the odd smile that appeared continually on his face. It was a smile that had in it something both of pain and weakness—a haggard, old man's smile; but there was, besides that, a grain of derision, a shadow of treachery, in his expression as he craftily watched, and watched, and watched me at my work.

## Chapter XXVI

## ISRAEL HANDS

THE wind, serving us to a desire, now hauled into the west. We could run so much the easier from the northwest corner of the island to the mouth of the North Inlet. Only, as we had no power to anchor, and dared not beach her until the tide had flowed a good deal farther, time hung on our hands. The cockswain told me how to lay the ship to; after a good many trials I succeeded, and we both sat in silence, over another meal.

"Cap'n," said he, at length, with that same uncomfortable smile, "here's my old shipmate, O'Brien; s'pose you was to heave him overboard. I ain't partic'lar, as a rule, and I don't take no blame for settling his hash; but I don't reckon him ornamental, now, do you?"

"I'm not strong enough, and I don't like the job; and there he lies, for me," said I.

"This here's an unlucky ship—the *Hispaniola*, Jim," he went on, blinking. "There's a power of men been killed in this *Hispaniola*—a sight o' poor seamen dead and gone since you and me took ship to Bristol. I never seen such dirty luck, not I. There was this here O'Brien, now—he's dead, ain't

213

he? Well, now, I'm no scholar, and you're a lad as can read and figure; and, to put it straight, do you take it as a dead man is dead for good, or do he come alive again?"

"You can kill the body, Mr. Hands, but not the spirit; you must know that already," I replied. "O'Brien, there, is in another world, and may be watching us."

"Ah!" says he. "Well, that's unfort'nate—appears as if killing parties was a waste of time. Howsomever, sperrits don't reckon for much, by what I've seen. I'll chance it with the sperrits, Jim. And now you've spoke up free, and I'll take it kind if you'd step down into that there cabin and get me a— well, a—shiver my timbers! I can't hit the name on't. Well, you get me a bottle of wine, Jim—this here brandy's too strong for my head."

Now the cockswain's hesitation seemed to be unnatural; and as for the notion of his preferring wine to brandy, I entirely disbelieved it. The whole story was a pretext. He wanted me to leave the deck—so much was plain, but with what purpose I could in no way imagine. His eyes never met mine; they kept wandering to and fro, up and down, now with a look to the sky, now with a flitting glance upon the dead O'Brien. All the time he kept smiling and putting his tongue out in the most guilty, embarrassed manner, so that a child could have told that he was bent on some deception. I was prompt with my an-

swer, however, for I saw where my advantage lay,
and that with a fellow so densely stupid I could easily
conceal my suspicions to the end.

"Some wine?" I said. "Far better. Will you have
white or red?"

"Well, I reckon it's about the blessed same to me,
shipmate," he replied; "so it's strong, and plenty of
it, what's the odds?"

"All right," I answered. "I'll bring you port,
Mr. Hands. But I'll have to dig for it."

With that I scuttled down the companion with all
the noise I could, slipped off my shoes, ran quietly
along the sparred gallery, mounted the forecastle
ladder and popped my head out of the fore companion. I knew he would not expect to see me there,
yet I took every precaution possible, and certainly
the worst of my suspicions proved too true.

He had risen from his position to his hands and
knees, and though his leg obviously hurt him pretty
sharply when he moved—for I could hear him stifle
a groan—yet it was at a good, rattling rate that he
trailed himself across the deck. In half a minute
he had reached the port scuppers, and picked out of
a coil of rope a long knife, or rather a short dirk, dis-
colored to the hilt with blood. He looked upon it
for a moment, thrusting forth his under jaw, tried
the point upon his hand, and then hastily concealing
it in the bosom of his jacket, trundled back again into
his old place against the bulwark.

This was all I required to know. Israel could move about; he was now armed, and if he had been at so much trouble to get rid of me, it was plain that I was meant to be the victim. What he would do afterward—whether he would try to crawl right across the island from North Inlet to the camp among the swamps, or whether he would fire Long Tom trusting that his own comrades might come first to help him, was, of course, more than I could say.

Yet I felt sure that I could trust him in one point, since in that our interests jumped together, and that was in the disposition of the schooner. We both desired to have her stranded safe enough, in a sheltered place, and so that, when the time came, she could be got off again with as little labor and danger as might be, and until that was done I considered that my life would certainly be spared.

While I was thus turning the business over in my mind I had not been idle with my body. I had stolen back to the cabin, slipped once more into my shoes and laid my hand at random on a bottle of wine, and now with this for an excuse, I made my reappearance on the deck.

Hands lay as I had left him, all fallen together in a bundle, and with his eyelids lowered as though he were too weak to bear the light. He looked up, however, at my coming, knocked the neck off the bottle like a man who had done the same thing often, and took a good swig, with his favorite toast of

"Here's luck!" Then he lay quiet for a little, and then, pulling out a stick of tobacco, begged me to cut him a quid.

"Cut me a junk o' that," says he, "for I haven't no knife, and hardly strength enough, so be as I had. Ah, Jim, Jim, I reckon I've missed stays! Cut me a quid as'll likely be the last, lad; for I'm for my long home, and no mistake."

"Well," said I, "I'll cut you some tobacco, but if I was you and thought myself so badly, I would go to my prayers, like a Christian man."

"Why?" said he. "Now you tell me why."

"Why?" I cried. "You were asking me just now about the dead. You've broken your trust; you've lived in sin and lies and blood; there's a man you killed lying at your feet this moment; and you ask me why! For God's mercy, Mr. Hands, that's why."

I spoke with a little heat, thinking of the bloody dirk he had hidden in his pocket and designed, in his ill thoughts, to end me with. He, for his part, took a great draught of the wine and spoke with the most unusual solemnity.

"For thirty year," he said, "I've sailed the seas and seen good and bad, better and worse, fair weather and foul, provisions running out, knives going, and what not. Well, now I tell you, I never seen good come o' goodness yet. Him as strikes first is my fancy; dead men don't bite: them's my views—amen,

so be it. And now, you look here," he added, suddenly changing his tone, "we've had about enough
of this foolery. The tide's made good enough by
now. You just take my orders, Cap'n Hawkins,
and we'll sail slap in and be done with it."

All told, we had scarce two miles to run, but the
navigation was delicate, the entrance to this northern
anchorage was not only narrow and shoal, but lay
east and west, so that the schooner must be nicely
handled to be got in. I think I was a good, prompt
subaltern, and I am very sure that Hands was an
excellent pilot; for we went about and about, and
dodged in, shaving the banks, with a certainty and a
neatness that were a pleasure to behold.

Scarcely had we passed the head before the land
closed around us. The shores of North Inlet were
as thickly wooded as those of the southern anchorage,
but the space was longer and narrower, and more
like, what in truth it was, the estuary of a river.
Right before us, at the southern end, we saw the
wreck of a ship in the last stages of dilapidation.
It had been a great vessel of three masts, but had
lain so long exposed to the injuries of the weather
that it was hung about with great webs of dripping
sea-weed, and on the deck of it shore bushes had
taken root, and now flourished thick with flowers.
It was a sad sight, but it showed us that the anchorage
was calm.

"Now," said Hands, "look there; there's a pet

bit for to beach a ship in. Fine flat sand, never a catspaw, trees all around of it and flowers a-blowing like a garding on that old ship."

"And, once beached," I inquired, "how shall we get her off again?"

"Why, so," he replied; "you take a line ashore there on the other side at low water; take a turn about one o' them big pines; bring it back, take a turn round the capstan and lie-to for the tide. Come high water, all hands take a pull upon the line, and off she comes as sweet as natur'. And now, boy, you stand by. We're near the bit now, and she's too much way on her. Starboard a little—so—steady—starboard—larboard a little—steady—steady!"

So he issued his commands, which I breathlessly obeyed; till, all of a sudden, he cried: "Now, my hearty, luff!" And I put the helm hard up and the *Hispaniola* swung round rapidly and ran stem on for the low-wooded shore.

The excitement of these last maneuvers had somewhat interfered with the watch I had kept hitherto, sharply enough, upon the cockswain. Even then I was still so much interested, waiting for the ship to touch, that I had quite forgot the peril that hung over my head, and stood craning over the starboard bulwarks and watching the ripples spreading wide before the bows. I might have fallen without a struggle for my life, had not a sudden disquietude seized upon me and made me turn my head. Perhaps I had heard a creak or seen his shadow moving with the tail of my eye; perhaps it was an instinct like a cat's; but, sure enough, when I looked round, there was Hands, already halfway toward me, with the dirk in his right hand.

We must both have cried out aloud when our eyes met, but while mine was the shrill cry of terror, his was a roar of fury like a charging bull's. At the same instant he threw himself forward and I leaped sideways toward the bows. As I did so I left hold of the tiller, which sprung sharp to leeward; and I think this saved my life, for it struck Hands across the chest, and stopped him, for the moment, dead.

Before he could recover I was safe out of the corner where he had me trapped, with all the deck to dodge about. Just forward of the mainmast I stopped, drew a pistol from my pocket, took a cool aim, though he had already turned and was once more coming directly after me, and drew the trigger.

The hammer fell, but there followed neither flash nor sound; the priming was useless with sea-water. I cursed myself for my neglect. Why had not I, long before, reprimed and reloaded my only weapons? Then I should not have been as now, a mere fleeing sheep before this butcher.

Wounded as he was, it was wonderful how fast he could move, his grizzled hair tumbling over his face and his face itself as red as a red ensign with his haste and fury. I had no time to try my other pistol, nor, indeed, much inclination, for I was sure it would be useless. One thing I saw plainly: I must not simply retreat before him, or he would speedily hold me boxed into the bows, as a moment since he had so nearly boxed me in the stern. Once so caught, and nine or ten inches of the blood-stained dirk would be my last experience on this side of eternity. I placed my palms against the mainmast, which was of a goodish bigness, and waited, every nerve upon the stretch.

Seeing that I meant to dodge he also paused, and a moment or two passed in feints on his part and corresponding movements upon mine. It was such a game as I had often played at home about the rocks of Black Hill Cove; but never before, you may be sure, with such a wildly beating heart as now. Still, as I say, it was a boy's game, and I thought I could hold my own at it against an elderly seaman with a wounded thigh. Indeed, my courage had begun to rise so high that I allowed myself a few darting thoughts on what would be the end of the affair; and while I saw certainly that I could spin it out for long, I saw no hope of any ultimate escape.

Well, while things stood thus suddenly the *Hispaniola* struck, staggered, ground for an instant in the sand, and then, swift as a blow, canted over to the port side, till the deck stood at an angle of forty-five degrees, and about a puncheon of water splashed into the scupper-holes, and lay in a pool between the deck and bulwark.

We were both of us capsized in a second, and both of us rolled, almost together, into the scuppers, the dead Red-cap, with his arms still spread out, tumbling stiffly after us. So near were we, indeed, that my head came against the cockswain's foot with a crack that made my teeth rattle. Blow and all, I was the first afoot again, for Hands had got involved with the dead body. The sudden canting of the ship had made the deck no place for running on; I had to find some new way of escape, and that upon the instant, for my foe was almost touching me. Quick as thought, I sprung into the mizzen-shrouds, rattled up hand over hand, and did not draw a breath till I was seated on the cross-trees.

I had been saved by being prompt; the dirk had struck not half a foot below me, as I pursued my upward flight; and there stood Israel Hands with his mouth open and his face upturned to mine, a perfect statue of surprise and disappointment.

Now that I had a moment to myself, I lost no time in changing the priming of my pistol, and then, having one ready for service, and to make assurance doubly sure, I proceeded to draw the load of the other, and recharge it afresh from the beginning.

My new employment struck Hands all of a heap; he began to see the dice going against him, and after an obvious hesitation, he also hauled himself heavily into the shrouds, and, with the dirk in his teeth, began slowly and painfully to mount. It cost him no end

Both My Pistols Went Off.

of time and groans to haul his wounded leg behind
him; and I had quietly finished my arrangements
before he was much more than a third of the way
up. Then, with a pistol in either hand, I addressed
him:

"One more step, Mr. Hands," said I, "and I'll
blow your brains out! Dead men don't bite, you
know," I added, with a chuckle.

He stopped instantly. I could see by the work-
ings of his face that he was trying to think, and the
process was so slow and laborious that, in my new-
found security, I laughed aloud. At last, with a
swallow or two, he spoke, his face still wearing the
same expression of extreme perplexity. In order to
speak he had to take the dagger from his mouth, but,
in all else, he remained unmoved.

"Jim," says he, "I reckon we're fouled, you and
me, and we'll have to sign articles. I'd have had you
but for that there lurch; but I don't have no luck,
not I; and I reckon I'll have to strike, which comes
hard, you see, for a master mariner to a ship's
younker like you, Jim."

I was drinking in his words and smiling away, as
conceited as a cock upon a walk, when, all in a breath,
back went his right hand over his shoulder. Something sung like an arrow through the air; I felt a
blow and then a sharp pang, and there I was pinned
by the shoulder to the mast. In the horrid pain and
surprise of the moment—I scarce can say it was by

my own volition, and I am sure it was without a conscious aim—both my pistols went off, and both escaped out of my hands. They did not fall alone; with a choked cry the cockswain loosed his grasp upon the shrouds, and plunged head first into the water.

## CHAPTER XXVII

## "PIECES OF EIGHT"

OWING to the cant of the vessel, the masts hung far out over the water, and from my perch on the cross-trees I had nothing below me but the surface of the bay.  Hands, who was not so far up, was, in consequence, nearer to the ship, and fell between me and the bulwarks.  He rose once to the surface in a lather of foam and blood, and then sunk again for good.  As the water settled, I could see him lying huddled together on the clean, bright sand in the shadow of the vessel's sides.  A fish or two whipped past his body.  Sometimes, by the quivering of the water, he appeared to move a little, as if he were trying to rise.  But he was dead enough, for all that, being both shot and drowned, and was food for fish in the very place where he had designed my slaughter.

I was no sooner certain of this than I began to feel sick, faint, and terrified.  The hot blood was running over my back and chest.  The dirk, where it had pinned my shoulder to the mast, seemed to burn like a hot iron, yet it was not so much these real sufferings that distressed me, for these, it seemed to me, I could bear without a murmur; it was the horror I had upon my mind of falling from the cross-trees into that still, green water beside the body of the cockswain.

I clung with both hands till my nails ached, and I shut my eyes as if to cover up the peril. Gradually my mind came back again, my pulses quieted down to a more natural time, and I was once more in possession of myself.

It was my first thought to pluck forth the dirk; but either it stuck too hard or my nerve failed me, and I desisted with a violent shudder. Oddly enough, that very shudder did the business. The knife, in fact, had come the nearest in the world to missing me altogether; it held me by a mere pinch of skin, and this the shudder tore away. The blood ran down the faster, to be sure, but I was my own master again, and only tacked to the mast by my coat and shirt.

These last I broke through with a sudden jerk, and then regained the deck by the starboard shrouds. For nothing in the world would I have again ventured, shaken as I was, upon the overhanging port shrouds, from which Israel had so lately fallen.

I went below and did what I could for my wound; it pained me a good deal, and still bled freely, but it was neither deep nor dangerous, nor did it greatly gall me when I used my arm. Then I looked around me, and as the ship was now, in a sense, my own, I began to think of clearing it from its last passenger —the dead man, O'Brien.

He had pitched, as I have said, against the bulwarks, where he lay like some horrible, ungainly sort of puppet; life-size, indeed, but how different from life's color or life's comeliness! In that position, I could easily have my way with him, and as the habit of tragical adventures had worn off almost all my terror for the dead, I took him by the waist as if he had been a sack of bran, and, with one good heave, tumbled him overboard. He went in with a sounding plunge, the red cap came off, and remained floating on the surface, and as soon as the splash subsided, I could see him and Israel lying side by side, both wavering with the tremulous movement of the water. O'Brien, though still quite a young man, was very bald. There he lay with that bald head across the knees of the man who had killed him, and the quick fishes steering to and fro over both.

I was now alone upon the ship; the tide had just turned. The sun was within so few degrees of setting that already the shadow of the pines upon the western shore began to reach right across the anchorage and fall in patterns on the deck. The evening breeze had sprung up, and though it was well warded off by the hill with the two peaks upon the east, the cordage had begun to sing a little softly to itself and the idle sails to rattle to and fro.

I began to see a danger to the ship. The jibs I speedily doused and brought tumbling to the deck, but the mainsail was a harder matter. Of course, when the schooner canted over, the boom had swung

outboard, and the cap of it and a foot or two of sail
hung even under water. I thought this made it still
more dangerous, yet the strain was so heavy that I
half feared to meddle. At last I got my knife and
cut the halyards. The peak dropped instantly, a
great belly of loose canvas floated broad upon the
water; and since, pull as I liked, I could not budge
the downhaul, that was the extent of what I could
accomplish. For the rest, the *Hispaniola* must trust
to luck, like myself.

By this time the whole anchorage had fallen into
shadow—the last rays, I remember, falling through
a glade of the wood, and shining bright as jewels on
the flowery mantle of the wreck. It began to be chill,
the tide was rapidly fleeting seaward, the schooner
settling more and more on her beam-ends.

I scrambled forward and looked over. It seemed
shallow enough, and holding the cut hawser in both
hands for a last security, I let myself drop softly
overboard. The water scarcely reached my waist; the
sand was firm and covered with ripple-marks, and
I waded ashore in great spirits, leaving the *Hispaniola* on her side, with her mainsail trailing wide upon
the surface of the bay. About the same time the
sun went fairly down, and the breeze whistled low in
the dusk among the tossing pines.

At least, and at last, I was off the sea, nor had
I returned thence empty-handed. There lay the
schooner, clear at last from buccaneers and ready for

our own men to board and get to sea again. I had nothing nearer my fancy than to get home to the stockade and boast of my achievements. Possibly, I might be blamed a bit for my truantry, but the recapture of the *Hispaniola* was a clinching answer, and I hoped that even Captain Smollett would confess I had not lost my time.

So thinking, and in famous spirits, I began to set my face homeward for the block-house and my companions. I remembered that the most easterly of the rivers which drain into Captain Kidd's anchorage ran from the two-peaked hill upon my left; and I bent my course in that direction that I might pass the stream while it was small. The wood was pretty open, and keeping along the lower spurs, I had soon turned the corner of that hill, and not long after waded to the mid-calf across the water-course.

This brought me near to where I had encountered Ben Gunn, the maroon, and I walked more circumspectly, keeping an eye on every side. The dusk had come nigh hand completely, and, as I opened out the cleft between the two peaks, I became aware of a wavering glow against the sky, where, as I judged, the man of the island was cooking his supper before a roaring fire. And yet I wondered, in my heart, that he should show himself so careless. For if I could see this radiance, might it not reach the eye of Silver himself where he camped upon the shore among the marshes?

Gradually the night fell blacker; it was all I could do to guide myself even roughly toward my destination; the double hill behind me and the Spy-glass on my right hand loomed faint and fainter, the stars were few and pale, and in the low ground where I wandered I kept tripping among bushes and rolling into sandy pits.

Suddenly a kind of brightness fell about me. I looked up; a pale glimmer of moonbeams had alighted on the summit of the Spy-glass, and soon after I saw something broad and silvery moving low down behind the trees, and knew the moon had risen.

With this to help me, I passed rapidly over what remained to me of my journey; and, sometimes walking, sometimes running, impatiently drew near to the stockade. Yet, as I began to tread the grove that lies before it, I was not so thoughtless but that I slacked my pace and went a trifle warily. It would have been a poor end of my adventures to get shot down by my own party in mistake.

The moon was climbing higher and higher; its light began to fall here and there in masses through the more open districts of the wood, and right in front of me, a glow of a different color appeared among the trees. It was red and hot, and now and again it was a little darkened as it were the embers of a bonfire smoldering.

For the life of me I could not think what it might be.

At last I came right down upon the borders of the clearing. The western end was already steeped in moonshine; the rest, and the block-house itself, still lay in a black shadow, checkered with long, silvery streaks of light. On the other side of the house an immense fire had burned itself into clear embers, and shed a steady, red reverberation, contrasting strongly with the mellow paleness of the moon. There was not a soul stirring, nor a sound beside the noises of the breeze.

I stopped, with much wonder in my heart, and perhaps a little terror also. It had not been our way to build great fires; we were, indeed, by the captain's orders, somewhat niggardly of firewood, and I began to fear that something had gone wrong while I was absent.

I stole round by the eastern end, keeping close in shadow, and at a convenient place, where the darkness was thickest, crossed the palisade.

To make assurance surer, I got upon my hands and knees, and crawled, without a sound, toward the corner of the house. As I drew nearer, my heart was suddenly and greatly lightened. It was not a pleasant noise in itself, and I have often complained of it at other times, but just then it was like music to hear my friends snoring together so loud and peaceful in their sleep. The sea-cry of the watch, that beautiful "All's well," never fell more reassuringly on my ear.

In the meantime there was no doubt of one thing:

they kept an infamous bad watch. If it had been Silver and his lads that were now creeping in on them, not a soul would have seen daybreak. That was what it was, thought I, to have the captain wounded; and again I blamed myself sharply for leaving them in that danger with so few to mount guard.

By this time I had got to the door and stood up. All was dark within, so that I could distinguish nothing by the eye. As for sounds, there was the steady drone of the snores, and a small occasional noise, a flickering or pecking that I could in no way account for.

With my arms before me I walked steadily in. I should lie down in my own place (I thought, with a silent chuckle) and enjoy their faces when they found me in the morning. My foot struck something yielding—it was a sleeper's leg, and he turned and groaned, but without awaking.

And then, all of a sudden, a shrill voice broke forth out of the darkness:

"Pieces of eight! pieces of eight! pieces of eight! pieces of eight! pieces of eight!" and so forth, without pause or change, like the clacking of a tiny mill.

Silver's green parrot, Captain Flint! It was she whom I had heard pecking at a piece of bark; it was she, keeping better watch than any human being, who thus announced my arrival with her wearisome refrain.

I had no time left me to recover. At the sharpclipping tone of the parrot, the sleepers awoke and sprung up, and with a mighty oath the voice of Silver cried:

"Who goes?"

I turned to run, struck violently against one person, recoiled, and ran full into the arms of a second, who, for his part, closed upon and held me tight.

"Bring a torch, Dick," said Silver, when my capture was thus assured.

And one of the men left the log house, and presently returned with a lighted brand.

# PART VI

## CAPTAIN SILVER

### CHAPTER XXVIII

## IN THE ENEMY'S CAMP

THE red glare of the torch lighting up the interior of the block-house showed me the worst of my apprehensions realized. The pirates were in possession of the house and stores; there was a cask of cognac, there were the pork and bread, as before; and, what tenfold increased my horror, not a sign of any prisoner. I could only judge that all had perished, and my heart smote me sorely that I had not been there to perish with them.

There were six of the buccaneers, all told; not another man was left alive. Five of them were on their feet, flushed and swollen, suddenly called out of the first sleep of drunkenness. The sixth had only risen upon his elbow; he was deadly pale, and the blood-stained bandage round his head told that he had recently been wounded, and still more recently dressed. I remembered the man who had been shot and run back among the woods in the great attack, and doubted not that this was he.

The parrot sat, preening her plumage, on Long John's shoulder. He himself, I thought, looked somewhat paler and more stern than I was used to. He still wore his fine broadcloth suit in which he had fulfilled his mission, but it was bitterly the worse for wear, daubed with clay and torn with the sharp briars of the wood.

"So," said he, "here's Jim Hawkins, shiver my timbers! dropped in, like, eh? Well, come, I take that friendly."

And thereupon he sat down across the brandy-cask, and began to fill a pipe.

"Give me the loan of a link, Dick," said he; and then, when he had a good light, "That'll do, my lad," he added, "stick the glim in the wood heap; and you, gentlemen, bring yourselves to!—you needn't stand up for Mr. Hawkins; *he'll* excuse you, you may lay to that. And so, Jim"—stopping the tobacco—"here you are, and quite a pleasant surprise for poor old John. I see you were smart when first I set my eyes on you, but this here gets away from me clean, it do."

To all this, as may be well supposed, I made no answer. They had set me with my back against the wall, and I stood there, looking Silver in the face, pluckily enough, I hope, to all outward appearance, but with black despair in my heart.

Silver took a whiff or two of his pipe with great composure, and then ran on again:

"Now, you see, Jim, so be as you *are* here," says he, "I'll give you a piece of my mind. I've always liked you, I have, for a lad of spirit, and the picter of my own self when I was young and handsome. I always wanted you to jine and take your share, and die a gentleman, and now, my cock, you've got to. Captain Smollett's a fine seaman, as I'll own up to any day, but stiff on discipline. 'Dooty is dooty,' says he, and right he is. You just keep clear of the cap'n. The doctor himself is gone dead agin you—the 'ungrateful scamp' was what he said; and the short and the long of the whole story is about here: You can't go back to your own lot, for they won't have you; and, without you start a third ship's company all by yourself, which might be lonely, you'll have to jine with Cap'n Silver."

So far so good. My friends, then, were still alive, and though I partly believed the truth of Silver's statement, that the cabin party were incensed at me for my desertion, I was more relieved than distressed by what I heard.

"I don't say nothing as to your being in our hands," continued Silver, "though there you are, and you may lay to it. I'm all for argyment; I never seen good come out o' threatening. If you like the service, well, you'll jine; and if you don't, Jim, why you're free to answer no—free and welcome, shipmate; and if fairer can be said by mortal seaman, shiver my sides!"

"Am I to answer, then?" I asked, with a very tremulous voice. Through all this sneering talk I was made to feel the threat of death that overhung me, and my cheeks burned and my heart beat painfully in my breast.

"Lad," said Silver, "no one's a-pressing of you. Take your bearings. None of us won't hurry you, mate; time goes so pleasant in your company, you see?"

"Well," says I, growing a bit bolder, "if I'm to choose, I declare I have a right to know what's what, and why you're here, and where my friends are."

"Wot's wot?" repeated one of the buccaneers, in a deep growl. "Ah, he'd be a lucky one as knowed that!"

"You'll, perhaps, batten down your hatches till you're spoke to, my friend," cried Silver, truculently, to this speaker. "Yesterday morning, Mr. Hawkins," said he, "in the dog-watch, down came Doctor Livesey with a flag of truce. Says he: 'Cap'n Silver, you're sold out. Ship's gone!' Well, maybe we'd been taking a glass, and a song to help it round. I won't say no. Leastways none of us had looked out. We looked out, and, by thunder! the old ship was gone. I never seen a pack o' fools look fishier; and you may lay to that, if I tells you that I looked the fishiest. 'Well,' says the doctor, 'let's bargain.' We bargained, him and I, and here we are; stores, brandy, block-house, the firewood you was thoughtful enough to cut, and, in a manner of speaking, the whole blessed boat, from cross-trees to keelson. As for them, they've tramped; I don't know where's they are."

He drew again quietly at his pipe.

"And lest you should take it into that head of yours," he went on, "that you was included in the treaty, here's the last word that was said: 'How many are you,' says I, 'to leave?' 'Four,' says he —'four, and one of us wounded. As for that boy I don't know where he is, confound him,' says he, 'nor I don't much care. We're about sick of him.' These were his words."

"Is that all?" I asked.

"Well, it's all you're to hear, my son," returned Silver.

"And now I am to choose?"

"And now you are to choose, and you may lay to that," said Silver.

"Well," said I, "I am not such a fool but I know pretty well what I have to look for. Let the worst come to the worst, it's little I care. I've seen too many die since I fell in with you. But there's a thing or two I have to tell you," I said, and by this time I was quite excited, "and the first is this: Here you are, in a bad way; ship lost, treasure lost, men lost; your whole business gone to wreck; and if you want to know who did it—it was I! I was in the apple barrel the night we sighted land, and I heard

you, John, and you, Dick Johnson, and Hands, who
is now at the bottom of the sea, and told every word
you said before the hour was out.  And as for the
schooner, it was I who cut her cable, and it was I
who killed the men you had aboard of her, and it was
I who brought her where you'll never see her more,
not one of you.  The laugh's on my side; I've had
the top of this business from the first; I no more
fear you than I fear a fly.  Kill me, if you please, or
spare me.  But one thing I'll say, and no more; if
you spare me, by-gones are by-gones, and when you
fellows are in court for piracy I'll save you all I can.
It is for you to choose.  Kill another and do yourselves no good, or spare me and keep a witness to save
you from the gallows."

I stopped, for, I tell you, I was out of breath, and,
to my wonder, not a man of them moved, but all
sat staring at me like as many sheep.  And while
they were still staring I broke out again:

"And now, Mr. Silver," I said, "I believe you're
the best man here, and if things go to the worst, I'll
take it kind of you to let the doctor know the way
I took it."

"I'll bear it in mind," said Silver, with an accent
so curious that I could not, for the life of me, decide
whether he were laughing at my request or had been
favorably affected by my courage.

"I'll put one to that," cried the old mahogany-
faced seaman—Morgan by name—whom I had seen

in Long John's public-house upon the quays of Bristol. "It was him that knowed Black Dog."

"Well, and see here," added the sea-cook, "I'll put another again to that, by thunder! for it was this same boy that faked the chart from Billy Bones. First and last we've split upon Jim Hawkins!"

"Then here goes!" said Morgan, with an oath.

And he sprang up, drawing his knife as if he had been twenty.

"Avast, there!" cried Silver. "Who are you, Tom Morgan? Maybe you thought you were captain here, perhaps. By the powers, but I'll teach you better! Cross me and you'll go where many a good man's gone before you, first and last, these thirty years back—some to the yard-arm, shiver my sides! and some by the board, and all to feed the fishes. There's never a man looked me between the eyes and seen a good day a'terward, Tom Morgan, you may lay to that."

Morgan paused, but a hoarse murmur rose from the others.

"Tom's right," said one.

"I stood hazing long enough from one," added another. "I'll be hanged if I'll be hazed by you, John Silver."

"Did any of you gentlemen want to have it out with *me?*" roared Silver, bending far forward from his position on the keg, with his pipe still glowing in his right hand. "Put a name on what you're at;

you ain't dumb, I reckon. Him that wants shall
get it. Have I lived this many years to have a son
of a rum puncheon cock his hat athwart my hawser
at the latter end of it? You know the way; you're all
gentlemen o' fortune, by your account. Well, I'm ready.
Take a cutlass him that dares and I'll see the color
of his inside, crutch and all, before that pipe's empty."

Not a man stirred; not a man answered.

"That's your sort, is it?" he added, returning his
pipe to his mouth. "Well, you're a gay lot to look
at, any way. Not worth much to fight, you ain't.
P'raps you can understand King George's English.
I'm cap'n here by 'lection. I'm cap'n here because
I'm the best man by a long sea-mile. You won't
fight, as gentlemen o' fortune should; then by thunder you'll obey, and you may lay to it! I like that
boy now; I never seen a better boy than that. He's
more a man than any pair of rats of you in this here
house, and what I say is this: Let me see him as'll
lay a hand on him—that's what I say, and you may
lay to it."

There was a long pause after this. I stood straight
up against the wall, my heart still going like a
sledge-hammer, but with a ray of hope now shining
in my bosom. Silver leaned back against the wall,
his arms crossed, his pipe in the corner of his mouth,
as calm as though he had been in church; yet his
eye kept wandering furtively, and he kept the tail
of it on his unruly followers. They, on their part,

"Did Any of You Gentlemen Want to Have it Out With Me?" Roared
Silver.

243

drew gradually together toward the far end of the block-house, and the low hiss of their whispering sounded in my ears continuously like a stream. One after another they would look up, and the red light of the torch would fall for a second on their nervous faces; but it was not toward me, it was toward Silver that they turned their eyes.

"You seem to have a lot to say," remarked Silver, spitting far into the air. "Pipe up and let me hear it, or lay to."

"Ax your pardon, sir," returned one of the men; "you're pretty free with some of the rules, maybe you'll kindly keep an eye upon the rest. This crew's dissatisfied; this crew don't vally bullying a marlin-spike; this crew has its rights like other crews, I'll make so free as that, and by your own rules I take it we can talk together. I ax your pardon, sir, acknowledging you for to be capting at this present, but I claim my right and steps outside for a council."

And with an elaborate sea-salute this fellow, a long, ill-looking, yellow-eyed man of five-and-thirty, stepped coolly toward the door and disappeared out of the house. One after another the rest followed his example, each making a salute as he passed, each adding some apology. "According to rules," said one. "Fok's'le council," said Morgan. And so with one remark or another all marched out and left Silver and me alone with the torch.

The sea-cook instantly removed his pipe.

"Now look you here, Jim Hawkins," he said in a
steady whisper that was no more than audible,
"you're within half a plank of death, and what's a
long sight worse, of torture.   They're going to
throw me off.  But you mark, I stand by you through
thick and thin.  I didn't mean to; no, not till you
spoke up.  I was about desperate to lose that much
blunt, and be hanged into the bargain.  But I see
you was the right sort.  I says to myself: You
stand by Hawkins, John, and Hawkins'll stand by
you.  You're his last card, and by the living thunder,
John, he's yours!  Back to back, says I.  You save
your witness and he'll save your neck!"

I began dimly to understand.

"You mean all is lost?" I asked.

"Aye, by gum, I do!" he answered.  "Ship gone,
neck gone—that's the size of it.  Once I looked into
that bay, Jim Hawkins, and seen no schooner—well,
I'm tough, but gave out.  As for that lot and their
council, mark me, they're outright fools and cowards.
I'll save your life—if so be as I can—from them.  But
see here, Jim—tit for tat—you save Long John from
swinging."

I was bewildered; it seemed a thing so hopeless he
was asking—he, the old buccaneer, the ringleader
throughout.

"What I can do, that I'll do," I said.

"It's a bargain!" cried Long John.  "You speak
up plucky, and by thunder, I've a chance."

He hobbled to the torch, where it stood propped among the firewood, and took a fresh light to his pipe.

"Understand me, Jim," he said, returning. "I've a head on my shoulders, I have. I'm on squire's side now. I know you've got that ship safe somewheres. How you done it I don't know, but safe it is. I guess Hands and O'Brien turned soft. I never much believed in neither of *them*. Now you mark me. I ask no questions, nor I won't let others. I know when a game's up, I do; and I know a lad that's staunch. Ah, you that's young—you and me might have done a power of good together!"

He drew some cognac from the cask into a tin cannikin.

"Will you taste, messmate?" he asked, and when I had refused, "Well, I'll take a drain myself, Jim," said he. "I need a caulker, for there's trouble on hand. And, talking o' trouble, why did that doctor give me the chart, Jim?

My face expressed a wonder so unaffected that he saw the needlessness of further questions.

"Ah, well, he did, though," said he. "And there's something under that, no doubt—something, surely, under that, Jim—bad or good."

And he took another swallow of the brandy, shaking his great fair head like a man who looks forward to the worst.

## CHAPTER XXIX

## THE BLACK SPOT AGAIN

THE council of the buccaneers had lasted some time, when one of them re-entered the house, and with a repetition of the same salute, which had in my eyes an ironical air, begged for a moment's loan of the torch. Silver briefly agreed, and this emissary retired again, leaving us together in the dark.

"There's a breeze coming, Jim," said Silver, who had by this time adopted quite a friendly and familiar tone.

I turned to the loop-hole nearest me and looked out. The embers of the great fire had so far burned themselves out, and now glowed so low and duskily, that I understood why these conspirators desired a torch. About halfway down the slope to the stockade they were collected in a group; one held the light; another was on his knees in their midst, and I saw the blade of an open knife shine in his hand with varying colors, in the moon and torchlight. The rest were all somewhat stooping, as though watching the maneuvers of this last. I could just make out that he had a book as well as a knife in his hand; and was wondering how anything so incongruous had come in their possession, when the kneeling figure rose once more to his feet, and the whole party began to move together toward the house.

"Here they come," said I, and I returned to my former position, for it seemed beneath my dignity that they should find me watching them.

"Well, let 'em come, lad—let 'em come," said Silver, cheerily. "I've still a shot in my locker."

The door opened, and the five men, standing huddled together just inside, pushed one of their number forward. In any other circumstances it would have been comical to see his slow advances, hesitating as he sat down each foot, but holding his closed right hand in front of him.

"Step up, lad," cried Silver. "I won't eat you. Hand it over, lubber. I know the rules, I do; I won't hurt a depytation.

Thus encouraged the buccaneer stepped forth more briskly, and having passed something to Silver, from hand to hand, slipped yet more smartly back again to his companions.

The sea-cook looked at what had been given him. "The black spot! I thought so," he observed. "Where might you have got the paper? Why, hello! look here, now; this ain't lucky! You've gone and cut this out of a Bible. What fool's cut a Bible?"

"Ah, there," said Morgan, "there. Wot did I say? No good'll come o' that, I said."

"Well, you've about fixed it now, among you,"

continued Silver. "You'll all swing now, I reckon.
What soft-headed lubber had a Bible?"

"It was Dick," said one.

"Dick, was it? Then Dick can get to prayers,"
said Silver. "He's seen his slice of luck, has Dick,
and you may lay to that."

But here the long man with the yellow eyes struck
in.

"Belay that talk, John Silver," he said. "This
crew has tipped you the black spot in full council, as
in dooty bound; just you turn it over, as in dooty
bound, and see what's wrote there. Then you can
talk."

"Thanky, George," replied the sea-cook. "You
always was brisk for business, and has the rules by
heart, George, as I'm pleased to see. Well, what
is it, any way? Ah! 'Deposed'—that's it, is it? Very
pretty wrote, to be sure; like print, I swear. Your
hand o' write, George? Why, you was gettin' quite
a leadin' man in this here crew. You'll be cap'n
next, I shouldn't wonder. Just oblige me with that
torch again, will you? this pipe don't draw."

"Come, now," said George, "you don't fool this
crew no more. You're a funny man, by your account;
but you're over now, and you'll maybe step down off
that barrel, and help vote."

"I thought you said you knowed the rules," returned Silver, contemptuously. "Leastways, if you
don't, I do; and I wait here—and I'm still your cap'n,

mind—till you outs with your grievances, and I reply; in the meantime, your black spot ain't worth a biscuit. After that we'll see."

"Oh," replied George, "you don't be under no kind of apprehension; *we're* all square, we are. First, you've made a hash of this cruise—you'll be a bold man to say no to that. Second, you let the enemy out o' this here trap for nothing. Why did they want out? I dunno, but it's pretty plain they wanted it. Third, you wouldn't let us go at them upon the march. Oh, we see through you, John Silver; you want to play booty, that's what's wrong with you. And then, fourth, there's this here boy."

"Is that all?" asked Silver, quietly.

"Enough, too," retorted George. "We'll all swing and sun-dry for your bungling."

"Well, now, look here, I'll answer these four p'ints; one after another I'll answer 'em. I made a hash o' this cruise, did I? Well, now, you all know what I wanted; and you all know, if that had been done, that we'd a' been aboard the *Hispaniola* this night as ever was, every man of us alive, and fit, and full of good plum-duff, and the treasure in the hold of her, by thunder! Well, who crossed me? Who forced my hand, as was the lawful cap'n? Who tipped me the black spot the day we landed, and began this dance? Ah, it's a fine dance—I'm with you there—and looks mighty like a hornpipe in a rope's end at Execution Dock by London town, it

**George Merry**

251

does. But who done it? Why, it was Anderson and Hands and you, George Merry! And you're the last above board of that same meddling crew; and you have the Davy Jones insolence to up and stand for cap'n over me—you, that sunk the lot of us! By the powers! but this tops the stiffest yarn to nothing."

Silver paused, and I could see by the faces of George and his late comrades that these words had not been said in vain.

"That's for number one," cried the accused, wiping the sweat from his brow, for he had been talking with a vehemence that shook the house. "Why, I give you my word, I'm sick to speak to you. You've neither sense nor memory, and I leave it to fancy where your mothers was to let you come to sea. Sea! Gentlemen o' fortune! I reckon tailors is your trade."

"Go on, John," said Morgan. "Speak up to the others."

"Ah, the others!" returned John. "They're a nice lot, ain't they? You say this cruise is bungled. Ah! by gum, if you could understand how bad it's bungled, you would see! We're that near the gibbet that my neck's stiff with thinking on it. You've seen 'em, may be, hanged in chains, birds about 'em, seamen p'inting 'em out as they go down with the tide. 'Who's that?' says one. 'That! Why, that's John Silver. I knowed him well,' says another. And you can hear the chains a-jangle as you go about and reach for the other buoy. Now, that's about

where we are, every mother's son of us, thanks to him,
and Hands, and Anderson, and other ruination fools
of you.    And if you want to know about number
four, and that boy, why, shiver my timbers! isn't he
a hostage?    Are we going to waste a hostage?    No,
not us; he might be our last chance, and I shouldn't
wonder.    Kill that boy? not me, mates!    And number three?    Ah, well, there's a deal to say to number
three.    Maybe you don't count it nothing to have
a real college doctor come to see you every day—
you, John, with your head broke—or you, George
Merry, that had the ague shakes upon you not six
hours agone, and has your eyes the color of lemon
peel to this same moment on the clock?    And maybe,
perhaps, you didn't know there was a consort coming,
either?    But there is, and not so long till then; and
we'll see who'll be glad to have a hostage when it
comes to that.    And as for number two, and why I
made a bargain—well, you came crawling on your
knees to me to make it—on your knees you came, you
was that downhearted—and you'd have starved, too,
if I hadn't—but that's a trifle! you look there—that's
why!"

And he cast down upon the floor a paper that I
instantly recognized—none other than the chart on
yellow paper, with the three red crosses, that I had
found in the oilcloth at the bottom of the captain's
chest.    Why the doctor had given it to him was more
than I could fancy.

But if it were inexplicable to me the appearance of the chart was incredible to the surviving mutineers. They leaped upon it like cats upon a mouse. It went from hand to hand, one tearing it from another; and by the oaths and the cries and the childish laughter with which they accompanied their examination, you would have thought, not only they were fingering the very gold, but were at sea with it, besides, in safety.

"Yes," said one, "that's Flint, sure enough. J. F. and a score below, with a clove hitch to it, so he done ever."

"Mighty pretty," said George. "But how are we to get away with it, and us no ship?"

Silver suddenly sprung up, and supporting himself with a hand against the wall: "Now, I give you warning, George," he cried. "One more word of your sauce, and I'll call you down and fight you. How? Why, how do I know? You had ought to tell me that—you and the rest, that lost me my schooner, with your interference, burn you! But not you, you can't; you ain't got the invention of a cockroach. But civil you can speak, and shall, George Merry, you may lay to that."

"That's fair enow," said the old man Morgan.

"Fair! I reckon so," said the sea-cook. "You lost the ship; I found the treasure. Who's the better man at that? And now I resign, by thunder! Elect whom you please to be your cap'n now; I'm done with it."

"Silver!" they cried. "Barbecue forever! Barbecue for cap'n!"

"So that's the toon, is it?" cried the cook. "George, I reckon you'll have to wait another turn, friend, and lucky for you as I'm not a revengeful man. But that was never my way. And now, shipmates, this black spot? 'Taint much good now, is it? Dick's crossed his luck and spoiled his Bible and that's about all."

"It'll do to kiss the book on still, won't it?" growled Dick, who was evidently uneasy at the curse he had brought upon himself.

"A Bible with a bit cut out!" returned Silver, derisively. "Not it. It don't bind no more'n a ballad-book."

"Don't it, though?" cried Dick, with a sort of joy. "Well, I reckon that's worth having, too."

"Here, Jim—here's a curiosity for you," said Silver, and he tossed me the paper.

It was a round about the size of a crown-piece. One side was blank, for it had been the last leaf; the other contained a verse or two of Revelation—these words among the rest, which struck sharply home upon my mind: "Without are dogs and murderers." The printed side had been blackened with wood-ash, which already began to come off and soil my fingers; on the blank side had been written with the same material the one word, "Deposed." I have that curiosity beside me at this moment; but not a trace of writing now remains beyond a single scratch, such as a man might make with his thumb-nail.

That was the end of the night's business. Soon after, with a drink all round, we lay down to sleep, and the outside of Silver's vengeance was to put George Merry up for sentinel, and threaten him with death if he should prove unfaithful.

It was long ere I could close an eye, and heaven knows I had matter enough for thought in the man whom I had slain that afternoon, in my own most perilous position, and, above all, in the remarkable game that I saw Silver now engaged upon—keeping the mutineers together with one hand, and grasping, with the other, after every means, possible and impossible, to make his peace and save his miserable life. He himself slept peacefully, and snored aloud; yet my heart was sore for him, wicked as he was, to think on the dark perils that environed, and the shameful gibbet that awaited him.

## Chapter XXX

## ON PAROLE

I WAS wakened—indeed, we were all wakened, for I could see even the sentinel shake himself together from where he had fallen against the door-post—by a clear, hearty voice hailing us from the margin of the wood:

"Block-house, ahoy!" it cried. "Here's the doctor."

And the doctor it was. Although I was glad to hear the sound, yet my gladness was not without admixture. I remembered with confusion my insubordinate and stealthy conduct; and when I saw where it had brought me—among what companions and surrounded by what dangers—I felt ashamed to look him in the face.

He must have risen in the dark, for the day had hardly come; and when I ran to a loop-hole and looked out, I saw him standing, like Silver once before, up to the mid-leg in creeping vapor.

"You, doctor! Top o' the morning to you sir!" cried Silver, broad awake and beaming with good nature in a moment. "Bright and early, to be sure; and it's the early bird, as the saying goes, that gets the rations. George, shake up your timbers, son, and help Doctor Livesey over the ship's side. All a-doin' well, your patients was—all well and merry."

So he pattered on, standing on the hill-top, with his crutch under his elbow, and one hand upon the side of the log house—quite the old John in voice, manner, and expression.

"We've quite a surprise for you, too, sir," he continued. "We've a little stranger here—he! he! A noo border and lodger, sir, and looking fit and taut as a fiddle; slep' like a supercargo, he did, right alongside of John—stem to stem we was, all night."

Doctor Livesey was by this time across the stockade and pretty near the cook, and I could hear the alteration in his voice as he said:

"Not Jim?"

"The very same Jim as ever was," says Silver.

The doctor stopped outright, although he did not speak, and it was some seconds before he seemed able to move on.

"Well, well," he said at last, "duty first and pleasure afterward, as you might have said yourself, Silver. Let us overhaul these patients of yours."

A moment afterward he had entered the blockhouse, and, with one grim nod to me, proceeded with his work among the sick. He seemed to me under no apprehension, though he must have known that his life, among these treacherous demons, depended on a hair, and he rattled on to his patients as if he were paying an ordinary professional visit in a quiet

English family. His manner, I suppose, reacted on the men, for they behaved to him as if nothing had occurred—as if he were still ship's doctor, and they still faithful hands before the mast.

"You're doing well, my friend," he said to the fellow with the bandaged head, "and if ever any person had a close shave, it was you; your head must be as hard as iron. Well, George, how goes it? You're a pretty color, certainly; why, your liver, man, is upside down. Did you take that medicine? Did he take that medicine, men?"

"Aye, aye, sir, he took it sure enough," returned Morgan.

"Because, you see, since I am mutineer's doctor, or prison doctor, as I prefer to call it," says Doctor Livesey, in his pleasantest way, "I make it a point of honor not to lose a man for King George (God bless him!) and the gallows."

The rogues looked at each other, but swallowed the home-thrust in silence.

"Dick don't feel well, sir," said one.

"Don't he?" replied the doctor. "Well, step up here, Dick, and let me see your tongue. No, I should be surprised if he did; the man's tongue is fit to frighten the French. Another fever."

"Ah, there," said Morgan, "that comed of sp'iling Bibles."

"That comed—as you call it—of being arrant asses," retorted the doctor, "and not having sense

enough to know honest air from poison, and the dry
land from a vile, pestiferous slough. I think it most
probable—though, of course, it's only an opinion—
that you'll all have the deuce to pay before you get
that malaria out of your systems. Camp in a bog,
would you? Silver, I'm surprised at you. You're
less of a fool than many, take you all round; but you
don't appear to me to have the rudiments of a notion
of the rules of health. Well," he added, after he had
dosed them round, and they had taken his prescrip-
tions, with really laughable humility, more like charity
school-children than blood-guilty mutineers and pirates, "well, that's done for to-day. And now I shall
wish to have a talk with that boy, please."

And he nodded his head in my direction carelessly.

George Merry was at the door, spitting and splut-
tering over some bad-tasted medicine; but at the
first word of the doctor's proposal he swung round
with a deep flush, and cried, "No!" and swore.

Silver struck the barrel with his open hand.

"Si-lence!" he roared, and looked about him positively like a lion. "Doctor," he went on, in his
usual tones, "I was thinking of that, knowing as
how you had a fancy for the boy. We're all humbly
grateful for your kindness, and, as you see, puts faith
in you, and takes the drugs down like that much grog.
And I take it I've found a way as'll suit all. Hawkins, will you give me your word of honor as a young
gentleman—for a young gentleman you are, although

poor born—your word of honor not to slip your cable?"

I readily gave the pledge required.

"Then, doctor," said Silver, "you just step outside o' that stockade, and once you're there, I'll bring the boy down on the inside, and I reckon you can yarn through the spars. Good-day to you, sir, and all our dooties to the squire and Cap'n Smollett."

The explosion of disapproval, which nothing but Silver's black looks had restrained, broke out immediately the doctor had left the house. Silver was roundly accused of playing double—of trying to make a separate peace for himself—of sacrificing the interests of his accomplices and victims; and, in one word, of the identical, exact thing that he was doing. It seemed to me so obvious, in this case, that I could not imagine how he was to turn their anger. But he was twice the man the rest were, and his last night's victory had given him a huge preponderance on their minds. He called them all the fools and dolts you can imagine, said it was necessary I should talk to the doctor, fluttered the chart in their faces, asked them if they could afford to break the treaty the very day they were bound a-treasure-hunting.

"No, by thunder!" he cried, "it's us must break the treaty when the time comes; and till then I'll gammon that doctor, if I have to ile his boots with brandy."

And then he bade them get the fire lighted and stalked out upon his crutch, with his hand on my shoulder, leaving them in a disarray, and silenced by his volubility rather than convinced.

"Slow, lad, slow," he said. "They might round upon us in a twinkle of an eye if we was seen to hurry."

Very deliberately, then, did we advance across the sand to where the doctor awaited us on the other side of the stockade, and as soon as we were within easy speaking distance, Silver stopped.

"You'll make a note of this here also, doctor," said he, "and the boy'll tell you how I saved his life, and were deposed for it, too, and you may lay to that. Doctor, when a man's steering as near to the wind as me—playing chuck-farthing with the last breath in his body, like—you wouldn't think it too much, mayhap, to give him one good word! You'll please bear in mind it's not my life only now—it's that boy's into the bargain; and you'll speak me fair, doctor, and give me a bit o' hope to go on, for the sake of mercy."

Silver was a changed man, once he was out there and had his back to his friends and the block-house; his cheeks seemed to have fallen in, his voice trembled; never was a soul more dead in earnest.

"Why, John, you're not afraid?" asked Doctor Livesey.

"Doctor, I'm no coward; no, not I—not *so*

much!" and he snapped his fingers. "If I was I wouldn't say it. But I'll own up fairly I've the shakes upon me for the gallows. You're a good man and a true; I never seen a better man! And you'll not forget what I done good, not any more than you'll forget the bad, I know. And I step aside—see here—and leave you and Jim alone. And you'll put that down for me, too, for it's a long stretch, is that!"

So saying he stepped back a little way till he was out of ear-shot, and there sat down upon a tree-stump and began to whistle, spinning round now and again upon his seat so as to command a sight sometimes of me and the doctor, and sometimes of his unruly ruffians as they went to and fro in the sand, between the fire—which they were busy rekindling—and the house, from which they brought forth pork and bread to make the breakfast.

"So, Jim," said the doctor, sadly, "here you are. As you have brewed, so shall you drink, my boy. Heaven knows I cannot find it in my heart to blame you; but this much I will say, be it kind or unkind, when Captain Smollett was well you dared not have gone off, and when he was ill, and couldn't help it, by George, it was downright cowardly!"

I will own that I here began to weep. "Doctor," I said, "you might spare me. I have blamed myself enough; my life's forfeit any way, and I should have been dead now if Silver hadn't stood for me; and, doctor, believe this, I can die—and I dare say I deserve it—but what I fear is torture. If they come to torture me——"

"Jim," the doctor interrupted, and his voice was quite changed, "Jim, I can't have this. Whip over, and we'll run for it."

"Doctor," said I, "I passed my word."

"I know, I know," he cried. "We can't help that, Jim, now. I'll take it on my shoulders, holus bolus, blame and shame, my boy; but stay here, I cannot let you. Jump! One jump and you're out, and we'll run for it like antelopes."

"No," I replied, "you know right well you wouldn't do the thing yourself; neither you, nor squire, nor captain, and no more will I. Silver trusted me; I passed my word, and back I go. But, doctor, you did not let me finish. If they come to torture me, I might let slip a word of where the ship is, for I got the ship, part by luck and part by risking, and she lies in North Inlet, on the southern beach, and just below high water. At half-tide she must be high and dry."

"The ship!" exclaimed the doctor.

Rapidly I described to him my adventures, and he heard me out in silence.

"There is a kind of fate in this," he observed, when I had done. "Every step it's you that saves our lives, and do you suppose by any chance that we are going to let you lose yours? That would be a poor return, my boy. You found out the plot; you found Ben Gunn—the best deed that ever you did, or will do, though you live to ninety. Oh, by Jupiter! and talking of Ben Gunn, why, this is the mischief in person. Silver!" he cried, "Silver! I'll give you a piece of advice," he continued, as the cook drew near again; "don't you be in any great hurry after that treasure."

"Why, sir, I do my possible, which that ain't," said Silver. "I can only, asking your pardon, save my life and the boy's by seeking for that treasure; and you may lay to that."

"Well, Silver," replied the doctor, "if that is so, I'll go one step farther; look out for squalls when you find it!"

"Sir," said Silver, "as between man and man, that's too much and too little. What you're after, why you left the block-house, why you've given me that there chart, I don't know, now, do I? and yet I done your bidding with my eyes shut and never a word of hope! But no, this here's too much. If you won't tell me what you mean plain out, just say so, and I'll leave the helm."

"No," said the doctor, musingly, "I've no right to say more; it's not my secret, you see, Silver, or, I give you my word, I'd tell it to you. But I'll go as far with you as I dare go, and a step beyond, for I'll have my wig sorted by the captain, or I'm mistaken! And first, I'll give you a bit of hope; Silver, if we both get alive out of this wolf-trap, I'll do my best to save you, short of perjury."

Silver's face was radiant. "You couldn't say more, I am sure, sir, not if you was my mother," he cried.

"Well, that's my first concession," added the doctor. "My second is a piece of advice. Keep the boy close beside you, and when you need help, halloo. I'm off to seek it for you, and that itself will show you if I speak at random. Good-by, Jim."

And Doctor Livesey shook hands with me through the stockade, nodded to Silver, and set off at a brisk pace into the wood.

## CHAPTER XXXI

# THE TREASURE-HUNT—FLINT'S POINTER

"JIM," said Silver, when we were alone, "if I saved your life, you saved mine, and I'll not forget it. —I seen the doctor waving you to run for it with the tail of my eye, I did—and I seen you say no as plain as hearing. Jim, that's one to you. This is the first glint of hope I had since the attack failed, and I owe it to you. And now, Jim, we're to go in for this here treasure-hunting, with sealed orders, too, and I don't like it; and you and me must stick close, back to back like, and we'll save our necks in spite o' fate and fortune."

Just then a man hailed us from the fire that breakfast was ready, and we were soon seated here and there about the sand over biscuit and fried junk. They had lighted a fire fit to roast an ox; and it was now grown so hot that they could only approach it from the windward, and even there not without precaution. In the same wasteful spirit, they had cooked, I suppose, three times more than we could eat; and one of them, with an empty laugh, threw what was left into the fire, which blazed and roared again over this unusual fuel. I never in my life saw men so careless of the morrow; hand to mouth is the

only word that can describe their way of doing; and
what with wasted food and sleeping sentries, though
they were bold enough for a brush and be done with
it, I could see their entire unfitness for anything like
a prolonged campaign.

Even Silver, eating away, with Captain Flint upon
his shoulder, had not a word of blame for their reck-
lessness. And this the more surprised me, for I
thought he had never showed himself so cunning as
he did then.

"Aye, mates," said he, "it's lucky you have Barbecue to think for you with this here head. I got
what I wanted, I did. Sure enough, they have the
ship. Where they have it, I don't know yet; but
once we hit the treasure, we'll have to jump about and
find out. And then, mates, us that has the boats, I
reckon, has the upper hand."

Thus he kept running on, with his mouth full of
the hot bacon; thus he restored their hope and confidence, and, I more than suspect, repaired his own
at the same time.

"As for hostage," he continued, "that's his last
talk, I guess, with them he loves so dear. I've got
my piece o' news, and thanky to him for that; but it's
over and done. I'll take him in a line when we go
treasure-hunting, for we'll keep him like so much
gold, in case of accidents, you mark, and in the meantime, once we got the ship and treasure both, and off
to sea like jolly companions, why, then we'll talk

Mr. Hawkins over, we will, and we'll give him his share, to be sure, for all his kindness."

It was no wonder the men were in a good humor now. For my part, I was horribly cast down. Should the scheme he had now sketched prove feasible, Silver, already doubly a traitor, would not hesitate to adopt it. He had still a foot in either camp, and there was no doubt he would prefer wealth and freedom with the pirates to a bare escape from hanging, which was the best he had to hope for on our side.

Nay, and even if things so fell out that he was forced to keep his faith with Doctor Livesey, even then what danger lay before us! What a moment that would be when the suspicions of his followers turned to certainty, and he and I should have to fight for dear life—he, a cripple, and I, a boy— against five strong and active seamen!

Add to this double apprehension the mystery that still hung over the behavior of my friends; their unexplained desertion of the stockade; their inexplicable cession of the chart; or, harder still to understand, the doctor's last warning to Silver, "Look out for squalls when you find it"; and you will readily believe how little taste I found in my breakfast, and with how uneasy a heart I set forth behind my captors on the quest for treasure.

We made a curious figure, had anyone been there to see us; all in soiled sailor clothes, and all but me armed to the teeth. Silver had two guns slung about him, one before and one behind—besides the great cutlass at his waist, and a pistol in each pocket of his square-tailed coat. To complete his strange appearance, Captain Flint sat perched upon his shoulder and gabbled odds and ends of purposeless sea-talk. I had a line about my waist, and followed obediently after the sea-cook, who held the loose end of the rope, now in his free hand, now between his powerful teeth. For all the world, I was led like a dancing bear.

The other men were variously burdened; some carrying picks and shovels—for that had been the very first necessary they brought ashore from the *Hispaniola*—others laden with pork, bread, and brandy for the midday meal. All the stores, I observed, came from our stock, and I could see the truth of Silver's words the night before. Had he not struck a bargain with the doctor, he and his mutineers, deserted by the ship, must have been driven to subsist on clear water and the proceeds of their hunting. Water would have been little to their taste; a sailor is not usually a good shot; and, besides all that, when they were so short of eatables, it was not likely they would be very flush of powder.

Well, thus equipped, we all set out—even the fellow with the broken head, who should certainly have kept in shadow—and straggled, one after another, to the beach, where the two gigs awaited us. Even these bore trace of the drunken folly of the pirates, one in a broken thwart, and both in their muddled

and unbailed condition. Both were to be carried
along with us, for the sake of safety; and so, with
our numbers divided between them, we set forth upon
the bosom of the anchorage.

As we pulled over there was some discussion on
the chart. The red cross was, of course, far too large
to be a guide; and, the terms of the note on the back
as you will hear, admitted of some ambiguity. They
ran, the reader may remember, thus:

> "Tall tree, Spy-glass shoulder, bearing a point to the N.
> of N.N.E.
> "Skeleton Island E.S.E. and by E.
> "Ten feet."

A tall tree was thus the principal mark. Now,
right before us, the anchorage was bounded by a
plateau from two to three hundred feet high, adjoin-
ing on the north the sloping southern shoulder of the
Spy-glass, and rising again toward the south into the
rough, cliffy eminence called the Mizzen-mast Hill.
The top of the plateau was dotted thickly with pine
trees of varying height. Every here and there, one
of a different species rose forty or fifty feet clear
above its neighbors, and which of these was the particular "tall tree" of Captain Flint could only be decided on the spot, and by the readings of the compass.

Yet, although that was the case, every man on
board the boats had picked a favorite of his own ere
we were halfway over, Long John alone shrugging his
shoulders and bidding them wait till they were there.

We pulled easily, by Silver's directions, not to
weary the hands prematurely; and, after quite a long
passage, landed at the mouth of the second river—
that which runs down a woody cleft of the Spy-glass.
Thence, bending to our left, we began to ascend the
slope toward the plateau.

At the first outset, heavy, miry ground and a
matted, marsh vegetation greatly delayed our progress, but by little and little the hill began to steepen
and become stony under foot, and the wood to change
its character and to grow in a more open order. It
was, indeed, a most pleasant portion of the island
that we were now approaching. A heavy-scented
broom and many flowering shrubs had almost taken
the place of grass. Thickets of green nutmeg trees
were dotted here and there with the red columns
and the broad shadow of the pines, and the first
mingled their spice with the aroma of the others.
The air, besides, was fresh and stirring, and this,
under the sheer sunbeams, was a wonderful refresh-
ment to our senses.

The party spread itself abroad, in a fan shape,
shouting and leaping to and fro. About the center,
and a good way behind the rest, Silver and I followed
—I tethered by my rope, he plowing, with deep pants,
among the sliding gravel. From time to time, indeed, I had to lend him a hand, or he must have
missed his footing and fallen backward down the
hill.

We had thus proceeded for about half a mile, and were approaching the brow of the plateau, when the man upon the farthest left began to cry aloud, as if in terror. Shout after shout came from him, and the others began to run in his direction.

"He can't have found the treasure," said old Morgan, hurrying past us from the right, "for that's clean a-top."

Indeed, as we found when we also reached the spot, it was something very different. At the foot of a pretty big pine, and involved in a green creeper, which had even partly lifted some of the smaller bones, a human skeleton lay, with a few shreds of clothing, on the ground. I believe a chill struck for a moment to every heart.

"He was a seaman," said George Merry, who, bolder than the rest, had gone up close, and was examining the rags of clothing. "Leastways, this is good sea-cloth."

"Aye, aye," said Silver, "like enough; you wouldn't look to find a bishop here, I reckon. But what sort of a way is that for bones to lie? 'Tain't in natur'."

Indeed, on a second glance, it seemed impossible to fancy that the body was in a natural position. But for some disarray (the work, perhaps, of the birds that had fed upon him, or of the slow-growing creeper that had gradually enveloped his remains) the man lay perfectly straight—his feet pointing in one direction, his hands raised above his head like a diver's, pointing directly in the opposite.

"I've taken a notion into my old numskull," observed Silver. "Here's the compass; there's the tip-top p'int of Skeleton Island, stickin' out like a tooth. Just take a bearing, will you, along the line of them bones."

It was done. The body pointed straight in the direction of the island, and the compass read duly E.S.E. by E.

"I thought so," cried the cook; "this here is a p'inter. Right up there is our line for the Pole Star and the jolly dollars. But by thunder! if it don't make me cold inside to think of Flint. This is one of *his* jokes, and no mistake. Him and these six was alone here; he killed 'em, every man; and this one he hauled here and laid down by compass, shiver my timbers! They're long bones, and the hair's been yellow. Aye, that would be Allardyce. You mind Allardyce, Tom Morgan?"

"Aye, aye," returned Morgan, "I mind him; he owed me money, he did, and took my knife ashore with him."

"Speaking of knives," said another, "why don't we find his'n lying round? Flint warn't the man to pick a seaman's pocket; and the birds, I guess, would leave it be."

"By the powers and that's true!" cried Silver.

"There ain't a thing left here," said Merry, still

feeling round among the bones; "not a copper doit nor a baccy box. It don't look nat'ral to me."

"No, by gum, it don't," agreed Silver; "not nat'ral, nor not nice, says you. Great guns! messmates, but if Flint was living this would be a hot spot for you and me. Six they were, and six are we; and bones is what they are now."

"I saw him dead with these here deadlights," said Morgan. "Billy took me in. There he laid, with penny-pieces on his eyes."

"Dead—aye, sure enough he's dead and gone below," said the fellow with the bandage; "but if ever sperrit walked it would be Flint's. Dear heart, but he died bad, did Flint!"

"Aye, that he did," observed another; "now he raged and now he hollered for the rum, and now he sung. 'Fifteen Men' were his only song, mates; and I tell you true I never rightly liked to hear it since. It was main hot and the windy was open, and I hear that old song comin' out as clear as clear—and the death-haul on the man already."

"Come, come," said Silver, "stow this talk. He's dead, and he don't walk, that I know; leastways he won't walk by day, and you may lay to that. Care killed a cat. Fetch ahead for the doubloons."

We started, certainly, but in spite of the hot sun and the staring daylight, the pirates no longer ran separate and shouting through the wood, but kept side by side and spoke with bated breath. The terror of the dead buccaneer had fallen on their spirits.

## CHAPTER XXXII

# THE TREASURE-HUNT—THE VOICE AMONG THE TREES

PARTLY from the damping influence of this alarm, partly to rest Silver and the sick folk, the whole party sat down as soon as they had gained the brow of the ascent.

The plateau being somewhat tilted toward the west, this spot on which we had paused commanded a wide prospect on either hand. Before us, over the tree-tops, we beheld the Cape of the Woods fringed with surf; behind, we not only looked down upon the anchorage and Skeleton Island, but saw—clear across the spit and the eastern lowlands—a great field of open sea upon the east. Sheer above us rose the Spy-glass, here dotted with single pines, there black with precipices. There was no sound but that of the distant breakers mounting from all around, and the chirp of countless insects in the brush. Not a man, not a sail upon the sea; the very largeness of the view increased the sense of solitude.

Silver, as he sat, took certain bearings with his compass.

"There are three 'tall trees,'" said he, "about in the right line from Skeleton Island. 'Spy-glass

276

Shoulder,' I take it, means that lower p'int there.
It's child's play to find the stuff now. I've half a
mind to dine first."

"I don't feel sharp," growled Morgan. "Think-
in' o' Flint—I think it were—'as done me."

"Ah, well, my son, you praise your stars he's
dead," said Silver.

"He was an ugly devil," cried a third pirate, with
a shudder; "that blue in the face, too!"

"That was how the rum took him," added Merry.

"Blue! well I reckon he was blue. That's a true
word."

Ever since they had found the skeleton and got
upon this train of thought they had spoken lower
and lower, and they had almost got to whispering
by now, so that the sound of their talk hardly interrupted the silence of the wood. All of a sudden,
out of the middle of the trees in front of us, a thin,
high, and trembling voice struck up the well-known
air and words:

> "Fifteen men on the dead man's chest—
> Yo-ho-ho and a bottle of rum!"

I never have seen men more dreadfully affected
than the pirates. The color went from their six
faces like enchantment; some leaped to their feet,
some clawed hold of others; Morgan groveled on the
ground.

"It's Flint, by ——!" cried Merry.

The song had stopped as suddenly as it began—
broken off, you would have said, in the middle of a
note, as though someone had laid his hand upon the
singer's mouth. Coming so far through the clear,
sunny atmosphere among the green tree-tops, I
thought it had sounded airily and sweetly, and the
effect on my companions was the stranger.

"Come," said Silver, struggling with his ashen
lips to get the word out, "that won't do. Stand by
to go about. This is a rum start, and I can't name
the voice, but it's someone skylarking—someone that's
flesh and blood, and you may lay to that."

His courage had come back as he spoke, and some
of the color to his face along with it. Already the
others had begun to lend an ear to this encourage-
ment, and were coming a little to themselves, when
the same voice broke out again—not this time singing, but in a faint, distant hail, that echoed yet
fainter among the clefts of the Spy-glass.

"Darby McGraw," it wailed—for that is the
word that best describes the sounds—"Darby
McGraw! Darby McGraw!" again and again and
again; and then rising a little higher, and with an
oath that I leave out: "Fetch aft the rum, Darby!"

The buccaneers remained rooted to the ground,
their eyes starting from their heads. Long after the
voice had died away they still stared in silence, dreadfully, before them.

"That fixes it!" gasped one. "Let's go."

"They was his last words," moaned Morgan, "his last words above-board."

Dick had his Bible out and was praying volubly. He had been well brought up, had Dick, before he came to sea and fell among bad companions.

Still, Silver was unconquered. I could hear his teeth rattle in his head, but he had not yet surrendered.

"Nobody in this here island ever heard of Darby," he muttered; "not one but us that's here." And then, making a great effort: "Shipmates," he cried, "I'm here to get that stuff, and I'll not be beat by man or devil. I never was feared of Flint in his life, and, by the powers, I'll face him dead. There's seven hundred thousand pound not a quarter of a mile from here. When did ever a gentleman o' fortune show his stern to that much dollars for a boozy old seaman with a blue mug—and him dead, too?"

But there was no sign of reawakening courage in his followers; rather, indeed, of growing terror at the irreverence of his words.

"Belay there, John!" said Merry. "Don't you cross a sperrit."

And the rest were all too terrified to reply. They would have run away severally had they dared, but fear kept them together, and kept them close by John, as if his daring helped them. He, on his part, had pretty well fought his weakness down.

"Sperrit? Well, may be," he said. "But there's

one thing not clear to me. There was an echo.
Now, no man ever seen a sperrit with a shadow.
Well, then, what's he doing with an echo to him,
I should like to know? That ain't in natur', surely."

This argument seemed weak enough to me. But
you can never tell what will affect the superstitious,
and, to my wonder, George Merry was greatly relieved.

"Well, that's so," he said. "You've a head upon
your shoulders, John, and no mistake. 'Bout ship,
mates! This here crew is on a wrong tack, I do believe. And come to think on it, it was like Flint's
voice, I grant you, but not just so clear away like it,
after all. It was liker somebody else's voice now—
it was like——"

"By the powers, Ben Gunn!" roared Silver.

"Aye, and so it were," cried Morgan, springing
on his knees. "Ben Gunn it were!"

"It don't make much odds, do it, now?" asked
Dick. "Ben Gunn's not here in the body, any more'n
Flint." But the older hands greeted this remark with
scorn.

"Why, nobody minds Ben Gunn," cried Merry;
"dead or alive, nobody minds him!"

It was extraordinary how their spirits had returned, and how the natural color had revived in their
faces. Soon they were chatting together, with intervals of listening; and not long after, hearing no
further sound, they shouldered the tools and set

forth again, Merry walking first with Silver's compass to keep them on the right line with Skeleton Island. He had said the truth; dead or alive, nobody minded Ben Gunn.

Dick alone still held his Bible, and looked around him as he went, with fearful glances, but he found no sympathy, and Silver even joked him on his precautions.

"I told you," said he, "I told you you had sp'iled your Bible. If it ain't no good to swear by, what do you suppose a sperrit would give for it. Not that!" and he snapped his big fingers, halting a moment on his crutch.

But Dick was not to be comforted; indeed, it was soon plain to me that the lad was falling sick; hastened by heat, exhaustion, and the shock of his alarm, the fever, predicted by Doctor Livesey, was evidently growing swiftly higher.

It was fine open walking here, upon the summit; our way lay a little downhill, for, as I have said, the plateau tilted toward the west. The pines, great and small, grew wide apart; and even between the clumps of nutmeg and azalea, wide open spaces baked in the hot sunshine. Striking, as we did, pretty near northwest across the island, we drew, on the other hand, ever nearer under the shoulders of the Spyglass, and on the other, looked ever wider over that western bay where I had once tossed and trembled in the coracle.

The first of the tall trees was reached, and by the bearing, proved the wrong one. So with the second. The third rose nearly two hundred feet into the air above a clump of underwood; a giant of a vegetable, with a red column as big as a cottage, and a wide shadow around in which a company could have maneuvered. It was conspicuous far to sea, both on the east and west, and might have been entered as a sailing mark upon the chart.

But it was not its size that now impressed my companions; it was the knowledge that seven hundred thousand pounds in gold lay somewhere buried below its spreading shadow. The thought of the money, as they drew nearer, swallowed up their previous terrors. Their eyes burned in their heads; their feet grew speedier and lighter; their whole soul was bound up in that fortune, that whole lifetime of extravagance and pleasure, that lay waiting there for each of them.

Silver hobbled, grunting, on his crutch; his nostrils stood out and quivered; he cursed like a madman when the flies settled on his hot and shiny countenance; he plucked furiously at the line that held me to him, and, from time to time, turned his eyes upon me with a deadly look. Certainly he took no pains to hide his thoughts; and certainly I read them like print. In the immediate nearness of the gold, all else had been forgotten; his promise and the doctor's warning were both things of the past; and I could not doubt that he hoped to seize upon the treasure, find and board the *Hispaniola* under cover of night, cut every honest throat about that island, and sail away as he had at first intended, laden with crimes and riches.

Shaken as I was with these alarms, it was hard for me to keep up with the rapid pace of the treasure-hunters. Now and again I tumbled, and it was then that Silver plucked so roughly at the rope and launched at me his murderous glances. Dick, who had dropped behind us, and now brought up the rear, was babbling to himself both prayers and curses, as his fever kept rising. This also added to my wretchedness, and, to crown all, I was haunted by the thought of the tragedy that had once been acted on that plateau, when that ungodly buccaneer with the blue face—he who had died at Savannah, singing and shouting for drink—had there, with his own hand, cut down his six accomplices. This grove, that was now so peaceful, must then have rung with cries, I thought; and even with the thought I could believe I heard it ringing still.

We were now at the margin of the thicket.

"Huzza, mates, all together!" shouted Merry, and the foremost broke into a run.

And suddenly, not ten yards farther, we beheld them stop. A low cry arose. Silver doubled his pace, digging away with the foot of his crutch like one possessed, and next moment he and I had come also to a dead halt.

Before us was a great excavation, not very recent, for the sides had fallen in and grass had sprouted on the bottom. In this were the shaft of a pick broken in two and the boards of several packing cases strewn around. On one of these boards I saw, branded with a hot iron, the name "Walrus"—the name of Flint's ship.

All was clear to probation. The *cache* had been found and rifled—the seven hundred thousand pounds were gone!

## Chapter XXXIII

## THE FALL OF A CHIEFTAIN

THERE never was such an overturn in this world. Each of these six men was as though he had been struck. But with Silver the blow passed almost instantly. Every thought of his soul had been set full-stretch, like a racer, on that money; well, he was brought up in a single second, dead; and he kept his head, found his temper, and changed his plan before the others had had time to realize the disappointment.

"Jim," he whispered, "take that, and stand by for trouble."

And he passed me a double-barreled pistol.

At the same time he began quietly moving northward, and in a few steps had put the hollow between us two and the other five. Then he looked at me and nodded, as much as to say: "Here is a narrow corner," as, indeed, I thought it was. His looks were now quite friendly, and I was so revolted at these constant changes that I could not forbear whispering: "So you've changed sides again."

There was no time left for him to answer in. The buccaneers, with oaths and cries, began to leap, one after another, into the pit, and to dig with their fingers, throwing the boards aside as they did so.

Morgan found a piece of gold. He held it up with a perfect spout of oaths. It was a two-guinea piece, and it went from hand to hand among them for a quarter of a minute.

"Two guineas!" roared Merry, shaking it at Silver. "That's your seven hundred thousand pounds, is it? You're the man for bargains, ain't you? You're him that never bungled nothing, you wooden-headed lubber!"

"Dig away, boys," said Silver, with the coolest insolence; "you'll find some pig-nuts, and I shouldn't wonder."

"Pig-nuts!" repeated Merry, in a scream. "Mates, do you hear that? I tell you now, that man there knew it all along. Look in the face of him, and you'll see it wrote there."

"Ah, Merry," remarked Silver, "standing for cap'n again? You're a pushing lad, to be sure."

But this time everyone was entirely in Merry's favor. They began to scramble out of the excavation, darting furious glances behind them. One thing I observed, which looked well for us; they all got out upon the opposite side from Silver.

Well, there we stood, two on one side, five on the other, the pit between us, and nobody screwed up high enough to offer the first blow. Silver never moved; he watched them, very upright on his crutch, and looked as cool as ever I saw him. He was brave, and no mistake.

At last, Merry seemed to think a speech might help matters.

"Mates," says he, "there's two of them alone there; one's the old cripple that brought us all here and blundered us down to this; the other's that cub that I mean to have the heart of. Now, mates——"

He was raising his arm and his voice, and plainly meant to lead a charge. But just then—crack! crack! crack!—three musket-shots flashed out of the thicket. Merry tumbled head-foremost into the excavation; the man with the bandage spun round like a teetotum, and fell all his length upon his side, where he lay dead, but still twitching; and the other three turned and ran for it with all their might.

Before you could wink Long John had fired two barrels of a pistol into the struggling Merry; and as the man rolled up his eyes at him in the last agony, "George," said he, "I reckon I settled you."

At the same moment the doctor, Gray, and Ben Gunn joined us, with smoking muskets, from among the nutmeg trees.

"Forward!" cried the doctor. "Double quick, my lads. We must head 'em off the boats."

And we set off at a great pace, sometimes plunging through the bushes to the chest.

I tell you, but Silver was anxious to keep up with us. The work that man went through, leaping on his crutch till the muscles of his chest were fit to burst, was work no sound man ever equaled; and so thinks the doctor. As it was, he was already thirty yards behind us, and on the verge of strangling, when we reached the brow of the slope.

"Doctor," he hailed, "see there! no hurry!"

Sure enough there was no hurry. In a more open part of the plateau we could see the three survivors still running in the same direction as they had started, right for Mizzen-mast Hill. We were already between them and the boats, and so we four sat down to breathe, while Long John, mopping his face, came slowly up with us.

"Thank ye kindly, doctor," says he. "You came in in about the nick, I guess, for me and Hawkins. And so it's you, Ben Gunn!" he added. "Well, you're a nice one, to be sure."

"I'm Ben Gunn, I am," replied the maroon, wriggling like an eel in his embarrassment. "And," he added, after a long pause, "how do, Mr. Silver! Pretty well, I thank ye, says you."

"Ben, Ben," murmured Silver, "to think as you've done me."

The doctor sent back Gray for one of the pick-axes, deserted, in their flight, by the mutineers; and then as we proceeded leisurely downhill to where the boats were lying, related, in a few words, what had taken place. It was a story that profoundly interested Silver, and Ben Gunn, the half-idiot maroon, was the hero from beginning to end.

Ben, in his long, lonely wanderings about the

island, had found the skeleton. It was he that had rifled it; he had found the treasure; he had dug it up (it was the haft of his pick-ax that lay broken in the excavation); he had carried it on his back, in many weary journeys, from the foot of the tall pine to a cave he had on the two-pointed hill at the northeast angle of the island, and there it had lain stored in safety since two months before the arrival of the *Hispaniola*.

When the doctor had wormed this secret from him, on the afternoon of the attack, and when, next morning, he saw the anchorage deserted, he had gone to Silver, given him the chart, which was now useless; given him the stores, for Ben Gunn's cave was well supplied with goats' meat salted by himself; given anything and everything to get a chance of moving in safety from the stockade to the two-pointed hill, there to be clear of malaria and keep a guard upon the money.

"As for you, Jim," he said, "it went against my heart, but I did what I thought best for those who had stood by their duty; and if you were not one of these, whose fault was it?"

That morning, finding that I was to be involved in the horrid disappointment he had prepared for the mutineers, he had run all the way to the cave, and, leaving squire to guard the captain, had taken Gray and the maroon, and started, making the diagonal across the island, to be at hand beside the pine.

Soon, however, he saw that our party had the start of him; and Ben Gunn, being fleet of foot, had been dispatched in front to do his best alone. Then it had occurred to him to work upon the superstitions of his former shipmates; and he was so far successful that Gray and the doctor had come up and were already ambushed before the arrival of the treasure hunters.

"Ah," said Silver, "it was fortune for me that I had Hawkins here. You would have let old John be cut to bits, and never given it a thought, doctor."

"Not a thought," replied Doctor Livesey, cheerily.

And by this time we had reached the gigs. The doctor, with the pick-ax, demolished one of them, and then we all got aboard the other, and set out to go round by the sea for North Inlet.

This was a run of eight or nine miles. Silver, though he was almost killed already with fatigue, was set to an oar, like the rest of us, and we were soon skimming swiftly over a smooth sea. Soon we passed out of the straits and doubled the southeast corner of the island, round which, four days ago, we had towed the *Hispaniola*

As we passed the two-pointed hill we could see the black mouth of Ben Gunn's cave, and a figure standing by it, leaning on a musket. It was the squire, and we waved a handkerchief and gave him three cheers, in which the voice of Silver joined as heartily as any.

Three miles farther, just inside the mouth of North Inlet, what should we meet but the *Hispaniola*, cruising by herself. The last flood had lifted her, and had there been much wind, or a strong tide current, as in the southern anchorage, we should never have found her more, or found her stranded beyond help. As it was, there was little amiss, beyond the wreck of the mainsail. Another anchor was got ready, and dropped in a fathom and a half of water. We all pulled round again to Rum Cove, the nearest point for Ben Gunn's treasure-house; and then Gray, single-handed, returned with the gig to the *Hispaniola*, where he was to pass the night on guard.

A gentle slope ran up from the beach to the entrance of the cave. At the top, the squire met us. To me he was cordial and kind, saying nothing of my escapade, either in the way of blame or praise. At Silver's polite salute he somewhat flushed.

"John Silver," he said, "you're a prodigious villain and impostor—a monstrous impostor, sir. I am told I am not to prosecute you. Well, then, I will not. But the dead men, sir, hang about your neck like millstones."

"Thank you kindly, sir," replied Long John, again saluting.

"How dare you to thank me!" cried the squire. "It is a gross dereliction of my duty. Stand back!"

And thereupon we all entered the cave. It was a large, airy place, with a little spring and a pool of

clear water, overhung with ferns. The floor was
sand. Before a big fire lay Captain Smollett; and
in a far corner, only duskily flickered over by the
blaze, I beheld great heaps of coin and quadrilaterals
built of bars of gold. That was Flint's treasure that
we had come so far to seek, and that had cost already
the lives of seventeen men from the *Hispaniola*.
How many it had cost in the amassing, what blood
and sorrow, what good ships scuttled on the deep,
what brave men walking the plank blindfold, what
shot of cannon, what shame and lies and cruelty,
perhaps no man alive could tell. Yet there were still
three upon that island—Silver, and old Morgan, and
Ben Gunn—who had each taken his share in these
crimes, as each had hoped in vain to share in the
reward.

"Come in, Jim," said the captain. "You're a
good boy in your line, Jim; but I don't think you
and me'll go to sea again. You're too much of the
born favorite for me. Is that you, John Silver?
What brings you here, man?"

"Come back to do my dooty, sir," returned
Silver.

"Ah!" said the captain, and that was all he said.

What a supper I had of it that night, with all my
friends around me; and what a meal it was, with Ben
Gunn's salted goat, and some delicacies and a bottle
of old wine from the *Hispaniola*. Never, I am sure,
were people gayer or happier. And there was Silver,

I Beheld Great Heaps of Coin and Quadrilaterals Built of Bars of Gold.

sitting back almost out of the fire-light, but eating heartily, prompt to spring forward when anything was wanted, even joining quietly in our laughter— the same bland, polite, obsequious seaman of the voyage out.

## CHAPTER XXXIV

AND LAST

THE next morning we fell early to work, for the transportation of this great mass of gold near a mile by land to the beach, and thence three miles by boat to the *Hispaniola*, was a considerable task for so small a number of workmen. The three fellows still abroad upon the island did not greatly trouble us; a single sentry on the shoulder of the hill was sufficient to insure us against any sudden onslaught, and we thought, besides, they had more than enough of fighting.

Therefore the work was pushed on briskly. Gray and Ben Gunn came and went with the boat, while the rest during their absence piled treasure on the beach. Two of the bars, slung in a rope's end, made a good load for a grown man—one that he was glad to walk slowly with. For my part, as I was not much use at carrying, I was kept busy all day in the cave, packing the minted money into bread-bags.

It was a strange collection, like Billy Bone's hoard for the diversity of coinage, but so much larger and so much more varied that I think I never had more pleasure than in sorting them. English, French, Spanish, Portuguese, Georges, and Louises, doubloons and double guineas and moidores, and sequins, the pictures of all the kings of Europe for the last hundred years, strange oriental pieces stamped with what looked like wisps of string or bits of spider's web, round pieces and square pieces, and pieces bored through the middle, as if to wear them round your neck—nearly every variety of money in the world must, I think, have found a place in that collection, and for number, I am sure they were like autumn leaves, so that my back ached with stooping and my fingers with sorting them out.

Day after day this work went on; by every evening a fortune had been stowed aboard, but there was another fortune waiting for the morrow; and all this time we heard nothing of the three surviving mutineers.

At last—I think it was on the third night—the doctor and I were strolling on the shoulder of the hill where it overlooks the lowlands of the isle, when, from out the thick darkness below, the wind brought us a noise between shrieking and singing. It was only a snatch that reached our ears, followed by the former silence.

"Heaven forgive them," said the doctor; "'tis the mutineers!"

"All drunk, sir," struck in the voice of Silver from behind us.

Silver, I should say, was allowed his entire liberty, and, in spite of daily rebuffs, seemed to regard him-

self once more as quite a privileged and friendly de-
pendent. Indeed, it was remarkable how well he
bore these slights, and with what unwearying polite-
ness he kept at trying to ingratiate himself with all.
Yet, I think, none treated him better than a dog,
unless it was Ben Gunn, who was still terribly afraid
of his old quartermaster, or myself, who had really
something to thank him for; although for that matter, I suppose, I had reason to think even worse of
him than anybody else, for I had seen him meditating
a fresh treachery upon the plateau. Accordingly, it
was pretty gruffly that the doctor answered him.

"Drunk or raving?" said he.

"Right you were, sir," replied Silver; "and
precious little odds which, to you and me."

"I suppose you would hardly ask me to call you a
humane man," returned the doctor, with a sneer,
"and so my feelings may surprise you, Master Silver.
But if I were sure they were raving—as I am morally
certain one, at least, of them is down with fever—
I should leave this camp, and, at whatever risk to
my own carcass, take them the assistance of my
skill."

"Ask your pardon, sir, you would be very wrong,"
quoth Silver. "You would lose your precious life,
and you may lay to that. I'm on your side now,
hand and glove; and I shouldn't wish for to see the
party weakened, let alone yourself, seeing as I know
what I owes you. But these men down there, they

couldn't keep their word—no, not supposing they wished to—and what's more, they couldn't believe as you could."

"No," said the doctor. "You're the man to keep your word, we know that."

Well, that was about the last news we had of the three pirates. Only once we heard a gunshot a great way off, and supposed them to be hunting. A council was held and it was decided that we must desert them on the island—to the huge glee, I must say, of Ben Gunn, and with the strong approval of Gray. We left a good stock of powder and shot, the bulk of the salt goat, a few medicines and some other necessaries, tools, clothing, a spare sail, a fathom or two of rope, and, by the particular desire of the doctor, a handsome present of tobacco.

That was about our last doing on the island. Before that we had got the treasure stowed and had shipped enough water and the remainder of the goat meat, in case of any distress; and at last, one fine morning, we weighed anchor, which was about all that we could manage, and stood out of North Inlet, the same colors flying that the captain had flown and fought under at the palisade.

The three fellows must have been watching us closer than we thought for, as we soon had proved. For, coming through the narrows we had to lie very near the southern point, and there we saw all three of them kneeling together on a spit of sand with

their arms raised in supplication. It went to all our
hearts, I think, to leave them in that wretched state,
but we could not risk another mutiny, and to take
them home for the gibbet would have been a cruel
sort of kindness. The doctor hailed them and told
them of the stores we had left, and where they were
to find them, but they continued to call us by name
and appeal to us, for God's sake, to be merciful and
not leave them to die in such a place.

At last, seeing the ship still bore on her course,
and was now swiftly drawing out of ear-shot, one
of them—I know not which it was—leaped to his
feet with a hoarse cry, whipped his musket to his
shoulder, and sent a shot whistling over Silver's head
and through the mainsail.

After that we kept under cover of the bulwarks,
and when next I looked out they had disappeared
from the spit, and the spit itself had almost melted
out of sight in the growing distance. That was, at
least, the end of that; and before noon, to my in-
expressible joy, the highest rock of Treasure Island
had sunk into the blue round of sea.

We were so short of men that everyone on board
had to bear a hand—only the captain lying on a
mattress in the stern and giving his orders, for
though greatly recovered he was still in want of
quiet. We laid her head for the nearest port in
Spanish America, for we could not risk the voyage
home without fresh hands; and as it was, what with

There We Saw All Three of Them Kneeling Together.

299

baffling winds and a couple of fresh gales, we were all worn out before we reached it.

It was just at sundown when we cast anchor in a most beautiful land-locked gulf, and were immediately surrounded by shore-boats full of negroes and Mexican Indians and half-bloods, selling fruits and vegetables, and offering to dive for bits of money. The sight of so many good-humored faces (especially the blacks), the taste of the tropical fruits, and above all, the lights that began to shine in the town, made a most charming contrast to our dark and bloody sojourn on the island; and the doctor and the squire, taking me along with them, went ashore to pass the early part of the night. Here they met the captain of an English man-of-war, fell in talk with him, went on board his ship, and in short, had so agreeable a time that day was breaking when we came alongside the *Hispaniola*.

Ben Gunn was on deck alone, and as soon as we came on board he began, with wonderful contortions, to make us a confession. Silver was gone. The maroon had connived at his escape in a shore boat some hours ago, and he now assured us he had only done so to preserve our lives, which would certainly have been forfeited if "that man with the one leg had stayed aboard." But this was not all. The sea-cook had not gone empty-handed. He had cut through a bulk-head unobserved, and had removed one of the sacks of coin, worth, perhaps, three or four hundred guineas, to help him on his further wanderings.

I think we were all pleased to be so cheaply quit of him.

Well, to make a long story short, we got a few hands on board, made a good cruise home, and the *Hispaniola* reached Bristol just as Mr. Blandly was beginning to think of fitting out her consort. Five men only of those who had sailed returned with her. "Drink and the devil had done for the rest" with a vengeance, although, to be sure, we were not quite in so bad a case as that other ship they sung about:

> "With one man of the crew alive,
> What put to sea with seventy-five."

All of us had an ample share of the treasure, and used it wisely or foolishly, according to our natures. Captain Smollett is now retired from the sea. Gray not only saved his money, but, being suddenly smit with the desire to rise, also studied his profession, and he is now mate and part owner of a fine, full-rigged ship; married besides, and the father of a family. As for Ben Gunn, he got a thousand pounds, which he spent or lost in three weeks, or, to be more exact, in nineteen days, for he was back begging on the twentieth. Then he was given a lodge to keep, exactly as he had feared upon the island; and he still lives, a great favorite, though something of a butt with the country boys, and a notable singer in church on Sundays and saints' days.

Of Silver we have heard no more. That formidable seafaring man with one leg has at last gone clean out of my life, but I dare say he met his old negress, and perhaps still lives in comfort with her and Captain Flint. It is to be hoped so, I suppose, for his chances of comfort in another world are very small.

The bar silver and the arms still lie, for all that I know, where Flint buried them; and certainly they shall lie there for me. Oxen and wain-ropes would not bring me back again to that accursed island, and the worst dreams that ever I have are when I hear the surf booming about its coasts, or start upright in bed, with the sharp voice of Captain Flint still ringing in my ears: "Pieces of eight! pieces of eight!"

## THE END

# GLOSSARY

# 304     GLOSSARY

Page 156 Line 19—**Log:** The official record of a boat.
"   176   "   20—**Doldrums:** A portion of the ocean abounding in calms, squalls, and light winds.
"   180   "   12—**Hanger:** A short curved sword.
"   189   "   12—**Thwart:** A seat in a boat extending from one side to the other.
"   189   "   15—**Coracle:** A light boat made by stretching a skin or piece of leather over a frame.
"   204   "   1—**Tiller:** A lever or handle to turn the rudder.
"   204   "   9—**Yawing:** Steering wildly or out of regular course.
"   217   "   6—**I've missed stays:** I've failed in the attempt.
"   221   "   27—**Puncheon:** Eighty gallons, sometimes one hundred twenty gallons.
"   229   "   5—**Halyard:** A rope for raising and lowering sails.
"   229   "   8—**Downhaul:** A rope for pulling down a sail.
"   261   "   28—**Gammon:** To cajole, flatter, keep on one's side.

# THE CHILDREN'S *Bookshelf*

## Books That Every Child Should Own

**BLACK BEAUTY**
Sewell. 15 full-page illus., 4 in color.

**THE STORY OF A BAD BOY**
Aldrich. 14 full-page drawings, 4 in color.

**KING ARTHUR AND HIS KNIGHTS**
Merchant. 16 full-page drawings, 4 in color.

**THE WONDER BOOK OF BIBLE STORIES**
Marshall. 4 full pages in color and 54 text illus.

**LAMB'S TALES FROM SHAKESPEARE**
Lamb. 12 full-page illus., 4 in color.

**THE ARABIAN NIGHTS**
Introd. by Orton Lowe. 63 illus., 3 in color.

**ROBIN HOOD**
Introd. by George C. Harvey. 20 full-page drawings, 4 in color.

**ALICE'S ADVENTURES IN WONDERLAND and THROUGH THE LOOKING GLASS**
Carroll. 89 illus. by Tenniel, 4 color plates.

**HEIDI**
Spyri. 25 illus., 4 in color.

**TREASURE ISLAND**
Stevenson. 15 full-page drawings, 4 in color.

**HANS BRINKER or The Silver Skates**
Dodge. 12 illus., 4 in color.

**ROBINSON CRUSOE**
Defoe. 9 drawings, 4 in color.

**PINOCCHIO**
Collodi. 32 illus. by Charles Folkard, 8 in color.

**KIDNAPPED**
Stevenson. 14 illus., 4 in color.

**LITTLE WOMEN**
Alcott. 12 full-page illus., 4 in color.

**PATRIOTIC AMERICAN STORIES**
    Including The Man Without a Country
Introd. by John M. Foote. 11 full-page drawings, 4 in color.

**LITTLE MEN**
Alcott. 15 illus., 4 in color.

**AN OLD-FASHIONED GIRL**
Alcott. 18 illus., 4 in color

**DICKEN'S STORIES about Children**
14 illus., 4 in color.

**THE WINGS OF THE MORNING**
Tracy. 4 full pages in color.

**THE BOY'S STORY OF LINDBERGH**
Beamish. 30 photographs.

**WATER BABIES**
Kingsley. 8 full pages in color.

**THE SWISS FAMILY ROBINSON**
Wyss. 12 drawings. 4 in color.

**MOTHER GOOSE NURSERY RHYMES**
Arr. by Marshall. 304 illus., 4 in color.

**FAVORITE FAIRY TALES**
Arr. by Marshall. 104 illus., 4 in color.

**GRIMM'S FAIRY TALES**
64 illus., 4 in color.

**ANDERSEN'S FAIRY TALES**
Andersen. 14 illus., 4 in color.

**FOLK TALES FROM THE FAR EAST**
Meeker. 11 illus., 1 in color.

**THE WONDER BOOK OF MYTHS AND LEGENDS**
Compiled by William B. Forbush. 14 drawings, 4 in color.

**FAIRY TALES OF MANY LANDS**
Illus. with 4 full pages in color.

**THE RED FAIRY BOOK**
Lang. 95 illus., 4 in color.

**THE BLUE FAIRY TALES**
Lang. 107 illus., 4 in color.

**A WONDER BOOK AND TANGLEWOOD TALES**
Hawthorne. 14 colored illus.

**GULLIVER'S TRAVELS**
Swift. 16 drawings. 4 in color, 39 additional illus.

**EIGHT COUSINS**
Alcott. 12 illus., 4 in color.

**THE THREE MUSKETEERS**
Dumas. 14 illus., 4 in color.

**THE ADVENTURES OF TOM SAWYER**
Twain. 44 illus., 4 in color.

**ROSE IN BLOOM**
Alcott 13 illus., 5 in color.

**NEW FOUND TALES**
Egan. 28 illus., 4 in color.

**WINGS OF FLAME**
Egan. 14 illus., 3 in color.

**THE PILGRIM'S PROGRESS**
Bunyan. 44 famous Frederick Barnard drawings, 4 in color.

**JOAN OF ARC**
Holmes. 12 illus., 4 in color.

**THE OREGON TRAIL**
Parkman. 16 illus., 4 in color.

**TWENTY THOUSAND LEAGUES UNDER THE SEA**
Verne. 36 illus., 4 in color.

**MOBY DICK**
Melville. 10 illus., 4 in color.

**UNDER THE LILACS**
Alcott. 12 illus., 4 in color.

**THE WORLD'S GREAT ADVENTURE—1000 Years of Polar Exploration**
Miller. 150 illustrations.

**THE LITTLE LAME PRINCE and THE ADVENTURES OF A BROWNIE**
Mulock. 30 illustrations, 4 in colors.

**THE PRINCE AND THE PAUPER**
Twain. Illus. in color and black and white.

**TOBY TYLER**
Otis. 28 illus., 4 in color.

» *These books are obtainable at all booksellers at the same price as this volume.* «

# THE JOHN C. WINSTON CO., Publishers, PHILADELPHIA